THE WAKE OF THE
GENERAL BLISS

THE WAKE OF THE GENERAL BLISS

Edward Lueders

University of Utah Press
Salt Lake City
1989

LIBRARY OF CONGRESS CATALOGING-IN-PUBLICATION DATA
Lueders, Edward G., 1923–
  The wake of the general bliss.
  I. title.   II. title: General bliss.
PS3562.U34W3   1989   813'.54   88-20687
ISBN 978-0-87480-927-5

The author thanks the National Endowment for the Arts,
a federal agency, for a fellowship grant, and the University
of Utah for a David P. Gardner Faculty Fellowship Award,
both of which assisted in the writing of this book.

I leave a white and turbid wake; pale waters, paler cheeks, where'er I sail. The envious billows sidelong swell to whelm my track; let them; but first I pass.

—Herman Melville, *Moby Dick*

Music is your own experience, your thoughts, your wisdom. If you don't live it, it won't come out of your horn.

—Charlie Parker

CONTENTS

PREFACE ix

PRELUDE 1

CHAPTER ONE 4

CHAPTER TWO 19

CHAPTER THREE 55

INTERMEZZO 62

CHAPTER FOUR 64

CHAPTER FIVE 103

CHAPTER SIX 145

CODA 186

— PREFACE TO THE PAPERBACK EDITION —

As the generation that fought in World War II ages into their 80s and 90s and their numbers dwindle, interest grows in recording their personal recollections of the wartime experience. The media have focused understandably on the life-and-death dramas of combat soldiering in European and Pacific battles. But the far-flung involvement of servicemen and women in a great variety of other locations and contributing roles is needed to complete and humanize our comprehensive picture of U.S. military service in World War II. Everyone in uniform disrupted the course of their lives to serve their country in the all-out war effort. In many cases, as in my own assignments in China, Burma, and India, the roles they were given to perform led them into situations as unexpected, exotic, and potentially dangerous as those of some combat troops. Theirs are war stories too—offstage, so to speak, but no less vital in being revived for the record after half a century. They deserve to be told.

I nursed my own World War II stories privately for some forty years before they came together coherently and thematically around the central event of my troopship's man overboard in mid-Pacific. Rather than writing a war memoir, I chose the challenging form of a novel. It was published in 1989 as *The Wake of the General Bliss* and is reissued here in paperback form. The stories it tells are quite autobiographical and seem to fit the old literary tradition of related tales-told-along-the-way. Chaucer's *Canterbury Tales*, Boccaccio's *Decameron*, and even *Scheherazade*, though hardly models, come to mind. I also wanted to integrate musical motifs to add appropriate color and period authenticity.

The wartime jazz trio I'd played with as both soloist and ensemble provided the means to split my story-telling three ways. I developed this trio freely as the characters in my novel, through their music as well as through my own recollected tales that I assigned to them. For the record, the real members of the GI trio were amplified-guitar innovator H. Ray Warren, from Georgia; on drums, occasional bass, and vocals was Norman Simpson from Massachusetts, who later wrote personable travel books as *The Berkshire Traveler*; and me on piano. To further disguise myself, I borrowed some background and professionalism from another close friend and buddy at Barrackpore, the concert pianist Leonard Pennario. Any similarities to their counterparts in the novel are both more and less coincidental.

We were pulled from our regular duties at Air Transport Command (ATC) and brought together at CBI headquarters near Calcutta. There, with the small group of GI entertainers who made up our troupe, we rehearsed the show we would take on tour to ATC bases throughout China, Burma, and India. The special service officer at headquarters was Major Melvin Douglas, the veteran Hollywood actor. Under him, and directly in charge of us, was Captain Larry Clinton, the big band leader best known in the Forties for his swing arrangement of "The Dipsy Doodle." The Noncom working most closely with our rehearsals was Staff Sergeant Tony Martin, the singer-actor, sleek and handsome in his well-pressed suntans. As I vividly recall, he always greeted me with a light clap on my back and mock Brooklynese. "Hey Eddie," he'd say, "How's ya motha?" It was a calm and cordial prelude to the rugged, demanding, often harrowing situations lying ahead on our catch-as-catch-can tours through Upper Bengalese Assam (now Bangladesh), Burma (now Myanmar), and over the Himalayas (the "Hump," as we called it) to General Chiang Kai-shek's Nationalist China—and the episodes that I recount in the book.

The fictional parts of the book that had to be researched and imagined into place were the navy personnel and their response to the emergency at sea. Our troopship was in fact the Tasker H. Bliss, named for the venerated World War I army general and statesman. For the particulars of naval procedures I consulted commissioned officer colleagues teaching military science at the University of Utah. I am indebted to them for the authenticity of ship operation and maneuver, but I am responsible for any aberrations experts may find. Although the ship's captain, his lieutenant, and their crew on the bridge are my invention, I trust they are valid characters in their own right and essential to the novel's design.

The troopship itself was indeed our world for the month at sea. Like my characters, I came to know it well. For the great majority of Americans soldiering in World War II, the passively intense, transitional troopship passage to the arenas of combat, and, for the survivors, back again to re-enter their civilian lives, was an intrinsic and unforgettable part of their war experience. I hope that this new paperback edition of *The Wake of the General Bliss*, available some sixty years after the tale it tells, will find its place in the annals of my generation and our Great War.

EDWARD LUEDERS
September 2007

−Prelude−

In the common dream of the four thousand GI passengers crammed on the USS *General Simon P. Bliss*, the shores of America lay waiting some fifteen days ahead. It was February of 1946. The Bomb had devastated Hiroshima and another had been dropped on Nagasaki. Japan had surrendered. The war was finished. The restless months of waiting and then the final weeks in the staging area at Kanchrapara lay well behind them. They were in the middle of the Pacific Ocean. In transit. In transition. Homeward bound, across the apparently boundless Pacific.

For these thousands of GIs being transported from ancient India to modern America, there was nothing to *do*. Turned inward, the troops took increasing comfort in the simple regularities of shipboard life. In the thirteen days since the vessel had cast off from Calcutta's King George Docks and steamed out of the brown waters at the mouth of the Hooghly River into the open sea, they accustomed themselves to the narrow, predictable world of the *General Bliss*. During this long lull of passage, this mean time, the ship became the only familiar environment in their lives.

Each GI, once he had taken his own measure of the vessel, found it somehow whole, somehow his. He knew its length and breadth and its series of levels, from the superstructure and the commanding bridge with its curving bay of expressionless windows and the antennae of electronic rigging searching the air above it, down through the entrails below decks to his troop mess hall and the maze of passageways through which his chow lines snaked to reach it. He knew the dim underworld concourse of the latrine and the darkened hold where he slept, sandwiched into an assigned slot among the narrow tiers of slung canvas. From the remote engine rooms even farther below, he felt the steady pulse of energy and power that turned the screws and drove his ship through the ponderous sea.

But beyond this, all that is real to him in mid-Pacific is the uninterrupted reach of ocean to the clear, arching horizon. It seems as though nothing will ever break the rhythm of the days, the cycles of shipboard routine, and the ceaseless movement of the troopship through the swelling Pacific seas. It even becomes possible during idle, unblinking, sunlit stretches to think of nothing but the massive ocean sweeping endlessly past the ship. At times a curious inversion makes it seem as if the shifting sea does all the moving while, except for a slight rolling in place to maintain its languid balance, the heavy, stolid troop transport remains stationary.

Out beyond the *General Bliss* there is the sea and there is the sky. The two come together at the encircling seam of the horizon to seal in the universe around the moving center of the ship. After so many consecutive brilliant Pacific days without landmarks, this union of sea and air seems to contain all. The eye grows hypnotized by the open panorama of the sea. Against it, the men and their ship become transfixed, become a constant. Even the dashing wash of the sea past the sleek metal sides becomes, for anyone looking straight down from the railing, an entrancing study of solids and liquids, a dance of endless complementary motion.

Yet there is one feature of the surrounding seascape that can break that spell and bring back the human realities of their passage. When the men let their eyes follow the swirling water back to the stern and then into the widening sea behind them, their ship leaves its turbulent white mark upon the ocean-air continuum. The wake of the *General Bliss* is its mark and its distinction.

Only the wake, after two weeks out of the sight of land, gives the ship and its passengers their direction. It is the wake that makes their passage possible, that gives meaning to their motion. It is the wake, from its immediate churning presence almost beneath them, stretching back as far as the eye can see, that marks their way. It is the wake that links their ship with the horizon and intersects its perfect circle; that connects their exotic experiences in a disappearing India, China, Burma, already fading beyond the curving horizon, with the years that await, with the lives to be taken up, with their dream-future back in America. The wake alone, it seems, both points and propels them.

CHAPTER ONE

The right to perish might be thought
An undisputed right—
Attempt it, and the Universe
Upon the opposite
Will concentrate its officers—
You cannot even die
But nature and mankind must pause
To pay you scrutiny.

—Emily Dickinson

THE SHIP

The time is 1:40 p.m.—or 1340 hours in the more efficient continuous military measure of the *General Bliss*. The chow lines for the
second meal will be called in two hours or so. The troopship is steam-
ing along its course in mid-Pacific at a steady fifteen knots, as it had an
hour before, two hours before, the day before, the week before. The
day is mild. In the small hours of the afternoon the sun is direct and
warm. There is no wind to speak of, yet the motion of the ship pro-
vides a steady breeze that keeps the flag over the mainmast at a constant snapping flutter.

The crew of the *General Bliss* are all but invisible to the troops.
Most are in their quarters or at their posts out of sight. It seems as if

the ship is running unmanned, following its own will and inclination. To a considerable extent at the moment, this is true. The Captain has retired to his quarters after a rather heavy lunch and, in his special solitude, is taking a nap. On the bridge, the Officer of the Deck has also yielded temporarily to a biological need. After a companionable remark and nod to his talker to make his need for relief known and in some sense official, he has gone off to the adjacent head. At his departure, the talker and the helmsman exchange smirks. Everyone on the bridge relaxes visibly.

Out over the ship, at quadrants from the communication center of the talker, the lookouts lounge at their posts, each on the eminence of a mount provided for the operation of a dormant gun. Each gun is plugged, sealed, and covered, quite docile now that the war is concluded. Like the lookouts near their mounts, the guns face idly out over their segments of sea.

Far below, the engine room crew slump at their stations, lulled by the steady pounding rhythms of their machinery. In the galley the cooks are taking their break between meals. The huge cooking vats stand empty and idle. The CPO has challenged four of his staff to a poker game on the cutting table and the others cluster around to offer commentary and taunts. The GIs on KP details are for the time being at ease, finished cleaning up after the first meal and not yet alerted for their duties during the second. In the smokey latrines below decks, as at all hours of the day, men in a languid parade shuffle in and out as the need moves them.

Above decks, activities are minimal. In a wardroom forward on the starboard side, a number of ranking Army officers, natty in their tailored uniforms, sit around an oval table collating the morning reports from all companies on the ship. Off the main deck on the port side, somewhat below and opposite them, a trio of GI musicians, having played improvised lunch-hour music for the transient officers' mess, rise, stretch, and begin to put away their instruments. A staff sergeant dressed in khakis sits alone at the desk in the Army Information Office amidships, copying out in hunt-and-peck fashion on a gray Royal Standard a digest of the world news passed along to him earlier from the radio room. When finished, it will replace the old one among the posters and notices of the bulletin board on the main deck.

Outside, the troops in their loose, lived-in, dusty-green fatigue clothes cover nearly all the exposed surface of the ship. Some stand. Some sit. Some sprawl. Some are solitary. Some are gathered in groups. Time, for a spell, is completely fluid and loose, without edge. None of the men quite believe it when the terse announcement over the ship-wide systems of speakers suddenly blares.

"*MAN OVERBOARD!*"

The bodiless voice is there and gone so quickly that it is hardly even an interruption. Only the unmistakable intensity of the words and their utterance persists. All the same, everyone grows still, if only out of startled curiosity, alert for what will follow.

Something about the blunt announcement is quite different from anything the men have heard over those speakers before. The general announcement system has long since become a regular feature of their benign passage, the shrill piping of the bo'sun's whistle a familiar prelude to the public notice of each day's orderly procedures — the routine announcements to "All transient personnel," the formation of chow lines, the ship's watches, and the calling of the ship's crew to their ritual duties. Compared to the familiar rigid "Hut-two-three-four" doggerel of the Army's close-order drill, these announcements came close to poetry: "*Wooo-EEEeee.' Now hear this: Sweepers, man your brooms. Sweepers, man your brooms. Cleansweep fore and aft on all weatherdecks. . . .*"

But there is no poetry as this cry rings out a second time, with the same suddenness.

"*MAN OVERBOARD!*"

The words break into the ease of the afternoon without prelude. No bo'sun's whistle. No "*now hear this.*" The cry hangs out on the air gracelessly and unadorned — a separate thing, a disorder. The volume is louder than usual. The voice that speaks the two words is not the regulated metallic voice of the public address system. It is a voice they have never heard on the ship before. It is a private voice, the voice of a person rather than of a speaker.

While the ship waits for the next words, the sharp actuality of the voice dwindles away. The reverberation of "*MAN OVER-BOARD!*" still echoes and turns in the minds of the thousands who heard it, but it is an echo with no palpable source. It could have been something each had thought independently, as thoughts will come at rare times, heard inwardly with amazing, sudden clarity, thoughts which speak through the blood and bone as well as through the brain.

The space of time lengthens. The *General Simon P. Bliss* continues to slice through its cleavage of the sea, its momentum unbroken. The men on board wait.

Then the speakers cut through the tense air again with the audible clack of a switch. For an awful extended moment the system is imminently *on* but without any voice, without any words to fill and animate its empty electronic hum. When the words do come, they are spoken by a new voice with a new manner — loud, abrupt, unnerved.

"*Man overboard. Port side.*" With the addition of this first specific detail, the familiar world of alternatives and opposites returns. The voice repeats its message: "*Man overboard. Port side.*"

These are the words one hears with the ears. This is a voice in motion and apparently at work; yet it is followed by another period of empty air which threatens to plunge everyone again into the whirlpool of his own private thoughts. Then the general address system crackles anew and the same voice, speaking rather than shouting now, issues a direction:

"*Duty boat crew, lay up to number two lifeboat.*" And it repeats, "*Duty boat crew, lay up to number two lifeboat.*"

The ship, after its timeless interlude of shock, prepares to turn back into the world of action and consequence.

THE LIEUTENANT

The lieutenant who was serving as Officer of the Deck was only a few steps from the bridge when he heard his talker's shout over the speakers.

"*MAN OVERBOARD!*"

For an instant, his reaction, like everyone else's on the ship, was one of disbelief. Almost at once, however, it changed to a flash of anguish at the realization that as Officer of the Deck he was responsible for what was happening. The anguish turned to energy and anger as he plunged through the doorway and into the center of the situation. Mordecai, his talker, had left his seat and was at the window with the others. Only the helmsman was at his post. The Lieutenant had never before seen confusion on the bridge of a Navy ship. He was vaguely frightened at the sight.

"All right, Mordecai, God damn it!" he barked, and was surprised to hear his own oath and the strange emotion in his own voice. "Give it to me."

"Yes, sir." The talker turned and looked at him hard but with obvious relief. "Haines reported a man overboard, sir. You weren't here. So I passed the word."

I know that, man, the Lieutenant thought wordlessly with a tightening of the lips. The ambiguous shout he had heard through the speakers rang again in his head. It still hung in the air over the whole ship. Then, aloud and to the point: "Who's Haines? What side? What side?"

"Port side, sir."

Where's the Captain? the Lieutenant thought. *The Captain should be here. I have to get the Captain.* He moved toward the phone to call the Captain's quarters. *No.* As OOD he was in charge, and the whole ship was waiting. He didn't need the Captain—didn't want to call him. He moved swiftly instead to the general announcement microphone and flipped the switch on. He swung around, microphone clutched in his hand. Everyone on the bridge was standing stock-still, staring at him. He felt the stillness among the thousands of men outside, waiting and listening. It was an immense moment, and, somehow, idiotic. It was wholly his, and yet he knew hysterically that he had nothing really to do with it. A dumb moment. They were still staring. Everyone was still staring, awaiting the word. He looked into the microphone and gave them these words:

"*Man overboard. Port side.*"

It sounded good to him. The words had a rightness, a power in them, and he repeated: "*Man overboard. Port side.*"

Then, with a strong sense of that power feeding back into the voice in which he spoke, back from that other disembodied voice heard almost simultaneously through the slight metallic ring of the speakers throughout the ship, he began to track. His mind, like an engine which has been racing in neutral, eased, toned down, and slipped into gear.

He spoke his next words evenly into the general announcement system and was reassured by the cadence of their Navy language.

"*Duty boat crew / lay up to number two lifeboat.*" And again. "*Duty boat crew / lay up to number two lifeboat.*"

He clicked off the microphone switch.

The Officer of the Deck, in charge now, glanced at the ship's clock, noted the time, and jotted it down on the pad next to the mike — 1343. He was functioning rather well and thinking rapidly. He knew the time would be important.

"Anybody see him?" he shouted to those still at the windows. A ragged chorus of negatives came back. *God*, he thought suddenly, *and me sitting in the head when it happened. They all know I was in the head.* He set his jaw.

"I want a fix on the spot, Mr. Martin. Check the course. We're making fifteen knots, and it's been . . . three minutes. And I want it on a dime."

"Aye-aye, sir," Martin replied, and got to it.

"Mr. Mordecai, call the Captain's quarters and report the situation . . . "

"Aye-aye, sir," from Mordecai. He turned to his apparatus, then paused. This was something the OOD should do himself.

" . . . and instruct the lookouts at all stations to report any sighting directly to the bridge. Do that first."

"Aye-aye, sir," from Mordecai, who got to it.

The bridge was in action now and humming. The helmsman had been calling the Lieutenant's name. The Lieutenant looked at him and was shocked by the agonized expression on his face until he realized *oh my God, we're still running!* "Left full rudder, Helmsman," he shouted in a fury of purpose. "Engines ahead flank!" The helmsman relayed his order almost as he was giving it.

Turning away, the Lieutenant glanced at his watch. 1344, it told him. Four minutes and how much ocean gone by? Four minutes at fifteen knots is . . . two thousand yards — a nautical mile. Too much to make the full circle of an Anderson turn effective. It would probably bring them back across the wake far short of the man in the water. Nobody sighted him, and they weren't likely to now, at this distance.

They'd need to estimate his position by backplot as accurately as possible and retrace their tracks to it. Better to execute a Williamson turn to reverse their direction and get back on reciprocal course. It would take longer, but it would be more accurate.

The Lieutenant picked up a pair of binoculars and moved toward the windows. On the way he passed his talker who, one hand pressing his earphone flat against his ear, was watching him cross the bridge.

"Anything yet, Mister?" the Lieutenant asked as he passed him.

"No, sir." Mordecai shook his head and averted his eyes.

"Have you reported to the Captain?"

"No, sir," Mordecai replied, still tentative. "Not yet."

"Well, do it, Mister," the Lieutenant said, then added, more companionably, "We don't want the Old Man on our back."

"Yes, sir," from Mordecai. He shrugged off his reluctance, reached for the s/p phone, and buzzed the Captain's cabin.

At the window, the Officer of the Deck confirmed what his seaman's expectations had anticipated. The huge ship was starting to nose slightly to the left, its beam sliding a bit to the right to compensate, as the remote shudder of the engines increased and the enormous screws labored and cut more aggressively into the dark undersea far below and behind him. His decision suddenly was clear. The accuracy of the ship's return to the point of the man overboard was more important than the few additional minutes in coming about. Feeling the power of the slightly canting *General Bliss* partly his now, the Lieutenant watched with strange exhilaration as the ship moved slowly broadside to its own previous direction and pushed bodily against the ponderous sea into the initial 60-degree arc of its Williamson turn.

THE CAPTAIN

The Captain of the USS *General Simon P. Bliss* was alone in his cabin, not so much sleeping as dozing fitfully, when the cry first went out:

"*MAN OVERBOARD!*"

If he had been fully asleep, he might have responded more directly, for he seldom slept at sea without some subverted level of apprehension ready to snap him into wakefulness. On this occasion, however, logy from lunch and the warm, still air of his quarters, he had stripped to his underwear and sprawled on his bed, where he lay in a kind of mental and emotional vacuum, lolling between vague consciousness and casual slumber. Along with everyone else on the ship, he hung in a strange suspension at the cry, eyes still closed, musing on what seemed an intrusion from within his subconscious.

Then again: "*MAN OVERBOARD!*"

The second time was another matter. He sat straight up on the bed, all his senses grasping for the whole moment, his hearing already anticipating the confirmation that must surely follow. He remained still, his mind groping, his pulse quickening, until it came:

"*Man overboard. Port side.*"

The Captain swung off the bed onto his feet, and started fumblingly to dress. He had a dull, stubborn erection, over which he paused for an inane moment of fond attention. It caused another moment's difficulty as he zipped his pants, which he managed with some hesitation and a neatly synchronized flex of the knees.

Sitting back on the bed to put on his shoes, he heard his Officer of the Deck give his directions over the speakers: "*Duty boat crew, lay up to number two lifeboat,*" and he reacted, half-aloud, "O.K. Ninety-Day-Wonder's on the ball." *Can't feel her coming about, though,* he thought. *Must still be half asleep.* He shook his head vigorously, partly as a gesture to accompany his response, partly as an overture to jamming on his cap and emerging from his quarters. As he dipped through his doorway, the phone was buzzing back inside. He hesitated momentarily, started back, then ignored it and strode ahead toward the bridge.

The Captain was not a vain man. If he seemed so to his crew, it was because his experience made him appear altogether at ease in command of the *General Bliss* without relaxing any of the discipline he demanded. He had no current need to prove himself. He had commanded one of the busiest destroyers in the war. He had even achieved some measure of military celebrity, having served under Captain Arleigh "31-Knot" Burke during the Battle of Cape St. George in the Solomons. This transition to a peacetime troopship was full of irritations and frustrations for him. Admittedly, though, the war was over and there was less apparent reason for vigilance and a strict concern for military order. Besides, it obviously needed doing. These Army and Air Force troops had fought their war, too. He was aware that they carried home with them vivid and unforgettable wartime experience in the CBI, that remote Asiatic corner of the war dedicated to flying vital material from India over "the Hump" of the Himalayas into beleaguered China and Burma. In fact, he had felt an unexpected warmth and comradeship as he watched the ranks of GIs mount the gangplanks of the *General Bliss*, stepping from the ancient shore of the subcontinent, out of the babble and rubble of Calcutta onto the orderly decks of his ship, into his trust and the competent hands of the U.S. Navy.

But in the days that followed, he found himself increasingly resentful of the mass of troops in their dull-green fatigues who swarmed over his ship, useless and indolent, and forever in the way. He was dissatisfied with most of the Navy personnel on the *General Bliss* as well. Like himself, many were newly assigned. They were a mixed and rather sloppy crew, hardly up to the tightly organized, snappy operation of the destroyer crews which for years had reflected and maintained his Navy pride. He was grateful he didn't have to face battle with such a ragtag bunch.

He understood all this and was prepared to be reasonable. Erosion in the line of command had become routine in every Navy captain's life in the months since V-J Day. He had joked with friends, when his orders for assignment to the *General Bliss* first came through, about heading up a trans-Pacific pleasure cruise; but as the crossing moved them farther from their exotic port of embarkation he had to resist— with less success each day—the inclination to look on his human cargo as so much obtuse cattle he had contracted to deliver to the Port of San Francisco.

He showed his irritation as little as possible. At times, though, he caught himself narrowing his eyes and holding them in a semisquint, his mouth pulled a notch tighter than usual. He had also developed the habit, when the slackness of the whole enterprise began to edge him toward ill temper, of retiring to his cabin—always, however, after establishing, as he had on this occasion, his own immediate availability on call.

Walking now with determination toward the bridge, the Captain felt sympathetically the series of slight shudders and arrhythmic pitches as the engines strained and the ship began to sluice toward a turn. *Goddam sluggish tub!* he thought. *It'll take her forever.* By the time he reached the bridge, he virtually felt himself, along with his ship, drifting at hard left rudder and beginning, almost as a matter of personal will, the slow transition of coming about.

He paused at the door to the bridge, his first glance going to the helmsman, who saw him at the same instant and straightened. The helmsman met the glance levelly, nodded, more with his eyes than with his head, and held steady at his post as he sang out, "Captain's on the bridge."

The Captain acknowledged with a slight nod in return. *Good man*, he thought. *Leave him there.*

The others, occupied with the search at the windows or out on either side on the bridge wings, had not yet seen him. It was a strangely quiet, static scene. The Captain had a curious presentiment in the stillness of that instant that it would all come to nothing, that actions, as in a dream, were detached from their consequences. He broke the moment by stepping formidably through the door. "All right, Lieutenant, what's the word?" he said. His voice was loud, his manner patient, routine. "Anyone seen him?"

The Lieutenant lowered the binoculars, wheeled about, and threw the gesture of a salute, all in one motion.

"No, sir," he replied. It seemed insufficient, almost childlike. The Lieutenant felt compelled to keep talking. "We're coming about at hard left rudder, sir. Williamson turn, sir. Duty boat crew is standing by."

The Captain, not bothering to return the salute, studied his OOD, dropped his eyes for a second, then looked sharply up. *Might as well let him run the show a while. He needs it. Might do him good.* "Very well," he said. "Carry on." He moved to the window and began to scan the water back, around, and below with the others.

"Who went over, Lieutenant? Army?"

"Yes, sir. Must be Army. Must be."

The Captain's eyes narrowed. "Where'd the report come from?"

"Port side, sir, from . . . what's his name, Mordecai?"

His talker came to life. "Haines, sir. Port side lookout. Main deck, aft."

The Captain looked down, then compressed his lips.

"Have you checked the report, Mister?"

It was clear that they hadn't.

"Better check it out. All the way. We're going to need all the information you can get."

Typical, the Captain thought. Without a sighting from the bridge this could turn into a lengthy business. Everything about this voyage seemed to him fated to take its own time—slow, relaxed, freighted. Why should he suppose the search for a man overboard would be any different?

His mind suddenly went out to the four thousand men below, out there listening. They were a volatile element in the situation that had to be considered. But they also provided four thousand pairs of eyes. He took up the IMC microphone, almost casually, and flipped the switch. The speakers mounted at overlapping intervals throughout the vessel then carried his unemotional, measured, slightly echoing words to the alerted troops:

"*This is the Captain speaking. . . . We have had a report of a man overboard, port side. . . . All transient personnel are requested . . . to stay . . . where you are. . . . Those on the port side: we ask your help in locating the man overboard.*"

The Captain set down the microphone. He checked himself. In another minute he would be taking over completely. *No need for that— yet. Let the OOD do it.* He turned to the Lieutenant again.

"Standard procedure, Lieutenant." He gestured at the rack to the left of the helmsman which held regulations and specifications, mounted under plastic on masonite board for immediate reference. It was obvious his presence was an encumbrance at this point unless he did take full charge. He picked up a pair of binoculars and moved to the doorway.

"Let's get that boat in the water as soon as we can," he shot back. "I'll be out on the flying bridge. Carry on."

THE FLYING BRIDGE

From the port side of the flying bridge, the Captain peers down at the mass of Army fatigues on the decks, then squints out over the brilliant glitter of sea. The sun is bright overhead, the air mild and benevolent. A few layers of stratus clouds are rising from the horizon. The steady breeze whistles past his ears and dims all background sounds. He looks to the side and back, where he can see the initial light blue arc of the ship's turn breaking from the white churn of its wake. He feels firm and alone.

Some poor damned soul out there, he thinks. *Hope he got past the screws.* He measures off the line of the ship's bearing and progress. *Should have. But that could be why they haven't sighted him. Well, it's too late to do anything about that.*

Life jacket. Did he have his life jacket on? For the first week out, the Captain had felt reasonably assured that the Transportation Corps and Army chain of command were enforcing the shipboard order that life jackets be worn at all times by transient personnel on all weather decks. But the troops had grown lax about the regulation in recent days under the steady, hot sun. Many of the GIs lolling about the decks had been carrying their life jackets in hand, and worse—strictly against orders—using them as props against the unyielding blue-gray steel of the deck. And this is what it came to—a man overboard maybe without a life jacket, and even if he had it, maybe ineffective from misuse. The Captain bites his lower lip. Too late to do anything about that either, at least for the man out there.

The Navy lookout must have thrown out a life preserver first thing. Automatic. Or should be. Drilled into them. Yet no one on the bridge had mentioned it. Shouldn't have to, of course. Still, you couldn't take anything for granted on this trip. If that lookout—what was his name? Haines—had forgotten the life ring, he'd have his ass. The Captain puts the glasses to his eyes and raises them slowly along the course of the ship's wake, now almost broadside to the position of the *General Bliss* in its turn. Nothing but rolling, dimpled, sometimes serrated sea. No sign of the doughnut-shaped object he is looking for, but this does not surprise him. Even if it were in range, it could well be hidden at this distance in the rolling waters of the wake.

His mind dismisses the object and returns to the man in the water. He drops the angle of the glasses back down again to a point off the stern, inhales full, then lets part out and holds it as he begins a second search along the ship's wake. His eyes strain at the flat, circular image through the lens, trying to pick up the dark dot prefigured in his mind, bobbing in the distance. Not likely he'll sight him, he knows, until the ship can recover its lost ground. *Lost ground!* He lowers the binoculars. The neat, hard focus of their lens falls away into the range of his own human vision as he looks over the mass of troops on the decks below and out to the spread of the incomprehensible blue Pacific. . . .

Man overboard! The Captain sets his teeth, allowing himself at last a moment of private anger. After the countless times he has expected to hear that cry and prepared himself for it! The times when it seemed incredible to suppose his ship could pull through without men — valiant men, *his* men — being pitched over; times during monumental storms when his suddenly tiny destroyer had been flung between mountainous walls of the savage ocean, its decks battered and violently awash; other times at the height of battle when man-made storms of exploding shells and acrid smoke closed in amid monstrous booming percussions and repercussions while he maneuvered the trim ship sharply through the fire, the geysers of shattered sea, and the imploding surges from the enemy's near misses — times that threatened to dislodge even the wariest seaman in a moment of imbalance and catapult him into the maw of the angry, violated sea. . . . But it had never happened. They'd come through. He'd helped bring them all through.

His mind moves back to the exhilarating runs with "31-Knot" Burke through the hellish night scenes of the Battle of Cape St. George. The wonder of that experience, without a single American fatality — not one man lost in the whole show! Not even any casualties other than, well, some ruptured eardrums and a few cases of battle fatigue. And now . . .

. . . in the midst of this damn pleasure cruise, in an operation so simple and routine that the ship could have run itself . . . some dumb GI goes over. Carelessness. That's what the ship's log will have to show, however it comes to be accounted for. Eventually *his* responsibility. Has to be. He hears an echo of himself back across the years as a plebe at the Academy, saying, tight-lipped, "No excuse, sir." His abstracted gaze wavers, then focuses again on the fatigue-green shapes massed on the decks below. How could anyone handle that ill-assorted, idle, sloppy swarm overrunning his ship? And yet: they are four thousand single, individual human lives. Hard for him to see them that way. Dangerous, too, as his training and implacable combat experience have taught him . . .

. . . but he visualizes one of them now — featureless, yet quite distinct in his mind — a single man out there, overboard, moving in his separate, isolated, slow-motion-frantic way to maintain himself on the immense rolling surface of the Pacific Ocean, with unspeakable depths slanting down and away beneath him, and nowhere, absolutely nowhere, to stand. One human life plunging into the shifting, insupportable world of water, where only motion counts. One solitary victim deprived of his human stance by some human error, by some irretrievable moment of inattention . . . *Or!* . . . was the man overboard by no accident, no casual moment's mistake or sudden vertigo, but rather by a willful, calculated plunge bent on self-destruction?

The thought strikes the Captain hard. It is too unreasonable — grotesque, even — to suppose that anyone having survived the war would corrupt that accomplishment with the desperation of a suicidal act. Yet the notion has arisen, and the Captain cannot readily dismiss it. It invades his mind, which moves at once to surround it as an alien, the way the body sends white corpuscles to resist infection. He summons his thoughts willfully back to the conditions at hand.

Question: Do the motives of the man overboard have any bearing on what is to be done — on the ship's procedures or on its Captain's initiatives? Only this, as he considers: If it was a suicidal leap, he may not stay afloat long enough for a boat to get back to him. Yet something deep in the Captain's own makeup will not support this. Once in the water, he thinks, no matter what the cause, a man will respond to the instinct for self-preservation. He will fight the sea and the threat of darkness while he can. . . .

With an effort, the Captain brings his thoughts again to the surface and fixes them on a line of reason. If the man went over from the main deck, the high freeboard of the huge vessel would have given him a hell of a long way to fall and to accelerate before impact. He could easily have been knocked cold first thing. In which case . . . And the screws . . .

Beside the point, goddammit! All of it. Beside the goddam point. Doesn't make a damn bit of difference. Man goes overboard, you lower the motor whaleboat, search, and recover him. Sensible and clear. You *do* it. That's what the goddam procedure is for!

The Captain feels braced again by the interior shift in his own spirit. He breaks his rather slack stance at the rail, swaying his body upward from the hips. He squints out. The ship has continued in the large, slow arc. The Captain estimates the swing of its bow from the initial heading at the start of the turn. Damn near sixty degrees, he figures. The OOD did say a Williamson turn, didn't he? Better shift your rudder, buddy, or you're going to waste time and a lot of ocean making the rest of the turn before you're back on reciprocal course. The Captain slaps his thigh. Then he'll have to get the motor whaleboat lowered right. Wonder if he's ever done *that*. He'll want calm water. He may need to kick away the stern at just the right time to set the boat down easy when it's least likely to capsize. If they didn't teach that to the ninety-day-wonder, he might put the damn boat crew in the ocean too.

The Captain wheels about, clearing his throat audibly, and strides back to the doorway of the bridge.

As he passes through, it seems to him the bridge is abnormally dark, the others still oddly stiffened in their positions. This could be a long and trying affair, he realizes. The thought discourages him, but he keeps his manner brisk.

"All right, Lieutenant," he announces in a tone more even and reassuring than peremptory. "I have the deck and the conn."

CHAPTER TWO

Life! Life! Thou sea-fugue, writ from east to west,
. . .

Though long deferred, though long deferred:
O'er the modern waste a dove hath whirred:
Music is Love in search of a word.

— *Sidney Lanier, "The Symphony"*

INTRO: KANCHRAPARA

On a warm day in late December of 1945, S/Sgt. LeRoy Warner received his orders sending him to Kanchrapara. He had spent the morning working at a makeshift table outside his basha, modifying the amplifier for his electric guitar to extend the range of its bass tones. He was reassembling the unit when Cpl. Wickham, who had pulled CQ for the weekend, hailed him from the path leading from the headquarters area to the mess tent.

"Hey, Warner. You lucky son-a-bitch!"

LeRoy looked up and squinted. Cpl. Wickham, a bunkmate in his basha, had stopped on the path and stood there, head cocked to one side, grinning. Behind him spread the clusters of huts and tents and dun-colored buildings of Chandranagar Air Base. Beyond were the maintenance hangars and the airstrip. Cargo planes of the Air Transport Command sat idle on their cement pads. The ATC base was nearly as quiet these days as the small Indian village a half mile away down a dusty road, the remote spot on the map of upper Assam from which the U.S. air base took its name.

"Yeah?" LeRoy said, and looked down again at his work. "What's up?"

"Orders, you lucky bastard," Wickham answered. "New list just went up. You're on it, buddy. You're shipping home."

LeRoy's heart skipped and he caught his breath, but he kept his eyes on the head of his screwdriver until the small screw it turned was seated snugly in place. Then he looked up.

"You goin' back to the Orderly Room?" he asked.

"Yeah. After chow."

"Well," LeRoy Warner said, bending down to his work again, "tell 'em I can't go until I get this amp fixed up, will ya?"

The corporal snorted his appreciation and started off again toward the mess tent. LeRoy threw another taunt after him.

"Tell 'em to cut another set of orders for my gui-tar, will ya? I ain't goin' nowhere she don't go too."

Actually, S/Sgt. Warner was having a difficult time hiding his elation. He had been stationed at Chandranagar for nearly two years as an electrical maintenance specialist, servicing the workhorse C46s and C47s that shuttled supplies from bases in the Brahmaputra Valley over the barrier of the Himalayas to China. In all that time he'd had only one extended period away from the isolation of Chandranagar. Just before the end of the war he'd been put on detached service to tour as a member of a jazz trio in one of the all-soldier shows the Air Transport Command recruited from their own CBI personnel. Together with a pianist and a drummer from the base at Barrackpore, LeRoy had rehearsed the show at headquarters near Calcutta and then circulated for performances at ATC bases throughout China, Burma, and India.

Back at his assignment on the flight line at Chandranagar, though, with operations cut to practically nothing after V-J Day, Sgt. Warner, like virtually all U.S. troops in the CBI Theater, merely went through idle routines while he waited out his turn, according to the Armed Services point system, to be shipped home for discharge.

By way of temperament and talent, however, Roy—as he had come to be called in the Army—was more fortunate than most. A lean, easy-moving Southerner from Waycross, Georgia, Roy Warner had a good-natured intensity which found its outlet in the concentration he gave to complex electrical systems and to the improvised jazz music he loved to play. While others loafed and complained about their lot as they sweated out the wait for their orders to ship home, Roy spent most of his time playing with and on his guitar. He had built and rebuilt his own electrical apparatus for the instrument, hunting up spare parts in the shop to alter one effect or another, as he was doing now.

Having secured the final screw in the housing of his amplifier, Roy gave it an affectionate pat and stood up. Cpl. Wickham had moved on to the mess tent, where most of the base personnel had already gathered for lunch. No one else was around. Midday, December 30, 1945, and he was headed home at last. He stretched both arms out straight and stiff from his sides, shut his eyes, and let his head fall back.

"Je-sus Chr-ist," he said aloud. "All-mighty!" he added after a pause.

He shook his head back into position, opened his eyes, and studied the dusty, earth-colored landscape he stood in. Chandranagar. Assam. Bengal. India. How familiar it was to him after all his time there. Two years of his life and how unlikely it still was, how strange, how alien.

"Lord, I'm ready," he said under his breath. "Get me out of here."

Orders. That would mean a staging area somewhere near a port before getting on a ship. He wondered how long that might take. No matter. He was on orders. At least his buddy, Wickham, had said so. S/Sgt. LeRoy Warner took a few tentative steps toward the Orderly Room, paused, then veered to the right instead and headed for the mess tent.

Sgt. Mark Reiter was playing the piano in the Barrackpore service club when the news reached him that he was on orders to ship home. He usually spent an hour or so at the keyboard before lunch. Mark thought of it as practicing, a habit he'd been able to carry over into the service from his years of classical training before he was drafted. But he liked to try all sorts of music when he practiced. To the off-duty GIs who liked to lounge in the service club in the late morning and listen, it was the real thing. Although he had a formal background in music, Mark Reiter had taken a general undergraduate degree in college in preference to the conservatory training his early teachers had recommended. From the beginning, his strong inclination toward improvisation had turned his musical interest into the possibilities of jazz.

That morning was typical. By mid-morning, Mark had finished his few routine clerical chores in the Special Service Office that adjoined the rec hall in the service club. Although there was nothing further for him to do, he stayed at his desk until Lt. Foley, the Special Service Officer at Barrackpore, came back from his hour-long coffee break. Shortly thereafter, Sgt. Reiter wandered out into the rec hall, stepped up onto the small platform stage where the piano stood, and began his morning practice.

Lt. Foley had been a small-time orchestra leader in New Jersey. He understood musicians. He also was a little in awe of Mark Reiter, not only because he recognized Mark's musicianship, but also because Mark was on call to play for the generals. The air base at Barrackpore, together with the larger air strip at Dum Dum, closer in, served the headquarters area of Calcutta. Sgt. Reiter was frequently summoned from command headquarters in Calcutta and across the river at Hastings Mill to entertain visiting brass and VIPs from the States. Besides, Lt. Foley enjoyed listening to Mark Reiter himself as a background to his own work during these morning practice sessions.

That morning Mark started off with some exercises — études, maybe, the lieutenant thought. Then Mark began to improvise on some chord progressions — his own ideas, probably, although the lieutenant detected some runs along a whole-tone scale that made him think of Debussy.

For his part, Mark Reiter was not thinking of Debussy or much of anything else. He didn't like to push himself very hard in these morning sessions. He let his fingers do the playing, finding their own patterns while he, too, listened. His full attention was on the keyboard when a voice almost at his elbow broke his concentration.

"Hey. Do you know *In the Mood?*"

Mark played on for a while, flicked off a few more runs, and finished with a rising arpeggio that went right off the top of the keyboard as he turned to face the questioner. He hated this sort of interruption and its presumption. At the same time, he disapproved of himself for letting it irritate him so much. The regulars who came to the rec hall to listen knew better than to butt in. This GI he'd never seen before. He looked newly minted in his fresh starched suntans. Are they still sending new replacements to the CBI? Mark wondered. He kept staring at the GI who merely grinned, unaffected, and tried again.

"You know, *In the Mood* by Glenn Miller . . . "

Mark shook his head slowly. "Yeah, I know it," he said. "That's why I can't play it. You get me the whole Miller band and maybe I'll try it. I just play the piano." He turned back to the keyboard, uneasy with his own inclination to sarcasm.

"I'm just fooling around, practicing, anyway," he added without looking back.

"You mean you just ain't in the mood yourself, Sergeant Reiter?" someone else said from behind him. Mark knew that voice. He spun around to face Sgt. Stanley Norman, physical education specialist in the Special Service Office. Stanley Norman's expression was more gleeful than wry.

"You in the mood for an ocean voyage, Sergeant Reiter?" he asked.

"Hunh?" Mark replied. "Come on. . . . " He hadn't tumbled.

"You're on orders, you old ratbone," Stanley said. "So am I."

Mark Reiter's eyes narrowed. Stanley Norman loved to joke.

"You're not kidding? You wouldn't kid me?"

"Just saw the list. You *maloom* Kanchrapara, Sahib?" Stanley's mock Hindustani had a Western drawl.

"How soon do we go?"

"Day after tomorrow," Stanley told him. "Soon as we clear the base."

Mark Reiter was suddenly aware that the GI who had interrupted his practice was still there, taking it all in. Mark swung around to the piano keyboard and struck up the rousing chorus of *The Stars and Stripes Forever*. "Three cheers for the red, white, and blue," he sang. Then he slipped neatly from the strict two-beat of the march into his own swinging version, his foot tapping out the easy 4/4 rhythm, of *In the Mood*.

Shortly after he and Mark Reiter arrived at Kanchrapara for processing, Sgt. Stanley Norman discovered that Roy Warner, the guitarist they had toured with, was already there.

Kanchrapara, an open, sprawling American base about thirty-five miles outside Calcutta, was a staging area packed with troops waiting to be assigned to ships that would carry them home. Every day new shipping orders were posted, and every day the troops crowded around the boards to search for their own names. Stanley didn't find his name or Mark's, but he did spot the name of Sgt. LeRoy Warner on the list. He wasted no time locating Roy's billeting unit and getting the three of them together again that same night for a spirited reunion. The arrangement that subsequently put the trio aboard the *General Bliss* together, despite the fact that only Roy had sufficient points at the time to qualify him for a shipping list, was also the doing of Sgt. Stanley Norman.

Stanley had a way of handling things, of getting things done. Most who knew him thought of him as an operator. Yet Stanley's dealings sprang from honest motives. It was his way to see that advantage was taken of opportunities and situations rather than of people. His family background was, rather loosely at this point, Mormon. He came from Las Vegas, Nevada, and he had a Westerner's openness about him to go with a rather bland, though not altogether innocent, optimism. Stanley did not think of himself as an operator. That was probably the secret of his small successes. A specialist in athletics and physical conditioning, he kept himself in shape and made a good appearance. As a musician he was more entrepreneur than artist, although he sang passably well and kept a fairly steady beat on the drums. He could also fake his way on string bass, as long as the tempo was reasonable and no one was listening too closely.

It didn't take long after the reunion of the trio at Kanchrapara for Stanley to engineer the deal. First he booked them to play at two Kanchrapara locations, the Red Cross and the Officers' Club. Having thus established "The Roy Warner Trio" as a performing group, Stanley went directly to the Transportation Corps Office to make his case.

Look, Stanley said in so many words, you need entertainment aboard the troopship. If we can ship out together as a trio, we'll play whenever and wherever you want us to. All we'll need is a small piano and drums — or a string bass if that would be easier. It was, and Stanley wound up plucking his fingers raw all the way across.

Somehow, Stanley made it altogether reasonable to ship them all out at once on the thin logic that they were the Roy Warner Trio, the name they had decided on because it sounded good and Roy generally stood in front when they played. The departure dates of the two recent arrivals at Kanchrapara would therefore have to be moved up to join that of their "leader."

"We'll be playing at the Officers' Club tonight," Stanley told the major in charge. "Why don't you come and hear us?" Thus Sgt. Stanley Norman banked the fires and saluted his way out.

The major did come, and, fortunately, the trio was in fine form that night. The crowd, too, was large, attentive, appreciative, and involved. Spotting the major at the rear of the club, Stanley responded by turning into a master of ceremonies and fronting the performance. Occasionally, with just enough showmanship, he switched from drums to string bass on the slow numbers, a few of which he also sang, with more taste and flair than he usually mustered.

With Stanley handling the audience, Roy and Mark felt free to improvise and explore new possibilities in familiar tunes. Roy's electrically amplified guitar, a novelty to much of his audience, filled the room with warm resonances. He spun out long choruses in his linear style, bending tones to widen his expression, especially with the blue notes he favored in his solos, the flatted thirds and fifths and sevenths he liked to linger on to tease the ear before resolving them into the following phrase.

On the piano, Mark chorded lightly behind Roy's good-natured meanders, setting up some of his sixteenth-note runs, now and then picking up and echoing an attractive figure or phrase Roy had fallen into.

At times, during his own solos, Mark was crisp, direct, playful, understated. At others, on tunes that invited extended improvisation — especially on "My Funny Valentine" and "Alone Together" and some Gershwin ballads — Mark took off into new patterns, building, working hard over the keyboard, always moving forward into his structure, increasing its complexity, searching up and farther into the tune until it soared and sang, until he and the audience who followed with him—chief among them Roy, who would be listening, intent—achieved a kind of rapture of promise fulfilled in the music. Then he'd fall back into the ensemble with Roy and Stanley that would take the tune out and give way to eager applause and shouts from their audience.

The major obviously approved, as he made clear when he summoned the trio into his office the next day to expedite arrangements. They would ship out together as an entertainment unit on the USS *General Simon P. Bliss*. In the end, as Stanley had assured everybody, it was indeed a good deal all around.

THE PLATFORM

The Roy Warner Trio had just finished playing through the lunch shifts in the transient officers' mess when the first cry of *"MAN OVERBOARD!"* went out. The room was nearly empty. Stanley had already pulled the cloth cover over the bass and zipped it up and laid the covered bass down behind the piano. He and Mark were standing to one side while Roy finished putting away his equipment. Roy squinted up at the two with a curious tilted grin but kept right on packing. Caught in the inertia of this familiar routine with him, they continued simply to watch. When the cry was repeated, though, Stanley and Mark reacted at once, looking sharply at one another.

"Jesus," Mark said.

"Let's see what's going on," said Stanley. "C'mon, Roy, let's cut out."

Roy gave his equipment a final shove into place and followed them out. The three moved rapidly through the open hatchway, down a set of ladders, through a short passageway, and out into the open air of the main deck, where they joined the numbers of GIs who were drifting along the deck and heading, in an almost leisurely fashion, toward the rail.

"Man overboard. Port side," the speakers announced. The movement to the rail quickened. Again: *"Man overboard. Port side."*

"God," Mark said, as they settled into space along the rail and peered over it at the indifferent sea. "Which side is port? Is this it?"

"Yeah," Roy told him. "Starboard's right side, port's left. This is it."

"Don't see anything," Stanley said in a moment. He leaned out over the railing and took an exaggerated look back along the stern of the ship, then back farther along its wake. All along the rail others were doing the same. When he pulled back in, he was aware of more men crowding up behind them and beginning to press forward in their attempt to see. There was curiously little talk above the level of murmur, only the common question here and there: "See him? Can you see him?" Stanley leaned back the other way and took stock of their situation.

"What do you say we get out of here," he said to his companions. "Can't see anything anyway. Let's go back to our place on the fantail. Ought to see good from there." He waited to leave until he got nods from both Roy and Mark.

It took some polite pushing and turning sideways to work their way through the GIs behind them who were pressing in to get the places they were vacating. When they reached the clearer inner section of the deck, GIs were milling and moving about in a confusion of purpose. The three had to wend their way through, bumping and side-stepping, one behind the other, toward the rear of the ship. They were weaving past a speaker when it blared with the instructions for the duty boat crew. Mark, still leading, held up while the other two came abreast.

"Still want to try to make it?" Mark asked.

"Sure," said Stanley. "Come on." And he moved ahead, Mark and Roy following.

The place on the fantail they had in mind was a kind of platform on a rise above the main deck, set back against the bulkhead and accessible only by a small, steep, open stairway which had a bar and latch obstructing passage at the bottom. Ordinarily, this barrier was sufficient to discourage transient personnel from entering. Apparently, the platform was for use in the line of some shipboard duty, although it was hard to imagine what since it didn't lead anywhere beyond itself and was clear of any kind of equipment. Earlier in the voyage, the Roy Warner Trio had been permitted to set up and play there a number of times. It had turned out well as an improvised bandstand with the listening troops gathered in the spacious area below where the main deck gave onto the open elliptical curve of the fantail.

The congestion on the deck increased as they got closer. As a result, the last dozen yards or so before the main deck opened onto the fantail became a bottleneck, and they simply moved along in a shuffling pack of fatigue-clad bodies, jammed too tightly together at that point to raise or lower an arm.

Yet there was no undue shoving, no pushing in that press, no complaint or even a sense of urgency. The atmosphere of regulated ease on the *General Bliss* prevailed in spite of this dramatic rupture of the shipboard routine. The GIs simply went with the crowd at the bottleneck.

Their patience may also have been the result of unreality and disbelief in the whole occasion. Maybe it was just a drill, like the lifeboat drill they had gone through on the second day out. There were not supposed to be real surprises in the military. Someone was always in charge. Man overboard? For the Navy that must be linked to military orders and regulations. "Duty boat crew, lay up to number two lifeboat," the general announcement system had said. Good. The Navy was already moving into its routine, even as the disorganized GIs crowded together along the decks seeking a vantage point. Crowded but orderly.

In time, the temporary bottleneck broke into the open deck area of the fantail, and each man was free once again, within the larger confines of the troopship, to move as an individual. The Roy Warner Trio, regrouping as they emerged from the anonymity of the pack, moved to the left along the bulkhead and pulled up at the barrier to the stairway leading up to the platform.

"C'mon," Roy said. Dropping to his hands and knees, he squeezed under the bar, onto the ladder-like stairs, and clambered up to the platform. There he stood, hands on hips, surveying the situation. The others followed suit until the three stood side by side, looking out, the solid bulkhead rising behind them. They couldn't see down the steep sides of the ship, as they had earlier at the railing, but they now had a prospect that commanded a continuous semicircle of ocean clear to the horizon.

Mark was the first to speak. "Doesn't look like anyone sees him," he said. Nothing in the actions of the GIs crowding at the rail around the fantail indicated a sighting. There was no focus of attention, no center of excitement, no concerted pointing or shouting.

"No," said Stanley, "but we're still turning around. Look at the wake." The churning white turbulence had spread over the most recent stretch of ocean and turned to a less agitated bluish-white where the wake continued to bend and sweep to the right. "Maybe they can see him from up where the Captain is. What do you call it?"

"The bridge," Mark told him. Earlier, as they had made their way from the railing, he had shot a glance up there, instinctively thinking that was where the responsibility that spoke in the disembodied voices should show itself, but no one had been visible from that angle. The blank, sun-reflecting windows had looked as opaque, indifferent, and inscrutable as ever.

Almost in league with his thoughts at that instant, the speakers came to life:

"*This is the Captain speaking.*"

Mark almost came to attention.

"*We have a report of a man overboard, port side. All transient personnel are requested to stay where you are.*" The message was repeated, with an addition: "*Those on the port side, we ask your help in locating the man overboard.*"

All transient personnel, Mark was thinking. That's every last one of us — you too, Mr. Captain of the *General Bliss* — we're all transient personnel. . . .

"There's your answer," Roy said. "Man overboard, and nobody's seen him. At least the Captain hasn't."

"Technically speaking, Mon Capitaine," Stanley said in a deferential tone, "we are no longer on the port side, but we'll try to locate your man anyway." Roy grinned.

Mark didn't. "God," he said, almost under his breath. "Can you imagine some guy out there in the ocean? Out there," he put a hand loosely across his mouth, "in all that . . . water?"

All three faced out and away, looking in long, slow sweeps across the wake, which continued to angle away as the *General Bliss* pushed farther into its turn. Their thoughts shuttled in silence. The scene before them seemed preternaturally bright. It was awesome. It was beautiful. It was a spectacle of frictionless stress. It was equally a vista of restless peace.

Roy Warner said, "You'd need binoculars to see anything out there."

Mark Reiter said, "You could never see that through binoculars."

Stanley Norman sighed and said, "Well, since we're supposed to stay where we are, we might as well get comfortable." He slumped gently to the platform and sat with his back against the bulkhead, his legs sprawled out in front of him. In a moment, Roy, and then Mark, did likewise. They continued to look out over the milling crowd of GIs on the fantail below them, and out to the sea beyond.

It was curiously similar to the times in the weeks before when they had been there above the fantail playing for the entertainment of the troops, only now the GIs gathered below were oblivious to them, their attention focused not on the jazz improvisations of the Roy Warner Trio but this time in the opposite direction, out toward the surrounding ocean and the dark phantasm of a man, quite like themselves, overboard and adrift in the illimitable, rocking, counter-rhythms of the sea.

For a while, except for the indistinct sounds of low conversations rising from the groups below, mixing with the cool whisper of the wind past their ears, there was stillness and silence on the platform. Then the Roy Warner Trio began to talk together, ad lib, opening up and following out their themes, as they often did. Deliberately. Almost in tempo.

TRIO

ROY (with a tilt of the head): Where do you suppose that boat is — that duty boat they said on the p.a.?

STANLEY (explaining): Must be one of those lifeboats with the cranes. The big ones, you know, with the hoists.

MARK (considering): Taking them a long time to get it launched. Looks to me like they should have done that first thing — get a motor launch out to find him and pick him up. You can't do that with the whole troopship.

ROY: We'll see it when they get it down. They must know what they're doin'.

MARK: God, there's a lot of water out there. Can you imagine being in the ocean and watching the ship pull away and leave you there? How far do you suppose we are from where he went over? I wonder if they have a system to figure that out. I don't see how they can. Everything drifts and moves around. How can you tell anything about where we are — or where we were then — or where he is by now? He may be a couple miles back by now. Even while we're turning we're slipping around.

ROY: Well, you can tell by the wake where we've been. He ought to be somewhere around that, right? Even if he's tryin' to swim, he can't move very far.

MARK: I don't know. There are currents out there. Even the wake is drifting. You can't trust that to be where it was at first. It's like vapor trails from planes.

ROY: But the wake stays straight out there, all the way — all the way back. Until where we started to turn, anyway.

MARK (abruptly): You know, I'll bet he jumped.

STANLEY: Why? He probably slipped and fell. That'd be easy.

ROY: Or someone could have pushed him over.

MARK: I'll bet he jumped.

STANLEY: Why would he do that?

MARK: I don't know. Maybe he doesn't know himself. Maybe there isn't any reason. But I'll tell you the truth: I've come close to jumping — a number of times. I couldn't tell you why. Haven't you?

STANLEY: Are you crazy? Of course I haven't. That's the last thing I'd do. What would I do that for? I'd push everyone else on this boat over before I'd go. You serious?

MARK: Sure I'm serious. Sometimes when I've been on the lower deck — you know, where you come out from chow. Looking at the water there, so close to it, rushing by. I don't have any trouble up on this deck, really. I'm no high diver. But I love that water. Especially down there, leaning over the rail, watching that water. I don't know why. It's like the water wants me. I've come pretty close to jumping. I really don't know why.

ROY: Yeah. I know what you mean. Me too, a couple of times. It's from bein' bored, I think. Was for me. At least goin' over would be — *doin'* somethin'. It'd be excitin'. Just to go over. You don't think of what would really happen. You just think for a minute you might do it. Go right over into the water. It's my legs, really, want me to do it.

MARK: I think he jumped. It's like being hypnotized and someone telling you to do something you wouldn't do otherwise, that wouldn't make sense if you were, ahh . . . I don't know. I think I could have done it. But I don't know. How can you tell? I think of a lot of crazy things I might do. I hardly ever do them.

STANLEY: Well, I don't think he jumped. Everybody thinks about doing things like that, but you've got to be out of your skull to really do them. Course, he might be a psycho. There's probably plenty of Section Eights on board. But I just think he slipped or something and fell. An accident. Four thousand dumb GIs, you're going to have some accidents. Horsing around, maybe. Or a fight, even. Someone could have pushed him. I just can't see how a guy who's going home would jump off the troopship that's taking him. It could have happened to anybody. To one of us, you know? It really could. You take your chances. You play the odds.

MARK: You can play those odds when you get back home to Las Vegas, Stanley. Different kind of odds here on the *General Bliss*.

ROY: Oddballs, you mean. Everybody on the ship mopin' around all day, jus' thinkin' his own thoughts.

MARK: Or not thinking about anything at all. No thoughts. Empty.

STANLEY: Or women, huh? What GIs are *always* thinking about. Women.

MARK: That what you mean by odd*balls*, Roy?

ROY: Could be. Some guy all worked up over his woman left him, took off with some other joe. Maybe got a dear john letter in that last mail call at Kanchrapara. Or fell for some Anglo-Indian chick and had to leave her behind. No joke. Jus' been mopin' around thinkin' about it ever since. That could do it. Finally gets on top of him and he jumps. Could be.

MARK: Yes. Yes. Love and death. The old one-two.

STANLEY: On the *General Bliss*? Come on!

ROY: Maybe if you'd seen a lot of action. Real stuff, I mean. If you earned your battle stars by real fightin'. Not like us, but puttin' it on the line every day, livin' with it — like those guys we talked to in Bhamo, remember? Man, that'd knock me all out of whack. Can you imagine sittin' on your tail on this boat all this time doin' nothin' all day — nothin' but thinkin' about that stuff. You'd have to do *somethin'*. Some of those guys I knew on the flight line at Chandranagar, I'm tellin' you, they were out of it most of the time, those old C46s and '47s gettin' older every time out, and we never had any chance to really check 'em out — did the best we could, that's all — and they'd have to rev 'em up and if a prop or somethin' didn't fall off, there they'd go, takin' off thinkin' how many more times can I push my luck before I go down in those damn Himalayas like so many guys already, how many more missions, haulin' junk to China — PX crap, for chrissake, that's what really got to 'em — Colgate's damn toothpaste and condoms and booze for the officers' clubs — well, the booze was worth it — the rubbers too, I suppose . . .

STANLEY: Us, too, huh, Roy? Hauling us over the hump, too.

ROY: Naw. Not the same. Those jockeys that flew us were on milk runs. No sweat. Like that hot-rod in Chungking. Captain Shanghai. Geez.

MARK: That lunatic. I wonder where he is by now.

STANLEY: You kidding? He's been stateside since August, I bet. He had the points then, didn't he? Just waiting around for Shanghai to open up. He's probably in Vegas, cleaning up at the tables.

MARK: How about Captain Shanghai for our man overboard?

ROY: Forget it.

STANLEY: He could have been the guy who pushed him.

ROY: Naw. I'm talkin' about these real pilots, the guys that took all the shit and kept on flyin'. The weird thing is that the more they flew, the more they had to keep 'em flyin' . . .

MARK: *Sustineo Alas.* Keesler Field, Mississippi.

ROY: . . . They could be real trouble when they weren't flyin'. Nothin' else to do on those bases up there in Assam. Flyin' the damn Hump got to be better than sittin' around thinkin' about it. I mean those guys would have a hell of a time sittin' it out on this boat. Hard enough for me.

STANLEY: Come on, Roy. We never had it so good. So lots of guys had it rougher than we did. So we didn't get shot at. So we play music for the guys who did. So maybe there's a difference and maybe there isn't. We all been in India and Burma and China and we all sweated the war and came out on this side and now we're going home. We're all in the same boat, you know? His Majesty's Ship, the USS *General Simon P. Bliss*, which I am mighty glad to be on. I mean, we all came up the same gangplank in Calcutta, didn't we? And if we are good lads and don't screw up by jumping, or f-a-l-l-i-n-g overboard, I figure we're all going to get off at the same place on the solid turf of the U. S. of A., every ratbone one of us, and there you are, Amen. . . . I'll go along with this much, though. I'm sure glad we worked this trio deal on the ship. I *would* hate to be putting in all of this time with nothin' to do but goof off and shoot the breeze or play cards like those zombies in the officers' mess . . .

MARK: . . . or shoot craps down in the head? . . .

STANLEY: . . . or watch the Pacific Ocean go past so you can think about jumping into it. We've got a good deal, lads, and you know it.

ROY: Yeah, yeah, O.K. But that's not what I'm talkin' about. I mean the way it got to be after a while in India. Everybody felt it after a while — you too, Stanley. I'm talkin' about some of those guys who really had it, that could have gone overboard just from doin' nothin'.

MARK: It was loneliness, Roy. That's what it was. That's really what it was. I'd get to feeling like everybody in the world was lonely for something they couldn't have, and that would become the thing they wanted most in the world, because of the war, because of being where they didn't want to be. Because I was lonely that way myself. Everybody was. . . . I think you're right about India, though. The loneliness was worse because of India. Sometimes I thought getting out of India was more important than getting out of the Army. Now I don't know. I've been thinking about it, and it's different already. I'm out of India all right, but I'm already lonely for *it*! I'm taking it home with me. Can't help it. I've been thinking more about India than I have about home. It just sticks with me. It's all tied up with that loneliness. For so long. How's anyone going to be when he isn't lonely anymore? I forget what it's like. I really forget. Maybe we'll always be lonely. Like India, even though we're back in the States.

STANLEY: You trying to tell me a GI jumps overboard because he's lonesome?

MARK: Not lonesome, Stanley. *Lonely*. There's a difference, I think. *Lonely* is more basic. Like the way it is, rather than just how you feel. No. That isn't right. It's just that you got so used to feeling you didn't belong in *India*. It made you all the more lonely for where you were thinking all the time you ought to be. And it's still here with us on the boat. Half way home — that's far enough so that India ought to be finished. But it's a lot more real to me than what I'm going home to. Everything that happened in India was real. The things that *didn't* happen, too. That's part of it. I think that's what Roy's talking about, aren't you, Roy? Like you've got to have something to do after a while to keep from being afraid of what hasn't happened yet. I think it's that loneliness we're afraid of. That's what it really is.

ROY: Think of it this way, Stanley: What if you were always goin' to feel like you felt durin' the war in the CBI. Or thought you couldn't ever get out of that . . . loneliness, or whatever it is, after you got back to the States.

STANLEY: So you jump overboard? In the middle of the Pacific Ocean?

ROY: Come on, Stanley. You know what we're talkin' about.

STANLEY (taking over): O.K. O.K. O.K. Sure I do. But I don't know if you guys do. What you're talking about is women, man. If you're really lonesome, that's what you're talking about. Why don't you just say so? Me, too, friends and neighbors. The United States of America is full of nice, pretty, soft, ever-lovin', female-type United States women. *That's* what they don't have in India. And that's what *this* ratbone was lonesome for all over the CB and I. You can call it loneliness or whatever you want. I call it women. And they're out there waiting for us. Sisters, mothers, aunties; girlfriends, ladies of the night, movi-stars, sweethearts; lover, when you're near me, I can hear you speak my name; wives, maybe, even, till death do us part, right, Mark? I love all them women and I'm ready to let them all love me, all day, all night, Marianne. And I don't think it can possibly be as good as I think it is going to be. It's all those women, waiting. The cause of all that loneliness; the cure for all that loneliness. Am I right? What do you say, Roy?

ROY (approvingly): I say you got a point.

MARK (ceremoniously): Sergeant Norman rides again. Look out, ladies. Here comes Norman the Mormon, Lord Stanley, the scourge of India, China, Burma, and all points East, sex-mad and love-starved. It'll be the second Norman Conquest.

STANLEY (nodding slowly): Think about it.

—STANLEY'S SOLO—

"It's all those women waiting . . ."

. . . All those women, hmm? Well, they're there all right, but there's only just those two kinds. Those who wait. Those who don't. The same old split right down the middle. Hah! that's a laugh. It shows which kind I've got on *my* mind—the whores of Babylon: "Sodom and Gomorrah / Who cares about tomorrah." That's old Brother Catmull and his Mormon humor. What a drag. "Stand firm against the Devil, young man!" he says, and all the time he's raking it in, putting up those motels and casinos: "See all that empty land out there to the south? You think that's just desert sand? I say it's lust dust. It's going to be bigger than Fremont Street. Going to be rich hotels, bright lights, and casinos." And naked women. And money. If there's anything more seductive than money, it's the women. Anything more seductive than women, it's the money. Put them all together they spell M-o-t-h-e-r, the name that means the world to me. Come, Come, Ye Saints. I'm Comin', Virginia. When You Come to the End of a Perfect Lay. Those showgirls, I'll never understand them. There's only one kind at night. On the job. Spangles and make-up and big gorgeous jiggling breasts. Those long legs. You just want to spread them. That soft inside part of the thighs. 'Creamy thighs' they always call them in those books. Creamy pants is more like it. Sitting there trying to think nice clean thoughts with a hard-on about to split your zipper. Beautiful female bodies. The Lord's blessed handiwork. Trying not to think "fuck" or anything else like the stuff all over the walls in the toilets. It felt good, though, when you really could crowd out those words. Nothing like righteousness, Brother Norman. Felt cheated, too. Felt false. Either way. You've Got Me in Between / The Devil and the Deep Blue Sea. Wayne Madsen—Brother Madsen—and me. That time just before we got drafted, way down in front, looking right up at them. I could hardly swallow all night. All the words—both kinds— stuck right there in my throat. Trying to be cool, with my eyes popping out. Afraid to blink. Or to cross my legs. Or uncross my legs. Wayne sitting there grinning, saying 'O My' every once in a while. All I could say, somewhere down inside my mouth, was Jesus. Jesus." That seemed all right. You could take it either way. . . . Sex . . .

. . . that GI and that little Anglo-Indian girl in the Barrackpore latrine. Jesus! I still can't believe it. Middle of the night. Half asleep. Trying to stay that way. I Didn't Know What Time It Was / Then I

Met You. Getting up to take a leak. Reach through the mosquito netting for the flashlight. Get up and stagger out of the basha. Only my shorts on. Dark. Warm. Humid. Night smells of India. Sweat. Along the path, following the ray of the flashlight. Still half-lidded, dreamy. Trying not to wake up too much. Holding back pressure on the bladder. Up the mound to the latrine. Step in the open doorway and get shocked awake. Just stand there, mouth open. There they are, screwing away like mad right on the can. Or he is. Her sitting, slumped leaning back. Painted up like a clown. I'll never forget her face—that lascivious girl-whore face. That slight smirk. My flashlight on them like a spotlight on a performance. Everything else dark, blackout. Song of India. The latrine smells. Her looking right at me, over his shoulder, while he pumped away. Her smoking that damn cigarette! Was that what he paid her with? She'd take a slow drag and hold it away while she blew the smoke out toward the ceiling. Her chin up. Her eyes on me. Eyes full of—what? Challenge? No. Indifference? Lust? No, that was him, the GI, grunting and humping away. Contempt. Was that it? How long did I stand there watching? Her watching me over him. Skirt way up. Legs spread. Creamy thighs. Supple, taking his grunting thrusts. Eyes looking at me. Blinking slowly, like a cat. Latrine stink mixing with the night air in the open doorway. My own body hot, damp. India. The GI with his pants and shorts down around his ankles. Khaki shirt soaked with sweat up the back. Skinny white buttocks coming up every time he arched his back. Head tucked down. Who was he? Then he pulls away. Rocks back on his haunches. Twists toward me, breathing hard. A guy I never saw before. Or after. He swallows hard. He says: "Hey buddy. Do ya mind?" Just like that. Can't look him in the face. Can only look down at his cock, blood red, wet, up like a fist, in the flashlight. "Oh," I think I said. "Sorry." Know I said something, but it was like a voice coming from outside me—I flipped off the flashlight. Still I couldn't move. It was hard to do anything. Just stood there in the doorway. Looking into the dark. He started grunting and moaning again. Nothing to see but the glow of the damn cigarette. Whenever she took a drag it lit her young whore face. Then it went up, a dull red point in the latrine air. Nothing else but sounds, smells, darkness. I backed out into the night. Stunned, the rest of that bad night. Still stunned thinking about it . . .

. . . in the daytime, though, everything's different. Like right now, in this bright daylight. Bright as Nevada desert. They ought to find that guy out there. They'll get him. But think if he went overboard at night. If he was out there in the dark. Las Vegas in the daylight — that's different. My Vegas. The colors of the desert. The sand hills, the mountains. Red rock, rust colors, tan khaki. Dry. The air on your skin. Nose, lips, breathing dryness. Those night women in the daytime, when you'd see them around town. Shopping for groceries. Or the drug store. Just walking on the sidewalk. Nice as pie, most of them. Some sluts, no matter what time of day. Most, nice, though, with the stage make-up off. Dancers, maybe, the way they moved, but that's all. Nice-looking girls. It made you wonder . . .

. . . the other kind. The LDS girls in the Ward. Sarah. Gertrude. Fern. LeeAnn. Marry them. Playing around with Sarah after Primary. Horsing around, but that's all. Wrestling, though, and their bodies. Mine too. But that's all. Well, that time with Gertrude in the grass behind the Ward House when I got to feeling her too much. She loved it. And then she got mad. Red-in-the-face mad. I'll never forget her. Suddenly beating me with her fist. The others watching. Marry them. What else? Temple wedding. For time and all eternity. How comforting. How ultimate. How reassuring. How dull.

That girl in Salt Lake City, though, while I was at Kearns. Carole. I could settle for someone like her. Lucky break meeting her at that dance hall. The Coconut Grove. Some deal: men on one side, girls on the other. "Want to dance?" Just like that. All those dumb ratbones standing around. Best-looking girl in the place. You just go over and ask her. What else? "Sure, that's what I came for," she says. Pretty sharp. Good kid. Nice body. Put it right up to me when we danced. Plenty of nerve. Not bold, though. Good Mormon girl. Good time. Good night. The next time the whole family. Always the family. Come in from the base on the Kearns bus, and she meets me at the depot. Great. What'll we do — show? eat? Sure, but first the family. First, a word from our sponsor. All night with the family — three brothers, two sisters, and another one coming. All night Monopoly with the family. Do not pass go. Do not make pass. Here comes Mother with the food. More punch and cookies, Stanley? What — a hotel on Park Place! That Carole was pretty sharp, though. She knew the whole deal.

Pretty good in the car, too, when she took me back to the depot. Face it: I loved the whole thing that night, once I got over the first sense of betrayal. Loved it. Great family. Neat girl. Until I was back out in the barracks in Kearns. Felt full. Felt empty. Lonelier than ever. Felt cheated. Marry them? Sure. What else? What I need, probably. Look up Carole again. Move to Salt Lake maybe. No. Too close. Better stay in Las Vegas. Sarah's ready. Marry Sarah. A piece of land north of town. Ranch. Start a business. Some kind of agency. Real estate, maybe, like Wayne's old man. "Can't miss with real estate in this town, boys. Best place in the country to make it big. Can't miss with the casinos. Just stay legitimate. All that money's going to need us Mormons. Home folks you can trust to take care of it." Everyone's going to need agents. I can represent entertainers. Make a pile booking musicians. Big bands. Singers. Movie stars. Radio comedians. Show girls. Get married and have my own family. Kids. Hell, I don't know. Better make up my mind. Look out, ladies. Here comes Lord Stanley. Norman the Mormon. Hah! Joseph Smith or Brigham Young, ladies? What'll you have? Two breeds of cat there. Heads, Brigham Young; tails, Joseph Smith. Or I could steal the coin, screw around, and go to the Devil. Which sounds better? I don't know. All those women. And only those two kinds. Somehow, somewhere, there ought to be a third.

—ROY'S SOLO—

"I say, you got a point. . ."

. . . Leave it to Stanley with the little dick and the big ideas, but he's got a point all right, there's goin' to be all those women, lord yes, and here we come. Still, that's not the whole thing either, it just stays on your mind. They think I was screwin' old Rita in the service club storeroom while we were rehearsin' the show in Barrackpore, well, let 'em go on thinkin', it didn't hurt 'em then and it won't hurt 'em now. She was nice all right, and she knew a thing or two, I'll say that, with those nice high, brown, Anglo-Indian tits, her skin all smooth brown like an all-over Florida tan, those dark nipples standin' out firm, almost as stiff as me, I wonder if it feels anything the same, that was a surprise when I opened her blouse, her nipples bein' so big and dark, and her with the British talk, "I cahn't let you dew that, LeRoy, I just cahn't." Nothin' else too big, she was tall, about to here, nice, and that tight skinny ass, all tensed when I'd slide down with both hands and pull her up close, hot dog, and rub slow back and forth, those big brown eyes, dark as her nipples, watchin' me close. She liked it fine, rather do it with me than that sorry excuse for a first lieutenant she worked for with his tongue hangin' out pantin' after her, tryin' to pat-ass every time she flicked by, the jerk. She liked me well enough right off I could tell, good thing, no need to waste time with old Rita, second mornin' is all it took, coffee break, huh! — was the storeroom her idea or mine, I can't remember. Didn't matter, probably both, she was pretty cute all right, knew a thing or two, nice girl, really, easy enough with me but made it tough on those poor Barrackpore bastards. She liked the guitar, always watched my fingers when I played, I could tell that really got to her, "those long ahtistic finguz," she'd say and I could hardly be anything but careful and gentle after that. She knew what she was doin' I guess, but why she wouldn't lay down on that old cot and why she wouldn't let me put it in, I suppose it really was some sort of principle like she always tried to say, but it didn't sound right, savin' herself for some British export businessman she was supposed to be engaged to — engaged, hell, and him due back from England any old time, like there wasn't even a war goin' on, I still don't know whether to believe that one, but she made it sound like she believed it all right, what a Limey con artist he must have been, if she was tellin' it straight . . .

. . . Poor Rita, anyway, what did she have goin' for her except that deep look in her eyes and that skin, so smooth and brown and nice all over, and those full tiltin' breasts swellin' up at you, and skinny legs, I didn't mind, and that tight skinny ass, and a nice easy way with everything. Never knew a woman could handle a man that nice, like she knew it as well as I did the way she played with it, lord, even if she wouldn't lay down, wouldn't let me put it in, who cares, the way she handled me, what she wanted to do with it, even that first time when I unbuttoned and she took it out, real cool, "What have yew gaht in theyah, Leroy?" smilin' that little smile, and then her eyes darker and deeper all of sudden when she saw me and her hands eager and full of gentleness and then leadin' my hand to her place, "your ahtistic finguz," and the other time later, that was really beautiful how she knew what would feel best, both of us so nice, lord, and her lettin' me, wantin' me to . . .

. . . Hell, she had a lot more goin' for her than she let herself believe, that was her trouble. Bein' Anglo-Indian though, what could she do, caught in the middle, dyin' to be British, no place with the wogs, nowhere to fit, what can you do, smart good-lookin' educated chick, talkin' British, *thinkin'* British, and all anyone'll do is use her and spit on her, like some Limey tells her they're engaged, what a crock, no British is goin' to engage any Anglo-Indian except for ass, Americans just as bad. Poor Rita, what's she got to hope for? Talk about *lonely*, you could see it in her dark eyes, not in the storeroom, maybe, but all the rest of the time, well, maybe there too, sad even when she smiled and kind of lookin' in as much as lookin' out most of the time — contempt too, a lot of the time, like when that fat-ass lieutenant thought he was crackin' wise and makin' points and she'd give it back so neat he didn't even feel the knife, she was cool all right, and what kind of a life has she got to hope for now the British and Americans are pullin' out and she's stuck in India, which is where I guess she belongs but she can't settle for that, there's nobody'll want her for good, really, unless maybe some Anglo-Indian guy, but he'd be in the same fix and she's got nothin' but contempt for all of them too, along with herself — that half and half business, it's almost worse than bein' one of those untouchable Hindus, well, no, I suppose she's got that British exporter at least, or says she does, and what else has she got to hang on to? Maybe it'll work, at least she's got to think so — even if she made him up, some kind of fantasy she needed to make up. Still, maybe she *could* get some British guy, she's sure good enough, lord, and he could export *her*. What I hope is that I helped make it OK for a while with her, anyway she liked me and we liked each other there, very hot, very nice, even with no screwin', who needs it with Rita, but you guys can think whatever you want, it's O.K. with me, I know she went into the storeroom with me because I was only goin' to be there a while. You guys were out of luck bein' stationed there, all she could do was tease the local crowd, but she did dig my guitar, that started it, and my long finguz. Poor Rita. If you're lookin' for a real long-term case of the lonelies, Mark, try old Rita—did I make her less lonely or more lonely I wonder . . .

. . . Don't have to wonder about that little Khasi woman at the rest camp in Shillong, that's for sure. Singin' that queer little song and grinnin' all the time we were goin' at it on the mat with that high little-girl voice in my ear and humpin' and buckin' in rhythm like she was just washin' clothes or somethin', that was a new one, while her old man who set me up took the loot and stood outside, I'd have liked it better without him around, damn pimps, especially the little kids, "jig-jig sahib?" every time they see an American uniform, what a bunch of suckers we are, I really hated that, but her singin' to me while we were doin' it, weird, that was nice . . .

. . . Nancy, though. What about Nancy? Findin' her there in the Red Cross at Tezpur, look up from the guitar and, lord, there is Nancy Hamilton herself smilin' at me like we neither one of us ever left Waycross, except for the uniforms, that was strange, her in the Red Cross uniform, I guess I said that too often, but she did look so neat in it like always—not exactly pretty, nobody in Waycross ever thought Nancy was pretty, exactly, but I always liked the way she looked. Well, I never thought about her that much in school, she was too smart and got good grades all the time and didn't go out like the rest of us much except to the big deal dances with long dresses like that last one when we were seniors, I remember her then with that poor jerk Ben Pimske, Ben Pimply we used to call him, he must have asked her and she was too nice to say no. She didn't need long dresses though, not with those legs, when we'd watch girls' gym classes and pick out the best, hah, like the dumb yearbook election—best dancer, best personality, best sense of humor, best dresser—only we made it best tits, best ass, best lay, etc., Nancy was always up for best legs, her and Gladys Neff. But that was all, you just didn't think of Nancy Hamilton that way, the way you *always* thought about old Glad-ass, those legs always leadin' you on to everything else, maybe Nancy was too neat or you thought she was too smart to get into that sort of stuff, as if maybe she never took her clothes off, even in those tight little gym suits it was like she was dressed up for school . . .

. . . but there she was in Tezpur, and what a difference, the years since I'd seen her, since she went to college, that really made a differ-

ence all right, anyway she wasn't a high school kid any more, that's
for sure. I didn't know until that night in Tezpur how much I missed
everybody back in Waycross, well it wasn't them as much as us, just
the two of us that night, it seemed so natural the two of us together
first there in the Red Cross, drinkin' coffee, talkin' about everybody
we could think of, where they were, what they were doin', like we'd
known each other all our lives, which we practically have, I guess, and
then back in her room talkin' all night long, findin' out everything
about each other, what we really thought about this and that, what
we wanted to do after the war. I never told anyone else before how it
feels with my guitar goin' through the amplifier like my whole damn
nervous system is turned on and the electricity alive all the way from
the music in my gut through all those tight circuits and hearin' my
sound — feelin' it, really — comin' back, bigger than I am, bigger than
life, like the electricity itself, out of that speaker — and me surprised all
night to hear myself sayin' those things, but she *knew* what I was sayin',
knew all the way. I never felt so good talkin' with anyone as that night
with Nancy. Guess I didn't know how homesick I was. Her too. She
came close to cryin' that once and I put my arms around her and we
held each other close for that long time without talkin', like we'd come
home again with each other. Well, I couldn't help gettin' ideas, she felt
so good, and I didn't know what kind of messages she was sendin'
when she went in to put on her robe, was she gettin' ready for bed and
if so were we supposed to go to bed together and live happy ever after,
or was I supposed to cut out, like she was afraid I might get out of
hand, she must have felt me gettin' hard while we were holdin' each
other so close so she was lettin' me know she was goin' to bed and it
was time for me to think about leavin', I don't know, as near as I can
figure she really just wanted to get out of that American Red Cross
uniform and into Nancy Hamilton of Waycross, Georgia, just like she
said, and I guess I *was* the only guy she'd felt that comfortable with
and able to be herself with since she'd got to India, and I believed her,
I guess I still do. If I missed some giant cue she was throwin' me with
that gettin'-into-something-more-comfortable business, I guess I must
have passed up the most glorious night of my life or somethin', but
no, that wasn't it, that just wasn't what we had goin' that night. If I'd
had the chance to stay around Tezpur though instead of moving out

with the show the next day we could have got on to a lot of things later, if I had any doubts that first letter when I got back to Chandranagar settled it. I never got a letter like that from anyone, she sure knows how to write, it's like listenin' to music readin' that letter, makes me feel all over again like the two of us talkin', laughin', cryin', holdin' on to each other that night, and like I felt when I finally left, the sky just startin' to get light outside, holdin' on to her again and tellin' her how good I felt and kissin' her and she was kissin' me just the same way, kind of tired, I guess, I know I was, and not sexy but real warm and relaxed and sleepy, like it ought to be when you kiss someone goodnight that you feel that good with, and you mean it . . .

. . . she didn't answer that last letter, but maybe she didn't get it before she left. That doesn't matter, she'll be in Waycross when I get home, she better be, I sure will be glad to see her. I wonder where we go with it, can't get back to that night in Tezpur, I suppose, it won't be like bein' in India together, it'll be back in Waycross, but I don't know — loneliness, huh — we both know somethin' about that. Could be even better. Nobody else in Waycross is goin' to know what the hell I'm talkin' about if I try to tell them — or hear what I'm tryin' to play for that matter, but Nancy will. Nancy Hamilton, maybe, knows what I mean already better than anyone else.

—MARK'S SOLO—

" . . . *sex-mad and love-starved. . .* "

. . . Think about it? Try *not* to think about it! It's always there, waiting. All that longing. Has the word *long* in it. Love is longing but sex is shorting. Sex comes in short pants. Jokes for Stanley, ONE-two-THREE-four, ONE-two-THREE-four. Sixteenth-notes streamlined in Roy's glissandos, take it, Roy, and run, I'll back you up and bring it all around. Take Rita, Roy. Take her on the run while I sit here and chord in E-flat major, backing up. Back and fill. The only time I thought I might, she smiled and said I was a child, said what I needed was "a stick of bahley sugah," then she patted me on the head. That should have hurt, but maybe she was right. Was I relieved? I probably liked it, but it didn't stop me thinking about it, wanting her to want me just as much. Want and need. Wanton need. The Lord is my shepherd; I shall not want. Suffer little children, and forbid them not, to come unto me. It's so much loneliness and having to be alone. All alone / by the telephone. In the morning sow thy seed, and in the evening withhold not thy hand . . .

. . . millions of lonely hard-up GIs all over the world, all jerk — no, *jacking* off, I never thought of it before, it's like a jack-in-the-box, no, a jack-*not*-in-the-box, jack-be-nimble-jack-be-quick, jack-without-jill-went-up-the-hill, but really, I never thought, it's like jack in jacking up a car, and when it gets there, the soft implosions inside your ears where only you can hear, how can you share that kind of inward climax with someone else? Like music, can you ever share the music that *you* hear with anybody else or is it always one and one, even if you're listening together? Or like Stanley counting, you can see him, ONE-two-THREE-four, ONE-two-THREE-four, how would he do a waltz I wonder, like "Lover" in three-four time the way it's written, it would come out two-beat somehow, three times four could always come out twelve, like those Indian percussionists — I'll swear they were working out their stuff in full sixteens while we do well to think in twos and fours, and here I'm thinking one times two can only stay two separate ones . . .

. . . Well I'm a ding-dong Daddy from Dumas / and you oughtta see me strut my stuff —

— a poor player who struts and frets his hour upon the stage and then is heard no more. 'Tis a tale told by an idiot, full of sound and fury —

— Roy's the one who plays on frets, who struts, his fingers long and bent and calloused, always working on his callouses, no wonder, grooving on those wire strings, sliding up and down those strings the way he chords, active with his mouth, almost saying the sounds as they occur, his shoulders too, the left one anyway, hunching up, and when he solos how the fingers of his left hand lift and fall so quick and taut, running like a nervous spider up and down those strings — they're really wires — like spiders strutting up and down those frets. My keyboard is a different world than his, the keys laid out in black and white, consecutive and clean. They formulate my mind, the way I touch and feel and hear and spread myself inside my music. To play guitar you have to handle music differently, like Roy. He holds his music in his arms, across his lap. He cradles it. He rocks it, jerks the neck around, moves it so they sway together, bends his notes until they seem to cry. I cry apart, more pure it seems to me; the cry within is coaxed from the piano. Still it's mine; that sound is not my voice, or me, but I am in it. And yet it's hard to make it sing. My instrument is heavy, mutant marble. I'm like a sculptor come to give it form and character, to teach it how to speak and feel and think. But when I'm through, it stays, we separate and I am simply me, detached and transient again, the music carried in my head, abstract, ideal, without the notes or keys. Every keyboard ever played reverts to ivory and wood, to stone, inert, mechanical, and dumb . . .

. . . Is it possible we only love ourselves? I love my music. Roy loves his. Yet what we play together moves and comes to know itself along the way. When it's going right we're both aware it's us and something more we both can feel: we're justified: our music is a kind of whole in motion, and when we're finished, done. *It's* done, no matter what. But what? There's something always echoing, something like . . .

. . . that Himalayan episode? That's pretty strange but yes it was, that time when Roy went out to find a Khasi woman, I lacked the guts to go along. Or did I have the wit to know it wouldn't do, that what I wanted — wanton needed — couldn't be bought with rupees in a Himalayan hut. Instead I took that trail off into the hills and climbed alone for miles until Shillong was far behind while all around me spread the open diapason of those dusty woods. Those Himalayan vistas, God, and me, a foreign body there, surrounded by the trees, the rocky ledges, moss and lichens, wildly flowering plants, the warming breeze, being sung to by exotic birds and me moving through those mountain meadows, skirting monstrous rock-falls, yearning always upwards toward the awesome heights, those distant peaks beyond, those snowbound rooftops of the world. Just me climbing there, perspiring in the sunlight on that flat projecting cliff I finally climbed to, taking off my damp fatigues and then my Army shorts and socks and shoes to let the timeless Asian sunlight bathe and love me whole and feel myself aroused and naked as a pilgrim there, the heavy sun suffusing through my blood and I agreeably and eagerly tumescent. How I tingled, swelling toward the sun in that expansive scene. How I loved my living body there, breathing ever deeper, tighter, reaching for the spasms that at last expressed it through my lonely wanton sex. There, a moment longer, limbo, trying to hold the peaks in sight beneath my lowered eyelids, glowing still with light. I wanted not to feel depleted. Then the world of rock and sky returned. There was that dryness high up in my throat. I got back in my Army clothes and had my bones again. I felt estranged, cut down to size, yet somehow justified. Estranged meant loneliness again. I left the Khasi hills and visions of the Himalayan peaks behind and walked back to the village of Shillong with the pianos of that mountain scene like quarried marble in my mind. Roy told me later, grinning, that his Khasi woman sang a curious little song to him. I told him only that I took a hike . . .

. . . Is it likely that we only love ourselves? Thinking so may be our darkest circumstance, the fetal loneliness that breeds in war the seed of later wars. I want to know. I want a woman who can know. Was I somehow thinking *woman* in that Himalayan scene or was it only all-engorging *me*? Is that what sex is destined, orchestrated, for? The cymbals at the climax flattening out the monumental final chord to a metallic shudder and diminished waves of ringing in our ears. In *our* ears. Things insist on coming up in twos! Marching onto Noah's Ark. Two by two / they go marching through / Those sweethearts on parade. ONE- two-THREE-four. HUT-two three-four / you-had-a-good-home-but-you-LEFT (you RIGHT!), and: tea (da-dum) for two (da-dum) and two (da-dum) for tea (da-dum), and me (da-dum) for you (da-dum) and you (da-dum) for me (da-dum)—followed by that nice bright modulation from A-flat to C. Middle C on the keyboard. Middle Sea. How deep is the ocean / how high is the sky (*man overboard*): that same electronic hum from Roy's guitar (*Now hear this*—), that blare that shatters from his speaker when he overloads, I don't accept that sound, it isn't even his. I don't know how to think about all that water and someone out there turning by himself in all that endless shifting contrapuntal movement without a voice or song, just melting into ceaseless time. Mother Earth is wrong; it's Mother Sea. He's lying back in Whitman's cradle rocking endlessly in seminal and amniotic liquids like all our sexual longing, all our tidal rhythms, a desperation of the glands in search of waves of neverlasting love . . .

. . . Think about it? Try not to think about it. Try scenarios where you can go right through and come clean out the other side. Try swimming in the summer waters at the lake, stroking hard two hundred yards or so across the bay, then moving only just enough to float yourself ashore. Or later, lying in the sun and drying off, breathing slow and steady, eyes turned in until you doze. That's not so different, is it? Besides, I know that sleep is not the answer. If it were, I wouldn't lie awake and wonder how it ought to be, or what a woman really wants and feels, and what to do to make it whole with her. There must be times when everything, like music, goes together, bubbles rising in a rushing stream, rivers of emotion flowing sweet and heedless through their chiseled banks—by yon bonnie banks and by yon bonnie braes / by the bonnie bonnie banks of Loch Lo-mond. My Bonnie lies over the ocean / My Bonnie lies over the sea. My Bonnie, once again and maybe ever, ah, the One who waits and writes, my Bonnie whom I want to love and love to want, touching her only through two years of shuttling letters, always out of phase, behind the beat, rushing the normal tempo, then delaying, bogus touchings through the tenuous reaches of the military mail, a piteous dependency on letters read in private, touching private parts with pen and ink and censors' eyes and sightings half the globe away, we keep in touch by mental sight alone— and insight such as words and sacrosanct imaginings can muster through the mail. But Bonnie's there and now I'm going back. Two years of fleshless words upon our pages fantasizing love, refracting longing from the loins into lexicons of head and heart, the promises that try to make the letters formulate a future for our words made flesh . . .

. . . made flesh: that other Bonnie, what's-her-name, in Arlington before I shipped, Camp Anza at the service club, the club with that Baldwin baby grand I used to write my letters on before I'd start to chord around and play. It might have been because *her* name was Bonnie too, but that's a poor excuse for anything I did. I shouldn't kid myself. I even tried to sing some Gershwin, probably a chorus of Embraceable before we left to catch a bite at her apartment, so naturally we ate and talked. And then. She wrote me something like my thing about the river in that only letter when it finally got to me in India, her writing almost like her body on the page, rounded, smooth, collected, open as I read it. How did it go? I just recall the figure: something about us being pebbles on the bottom of a stream that rippled clean and clear. Not bad. Especially from her. But that was probably like her, even though I don't know what she's really like. It's just as well I'll never know. She certainly wasn't the artistic type, and yet it was my playing at the service club that first attracted her. They always seem to think musicians . . . well, if she expected some hot-stuff lover, she must have been surprised. Still, she wanted me to stay. She liked me well enough to make me comfortable. No question or I wouldn't have done it, wouldn't have dared to disappoint us both. But mostly her. She must have understood. She might have even been relieved. Who knows? She wanted me to stay and so I did. Lonely, both of us. But different in our loneliness. Nothing really desperate in either case. Two's company. There's no disputing that. Stay with me if you would like. I'd like you to. I sleep lots better when I'm not in bed alone. Whatever you want's O.K. with me. No clothes. Don't worry, nothing crude, I said. My nervous cool bravado. Somehow, though, she made it feel all right . . .

. . . but how she made my body warm all night! my mind a sieve of vivid fluttering chords, arpeggios, and long legato passages, my rhythmic beating pulse a steady throb against the rising/falling of her sleeping breath, so innocent! I simply held her, kissed her, held her, and she simply went to sleep, I know I must have dozed off too, but all I can remember is my yearning and her yielding flesh, only that tortuous felicity the whole night long in Arlington, the single bed, the almost dark, the corners of the walls and ceiling in her apartment softly flat while we were softly rounded, the whole night long with Bonnie what-was-her-last-name, never mind, together there in her bed while she slept and turned and slept and turned again. I must have held my breath for hours beside her, wanting her not to wake, moving (my hands!) only enough to keep my joy alive with questions for her woman's body, oh, her skin was such an exquisitely yielding answer that I almost turned to liquid, turned to milk beside her, moving ever so slightly so I'd know and go on knowing my delight, my breathing high and hollow, catching dryness in my throat, pulses pounding in my ears, I trembled like a child throughout that night, churning in the ecstacy of full desire in perfect focus, nerves in harmony at every touch . . .

. . . I guess she didn't know. What does a woman know or want to know? Obviously she was content. She slept. I held her close and stayed afloat on awesome waves of pleasure while she simply slept. But how she'd breathe and sigh within her blessed sleep, so rhythmically it hardly qualified as sound. She was so lambent in her sleep and, sleeping, yearned from time to time within my arms, my legs against her legs, sometimes bent to fit whatever curl her sleep required. I held her breasts and oh! her breasts, I'd never held so full and sweet a woman's naked breasts in these two hands before. I held her lovely breasts and suffered such tumultuous delight I prayed, I almost swore. I couldn't bear to move, until I had to, then at last I dared to let my hands complete her shape, exploring female glories in the dark, lightly lightly those melodic curves and hollows with all the wildest harmonies imaginable colliding in my heart, swelling through my pounding bloodstream, rising from the core . . .

I must have slept at times, but thin, with vast auroras glowing underneath my eyes and rich continuous dreaming chords resounding far below with echoes of her form, the pleasures of our double flesh. Then in the morning light she finally stirred for good and woke. We smiled in one another's eyes. She kissed me then and in her quick embrace, as if I saw a sudden surging peak, I yearned my last, and I was done. And we were done, the night a languid, melting memory, a past mystique, the business of a new and separate day begun. And it was done.

−ENSEMBLE−

Hey! The boat! There it goes. Hot dog.

The duty boat, the duty boat. Duty boaty number two.

Duty boat, do your duty.

Boat*swain*, do your duty.

Duty Number Two. Go get 'im.

Wonder what they use duty boat number *one* for.

They must save that to look out for Number One.

Look at 'em go. That thing moves pretty good.

Inboard engine. Lotsa power.

Duty boat, huh? It's more like a launch.

How many men in it? Can you tell?

Ahhh . . . six-seven. Maybe eight. Can't tell from here.

That's more than they'd need to go after Moby Dick. Some of them must be along for the ride.

Duty boat crew, man. They probably got a load of equipment on that baby. Communication gear. Medical. Engineers. Bunch of specialists. One for each job.

Like a damn union. Couple of officers along to keep 'em honest.

Look at 'er take those waves. Go get 'em, baby.

Look at the water. Out there. The wake. We're almost moving straight again. See? Look, over there.

You can see the whole way we turned now. All that smooth part.

They must have the engines on full speed now. Can you feel 'em?

Sure can. We're really movin'. Look at that wake. It's gettin' pure white again.

How they goin' to figure out where he is by now? How far to head back? Or where they calculate he ought to be?

I bet they've got it all figured. They probably got that boat headed right at 'im.

Maybe they know, maybe they don't. It all looks the same out there. Except for that wake. Goin' back right over our own wake.

Pretty weird if you think about it. *His* wake now, too, the guy overboard. Belongs to him.

He belongs to it, you mean.

The thing out there we got in common, him and us. The only thing in the whole ocean that can tell us where to look.

Forget it. They got electric equipment and compasses and ways to navigate and figure the variables. They can pinpoint the spot, I bet. Radar.

Sonar too. That's how they locate subs. They can even hunt whales with it.

So much for Moby Dick, huh?

Not that easy with Moby Dick. Not with the old white whale. Read the book.

Book schmook. Tried to read it once. Couldn't stay with it. This hunt's easier. Bet they get 'im.

Not so easy. Look at all that ocean.

What if he didn't have his life jacket on?

What if he can't swim? Have you ever tried to swim with your clothes
  on?

Not that hard in salt water. Holds you up as long as you keep moving.
  Keep air in your lungs.

Smart thing to do would be to get those clodhopper GI shoes off.
  First thing.

Smart thing would be to keep from going over in the first place.

Not . . . that . . . easy.

Watch the boat. They know what they're doin'. Watch.

CHAPTER THREE

Men looking into the sea,
taking the view from those who have as much right as you
*   have to it yourself,*
it is human nature to stand in the middle of a thing,
but you cannot stand in the middle of this;
the sea has no thing to give but a well-executed grave.

—Marianne Moore

THE BRIDGE

One of the Captain's first moves when he took over the conn from the OOD was to dispatch two junior officers to the lookout post from which the initial report of the man overboard had come. They were to determine all the details which might aid the search and rescue operation and which eventually would be needed for the full official report. He specifically charged the officers to learn the identity of the man himself. From the beginning, that seemed to him essential. He had to have a name, a rank, a serial number.

The results, unfortunately for the Captain's state of mind, were minimal, at least initially. The officers phoned in their preliminary findings, none of which added much to what was already known on the bridge. Haines, the lookout who first passed the word, had not himself seen the man go over the side, nor, when pressed, was he able to testify unconditionally that he had seen him in the water. He clearly thought he had, although he was anxious to point out the difficulty of seeing *anything* clearly as he tried to follow it back in the slipstream of foam before it merged into the wake and the whole spreading surface of the ocean behind. He had been roused from the lethargy of the afternoon by an outcry from a small group of GIs at the railing a little way off from his post—discordant shouts in which he heard, repeated in the chorus of voices, "Man overboard!" "Man overboard!"

Haines said he had stood up at once and looked from the group down into the water. He had seen something bulky in the wash of the ship, visible only at intervals as it swirled back, a dark object, not so much black as dark green, he thought—clearly darker than the sea it was carried in. It was roughly the size of a man, but it was tumbling erratically and he had never seen it wholly surfaced.

When questioned specifically he admitted that he had not thrown over the life preserver from his station at once. In fact, he was unhappily vague about just how long it was before he got around to it. The officers suspected that it might have been delayed even longer than the beleaguered Haines was willing to admit.

Neither had he used his binoculars until later—much later. As Haines explained it, he had been reluctant to do anything that might jeopardize his eye contact with the intermittent appearances of the dark object—the man overboard, as he assumed it to be. Only when he felt his chances for a direct, clear sight of the object were lost did he try the binoculars. By then the word had been passed to the whole ship over the speakers and the surge of the passengers to the rail had begun. When Haines looked back at last for the group who had first given the cry, they were indistinguishable in the crowd of men in fatigue uniforms bunching three and four deep at the rail.

Yes, he had thought about seeking them out for questioning then, but it would have been against orders to leave his post—especially at such a time of emergency. He had therefore remained steadfastly where he was, at his station, with his phone. The identity of the GIs who had initially raised the shout of "Man overboard," or where they might be found for questioning, were matters— along with the identity of the victim himself—about which the junior officers' investigation offered no real help at all.

Some time later, though, there was reason for elation on the bridge. Mordecai received a report from another lookout post, one forward of Haines, that the man overboard had been sighted off the port bow. Since the ship had recovered most of the distance lost in its long turn, the sighting seemed altogether credible. There was an atmosphere of high anticipation. Binoculars were trained intently on the ocean ahead and to the left. Mordecai, equally intent, listened with both hands cupping his earphones for confirmation and further information. Out on the bridge wing, the signalman waited, ready to relay directions to the alerted motor whaleboat.

But no confirmation came. Instead, Mordecai received from his chagrined source a clarification and a denial. The sighting had been the aberration of a single GI squinting off the port bow into the afternoon sun. The lookout had to report, finally, that he could see nothing in the area, to confess that he had too eagerly picked up and transmitted what he now regarded as a false report. Whatever the GI had seen or thought he had seen bobbing on the surface, he was quite alone.

The letdown on the bridge was almost palpable and a low murmur of exclamations greeted the news. Even the Captain groaned audibly and shook his head.

Some moments later, though, Ensign Martin sang out from the port bridge wing. He had raised something in the same area as the earlier report. In another moment others chimed in. The level of excitement rose again, although this time rather more cautiously.

"It's the life ring, I think," Martin added after a few seconds. Almost at once, others with their glasses fixed on the object agreed, and the bridge was alive with comment, exchanges, and conjecture. Another minute of intense scrutiny, however, settled the question no one had asked. The life preserver, which they could see better all the time, was apparently floating free and unencumbered. Their eagerness once more went unfulfilled. There was no sign of a man with it or in its immediate vicinity. *Well*, the Captain thought, *there's no telling how long it took that greenhorn lookout to get the thing in the water, but at least we must be somewhere near.* He glanced at the ship's clock. It was 1356 — some sixteen minutes from the time the ship's log would show that the man overboard report had first been passed. According to the plot they had run in the Combat Information Center, calculated from the ship's speed and turning radius, they would close in on the spot in another two or three minutes. The Captain had personally checked and therefore trusted the calculations. The life preserver now was further confirmation. But where was the man?

The Captain had already cut the engines back in the last leg of their return. In anticipation, he had maneuvered that return a bit to the windward to allow for drift and to provide some windbreak for the search. It was now time to stop altogether and drift without power into position for the concentrated search. He gave the order in his firm routine voice.

"Stop all engines."

The helmsman relayed the order crisply to the engine room. The Captain pictured the activity there as the engineers responded far below, closing the throttle which would still the last pulsing revolutions of the gigantic screws and commit the ship in silence and acquiescence to the larger impulses and motive power of the sea.

With an assuring nod to the helmsman, he added, "Steady on course. Zero-zero-seven."

It was done. He was uncomfortably aware of his arms hanging loose and useless at his sides. His hands seemed abnormally large, his fingers oddly splayed. He shook them at the wrists, then clenched them into fists. Still uncomfortable with them, he folded his arms, almost in the same movement spreading his legs into a firmer stance.

THE CAPTAIN

Although he is determined that his outward appearance and demeanor should not show it, the Captain is perplexed. He is unable to respond to the "man overboard" incident wholly in terms of Navy procedure and his duties of command. In a subversive manner the situation has invaded his personal emotions. The premature excitement he had shared with the others on the bridge had come with great relief. Now that the report has turned out to be erroneous, he is genuinely unnerved, as if he has been personally duped and betrayed. His uneasiness increases. He wants the whole troublesome episode finished — responsibly and successfully dealt with — but finished. Like a battle.

That, as he indistinctly understands, is at the root of his trouble — that and the general slackness he feels throughout his ship. His experience with emergency at sea has been framed by the conditions of war and combat. That means dealing with an adversary, besting an enemy by courage, wit, strength, coordination, steadfastness, strategy, maneuver, plan, firepower. But who or what is the enemy here? The ocean? The inexorable passage of time? Fate?

The Captain struggles against the notion that it is the anonymous man overboard himself, who seems as much a specter to be exorcised as a flesh-and-blood being to be restored. The image of this man overboard has become a sort of invisible antagonist, an incubus who entered his unguarded consciousness while he slept, as, in fact, it has taken over the mission and, for the time being at least, the destiny of the whole ship. He knows that the longer the search goes on, now, the less likely it is that they will raise him. Oddly appropriate, that nautical phrase, the Captain thinks, "to raise him." Like Lazarus from the tomb.

His mental image shifts from the body in the water to the decks of the ship, alive and covered with the unmanageable, curious hordes of GI troops. Even with the engines stopped and the ship adrift, a low level of noise persists — the inevitable noise of machinery and motion of humanity. He considers for a wild moment that he might turn off all the ship's machinery — at least the ventilator blowers — that he might send all transient personnel below decks, banish them and order absolute silence throughout his ship so that he might hear, however remote and thin, the faintest cry for help from the man overboard. It is impractical, of course, but nonetheless desirable.

Yet something has to be done. Now. He feels his moment. Impulsively but quite under control, he calls out to everyone on the bridge, requesting their close attention. As those on the bridge wings scurry in, the Captain turns calmly to Mordecai, who sits nervously fingering his chest phone.

"Mister Mordecai," he says to the talker, "Pass the word to all stations that we are back at the point where the man went overboard. I want everyone to redouble the effort to raise him. Their orders are to report anything and everything they see that might be our man and we will signal the boat crew at once to check it out."

Then, swinging his glance around the semicircle of the bridge, he takes them all in with a resoluteness that could have been either threat or encouragement but somehow communicates a compelling fusion of the two.

"That goes double for you men here on the bridge! I want everyone but the helmsman on lookout. I want every inch of that ocean scoured."

He is surprised and rather pleased to hear his voice take on a slight dramatic tremor.

"I want that man raised. Let me repeat that. I want that man raised, and *I expect one of you to raise him*."

They all stare back at him, alert to the new intensity in his manner. For the first time since he assumed command of the *General Bliss* he has the feeling that they are a unit with common purpose and spirit, as if there were an adversary out there after all. As he speaks, his glare fixes first one man, then another.

"We can't miss him from up here, unless he's under our goddam keel. If he's out there, we've got him in our reach now. So skin your eyes for him, men. I'm counting on you! Don't let me down!"

Let *me* down? Had he really said that? He blinks and swallows hard behind gritted teeth, the hinges of his jaw flexing visibly—a gesture which the others read, fortunately, as one of determination.

"All right," he says into the hush. "Take your places. And if you see anything, I don't care if it turns out to be a goddam bubble, sing out!"

There is an instantaneous bustle as they turn, almost as one, back to their vigil, some at the windows, most spilling out onto the bridge wings. The Captain's moment of exhilaration fades. He drops his eyes to the floor and breathes—inhaling, exhaling—deeply. When he looks back up, his eyes narrow and seek out the OOD at the window beside his talker. He calls to him by name. The Lieutenant wheels and returns the look, quizzical but compliant.

"Yes, sir?"

"Is that second boat crew standing by?"

"Yes, sir."

"All right. I want a second boat to join the motor whaleboat in the water as soon as you can man and lower it. Then I want those two boats to run an expanding square pattern at high speed over the whole critical area we mapped out from the plot. I want each boat to run that course independently and continuously unless we interrupt it with orders from the bridge to dispatch them to another sector. We've got to maximize their search potential on the surface. I want those boats in constant touch with our signalman on the bridge. Tell them to forget about radio transmission. Those damn battery line-of-sight units are nothing but static and interruption. All communication will be by semaphore and signal light. Got that?"

"Aye-aye, sir," the Lieutenant replies. He turns at once to give his talker the order for the waiting second boat crew.

His seaman's sense tells the Captain that the *General Bliss* has reached the end of its own momentum. It is a sensation he quite dislikes. His ship is now wholly adrift, dead in the water. For all its size and weight and substance, it is as much merely afloat and subject to the whim and drift of the impassive ocean as is the man himself out there. Dead in the water.

Well, not quite. The ship might be equally adrift and powerless, but at least the Captain can maintain his bearing. He has already, almost instinctively, made a judgment of the elements involved in their heading, the light, rising wind, and the condition of the seas. Now, as he feels the bow of the ship begin, very slightly, to swing toward the left, the course he has been holding is no longer a factor. He is pleased to note the helmsman's eyes on him, anticipating the order. Good man.

"Right full rudder," the Captain says to him with quiet finality, almost as if it concluded a private conversation between the two.

He stands mute and preoccupied in the silence that follows, a silence which seems to fall sympathetically over the entire troopship in the quiet equipoise of the moment. The Captain gazes ahead almost absently, considering the narrowing options ahead, reaching mentally forward toward — what? The consequences of his conduct in the search, now moving into its critical stage, perhaps. Or the lack of consequences. That, too, difficult as it is to grasp.

For an interval he stands there quietly, immobile, abstracted. Then one hand goes to the binoculars at the end of their cord around his neck. Energized by the contact, he straightens up and surveys his bridge crew deployed on lookout, intent at the windows and out on the bridge wings. Restored and full of resolve, he moves smartly through the doorway, out, and up to the flying bridge. Once again semi-detached and solitary, he raises the glasses to his eyes and joins in the alliance of searchers.

—INTERMEZZO—

It was hard for anyone who was not constantly checking the time to tell how long the *General Bliss* had been drifting without power. For the troops on deck, especially, the passing time had lost its strict relation to units ticking off a clock. The ship had yielded itself slowly — almost gratefully, it seemed — to the larger, encompassing rhythms of the sea. For the men aboard there was a curious and unexpected release in feeling themselves, as a part of the ship that bore them, adrift and abandoned to the complex but gentle whims of the Pacific. The man-world of the ship had surrendered its will to the natural permutations of the whole.

There was a strange peace in this surrender, a peace which virtually becalmed the already muted and offstage lives behind them in India and ahead of them in the United States. It was as if they had reached some still, balanced center of things, where life expanded to join with the total seascape and its perpetual undulations.

They had, quite literally, given up direction. Matters of motion and progress had become less clearly relative as they joined with the movements of the swelling ocean and its endless tidal rhythms. The idea of landforms and solid earth retreated far into the distant imagination. Even there it was alien, like another world, another life than the one they were now accepted in.

Curious inversions were at play. Powerless in the middle of the Pacific Ocean, the vessel now took its direction not from the presiding Captain and the technologically sophisticated machinery of his mid-twentieth century ship, but rather from a direct reading of the natural elements themselves, with the sovereign sun midway between the zenith and the western horizon, dropping toward the sea behind them.

But the sun was now *before* them. By coming about to search for the one soul lost out of the four thousand — the one eccentric particle flung radically off from the nucleus of human society on the ship — the men of the *General Bliss* now faced back toward the Orient, pointing westward *into* the afternoon sun.

Even the wake of the *General Bliss* — interrupted, altered, and askew since the ship's turnaround had begun — was no longer a clear connection, no longer their arrow across the trackless sea, their sign of deliberate power and direction within the encircling horizon. Instead, the wake had itself revolved during their turn, had moved broadside and was now ahead of them. There they watched it grow gradually less distinct as they searched the surface. The wake was no longer the bold, confident mark of their passage across the Pacific, but a token spoor slowly being obliterated by the ceaseless countermovement and unconditional accommodation of the sea.

Chapter Four

I . . . go to my well for water, and lo! there I meet the servant of the Brahmin, priest of Brahma, Vishnu and Indra, who still sits in his temple on the Ganges reading the Vedas, or dwells at the root of a tree with his crust and water jug. I meet his servant come to draw water for his master, and our buckets as it were grate together in the same well. The pure Walden water is mingled with the sacred water of the Ganges.

—Henry D. Thoreau

The Platform

Stanley was the only one of the Roy Warner Trio who was keeping track of the time. It was practically a tic of his anyway, flipping his wrist over every few minutes and checking his watch. What he had in mind that gave him further motivation now was the approaching hour for his mess call. The chow line for the second meal customarily began to form in a half-hearted way around mid-afternoon in anticipation of the general announcement that came over the speakers at 1530 hours. His habit was to be in the forefront. This didn't save him any time waiting, for he merely exchanged about the same length of pre-announcement time standing in the anticipatory line for the slow-moving accordion shuffle of the regular line later. But it did get him fed earlier, and Stanley was the type whose hunger pangs were almost continuous. If he was awake, he was hungry.

This procedure also set him up favorably for the ice cream window line, which was open to the elect twenty minutes or so after the evening chow lines were called. This ice cream was available only to the ship's crew and the privileged few among the troops who assumed shipboard responsibilities of some onerous sort. A turn at KP or some other special duty was rewarded by one ticket for ice cream. This could be redeemed during certain hours at the small window opening in the stores area below decks for a generous single-dip cone of smooth, premium-grade, stateside vanilla ice cream, a delicacy most of the troops scattered at remote bases throughout the CBI had craved and gone without for months, some for years.

Stanley Norman had learned of this opportunity while hobnobbing with some sailors in the crew early in the voyage. He had gone at once to the Army Transportation Officer to whom they reported and successfully cadged ice cream tickets for the Roy Warner Trio through him—a considerable coup, since theirs, like those of the Navy crew members, were good for the entire voyage with thirty numbered squares around the edges to be punched out as they exercised their privilege, one delectable ice cream cone per day. It was legitimate enough, Stanley had pointed out, since as special service entertainers they were working their way across.

His check of his watch gave him the current time: 2:45, it read; 1445, he translated. Ordinarily that would be time for him to start ambling toward the bulkhead door amidships with the chain looped across it, where the chow lines commenced. But little was ordinary about this afternoon, except for the automatic urgings of his stomach and an appetite that not even the colorless, viscous food ladled out at the transient personnel serving line could discourage.

"I wonder if they'll go right ahead with chow this afternoon," he said.

His companions did not comment.

"They'll have to," he offered. "It seems strange, though. Like we ought to wait until they find him."

The three had lapsed into silences as the search for the man overboard progressed. With the rest of the GIs, but separate on their platform, they had watched the motor whaleboat skimming this way and that. At times when it neared the mother ship, the altering pitch of its whining motor as the boat sped from swell to swell would grow barely audible. Most of the time it was far off and moved in silence.

Now a second boat had joined it — a surprise since there had been no general announcement, and it had been launched, for those who were port side or aft, from a blind part of the ship.

With the huge troop transport motionless in the water, it was fascinating to watch the agile small powerboats speeding in what seemed a haphazard, almost playful fashion around them and over the surrounding seas. Now that there were two of the boats, it became even more engaging as their contrary movements competed for the attention of the watching troops. For a while it was like a bizarre sporting event. The boats scurried about like nervous water-striders in a kind of inane competition, speeding, almost stopping, then turning sharply, changing course, and racing off at a new slant. In the middle of their play, the four thousand spectators followed the game from the tiered grandstand decks. They made a strangely attentive audience, thankful for the diversion but still under the disquieting spell of the occasion. Beneath their sporting responses to the antics of the careening boats — concern as one would execute a tight turn at a far corner of its run, an approving chorus of cheers when one would speed by broadside in a straightaway spurt — they were aware that human life was at stake, that the life and death theme of the chase involved one quite like themselves.

But hope was dwindling. The surface diversions of the boats were helpful for a while in rallying the common spirit on board, but as their whirligig movements across their patches of ocean continued and began to repeat themselves, attention began to wane. The focus and cogency of the search itself began to fall slowly away, and the watchers gradually retreated to the privacy of individual reflection.

The members of the Roy Warner Trio were not altogether representative of the multitude of GIs watching the search from the decks of the *General Bliss*. Their vantage on the platform overlooking the fantail gave them a physically separate and superior attitude toward the proceedings — watching the watchers as much as the performance of the boats. In at least one respect, however, the superiority of their outlook was limited and, in part, illusory. The trio enjoyed full vision looking east over the hemisphere to the rear of the ship, but the solid bulkhead at their backs cut off their view of the complementary half to the front and ahead. They could not see, for instance, as could those looking out from either the bridge or the railings on deck, that the layers of clouds moving in from the west were now solid above the horizon and had already taken over most of the afternoon sky.

The GI troops on the fantail had begun to move about again. Many were shifting from one side to the other, as if there might be something new to be seen from there. Their crossover was causing congestion in the middle of the broad deck area. Tired of standing in the dense pack against the railings while straining to see over the heads and shoulders of others, many had settled back and were clustered in small conversational groups, some of them sitting.

Apart and above them, the Roy Warner Trio also sat. Stanley flipped his wrist again and checked the time: 2:48 — 1448 hours. He looked back down at the troops.

"The natives are getting restless," Stanley Norman said.

"Short attention span," Roy Warner said. "They're gettin' bored."

A wide, sweeping shadow fell over the clumps of GIs nearest them and spread quickly over the whole fantail. The first of the clouds advancing from the west had overtaken the afternoon sun. The bright tableau below them cooled and went flat as the shadow absorbed its color and contrast. The human figures in their fatigue green faded, lost their edge, blended with the battleship gray of the deck. The cloud shadow moved out over the ocean behind — that is, the ocean still ahead of them — erasing the glitter from the tips of the waves and turning the surface sullen.

All three of the musicians looked overhead, their mouths falling open. They were as yet unable to see the source of the enveloping shadow.

"They're not bored," said Mark Reiter after a moment. He gazed off over the water where he could see the rapidly advancing line of the cloud shadow wiping out the dancing reflection of sunlight on the sea beyond. "They're like me," he added. "They're nervous. They don't want to think about it."

"They're probably like me," said Stanley. "It's almost three o'clock. They're getting hungry."

LULIANG

Mark was still following the enveloping shade as it spread far out to sea. "Like the shadow of death," he said.

"Nothin' new there, man," Roy replied. "It's always comin'. Right around the corner."

"Love is just around the corner . . . " Stanley sang.

Mark picked up the second line, " . . . Any cozy little corner . . . "

"No, really," Roy said. He drew up his knees and folded his hands around them. "Think of how many times we came close to gettin' killed. Without tryin'. I mean when you would have thought there wasn't any danger, nothin' to worry about."

"Like when?" Stanley asked.

"Well, like that landin' in Chungking, that crazy Captain Shang-hai bankin' us into that airstrip the Chinese were buildin' up on the hill."

"Jesus," Mark said, remembering. "That was hard to believe. Those coolies pulling that huge stone roller. I'll never know how we missed them."

"Or how we kept from blowin' a tire or slippin' over on those rocks, that crazy hot-rod," Roy said, shaking his head.

"How about those poor coolies on the runway?" Stanley added. "Talk about the shadow of death. We couldn't have missed them by more than ten feet."

"Well, that's what I mean," Roy said. "You never know when it's comin'. No matter who you are, what you're doin'."

Mark looked across at him. "The chances go up considerably if you're in a war."

"I don't know about that," Roy said; "not for us, anyway, I don't think they did." He picked at a nub on the knee of his fatigue pants. "Well, maybe some. Just bein' in India and China and movin' around made a difference, I know that."

"Burma too, Roy," Stanley offered. "How about those leeches when we took that swim in the Irrawaddy River—where was it? Mytkiyina, right? I get the shivers thinking about that, even now."

"Yeah, me too," Mark said.

Roy did not altogether agree. "No harm if you see 'em and get 'em off soon enough. Same with ticks. I've had leeches on me in Georgia. Not as big as those suckers, though. But think of those CIA guys in our basha in Bhamo. All that behind-the-lines stuff they'd been through. Or the guys who had to fight hut by hut to get Bhamo back from the Japanese."

"What about them?" Stanley wanted to know.

"Well, I mean those guys were really in the war. Like the flight crews back and forth over the Hump in those old crates. They all knew they might get it any time. But then the rest of us, too, even though we weren't commandos or doin' anything you'd consider dangerous. Maybe that GI that went overboard was just like us, you know? Only today *he's* the one. I've been thinkin' back, how many times it could have been us, how many times we could have got killed."

"Sure. That's why we got those points for battle stars, lads. Let's not knock it. That's just the way it is if you're not paying attention— anywhere. You can get hit by a truck in Reno or catch cold and die from pneumonia in Ratbone, Idaho. Who knows?"

"That's just what I mean, Stanley. That's the point."

" . . . Or fall off a ship in the middle of the Pacific Ocean, huh? Is that it?"

Mark looked up and out and spread his hands in mock benediction. "In the midst of life . . . " he said.

"Well, if you want some more," said Stanley, looking back and forth between the two, "there's that wild trip in the six-by-six up that narrow mountain road to Shillong."

Mark joined him. "That's right." He pulled at an ear lobe and shook his head. "With a bus coming down that one-way stretch."

"Never forget," said Stanley. "Chicken coops, all that old beat-up luggage strapped on, Indian people hanging all over it, and barely enough room for *one* vehicle. I don't know how we made it. I'll swear we had three wheels over the side to let them go joy-riding past."

"Karma, Stanley," said Mark with a smile. "It wasn't the chickens' time."

"Come to think of it," Roy said, "we probably owe our lives to you, Stanley. If we didn't have you to drive us back to Barrackpore after those crazy jobs we played in Calcutta . . . "

"Right you are, lads," said Stanley, brightening and nodding his head elaborately. "Very nice to have Sergeant Norman sober to beat the fierce Sikh taxi drivers of Greater Calcutta at their own game. Fear not. Norman the Mormon will get you sots home to sleep it off and live to drink another day." His tone relaxed. "I didn't mind, though. I kind of liked to drive that weapons carrier. I only wish they'd let me drive it on the right side of the road." He grew serious. "There *was* one time we almost got it, though. I never told you guys."

"No time like the present," said Mark, his gaze still out over the sea.

"It was on the Barrackpore Road about two-thirds of the way back to the base. New Year's Eve. Or morning. After that New Year's job we played for that Anglo-Indian guy on the make. All the British and American officers and those gorgeous Anglo-Indian women for dates. Remember? That guy I had the trouble with, after — didn't want to pay us if we wouldn't play for an extra hour. What a creep. I finally had to take the rupees out of his wallet myself. He wasn't much drunker than you two guys, though — and everybody else in that lousy place."

"I didn't have any choice!" Mark broke in. "Those dumb officers trying to show off for their Anglo-Indian babes. Getting drunk trying to get *them* drunk. And then taking it out on us. That one British officer — remember, Roy? — with the moustache?"

Roy nodded, looking glum.

"Wouldn't leave us alone," Mark went on. "Kept bringing rounds of drinks, one on the piano, one on your speaker. You were lucky, Stanley, he ignored you. Nowhere to put them back there on the drums. Then he'd stand there right in front and threaten us if we didn't drink it. I guess he figured if he could get us drunk he could get his woman drunk along with us."

"Naw," Roy said. "He was the one without a woman. Don't you remember? The poor sucker. His woman had taken a shine to some hotshot American officer and ditched him — left the party. That's what was eatin' him. He was mad as hell and tryin' to act cool. I had to buddy-buddy with the creep to keep him from bustin' up the place." Roy shook his head. "The thing is, I remember, he really liked our music. Wild night."

Mark was watching him. "I don't remember that. Can't remember much of anything after—what was it?—that crazy grand march they wanted us to play at midnight! And nobody could even stand up. Jesus. Isn't that right? It's really foggy. All I remember is people falling on each other and that British officer getting nastier with every drink he'd bring me. I had to chug-a-lug right with him every time or it was a vile insult to the Queen and he'd jolly well have to thrash me right there and take on every 'Yahnkee bahstahd' in the place. So there I am drinking to keep the peace and prevent an international incident. That godawful Indian gin. I've never been so drunk in my life. Or so sick afterwards. Never before, never again. I thought I was going to die. See? There you are, Roy. I could have died right there. A drunken hero's death. Sergeant Mark Reiter. The Distinguished Service Cross. Died valiantly from an involuntary excess of godawful Indian gin, January 1, 1946, while preserving the honor and integrity of the Allied Front."

"The enemy having surrendered," Stanley added, mimicking Mark's tone, "and the war being over some months heretofore."

Mark raised his eyebrows. "I do remember sitting around waiting for you to get the loot so we could take off. Very vague. Very tired." He sighed. "Very long ride back to Barrackpore, about which— you're absolutely right, Stanley—I remember nothing, being some kind of dead. Awful!"

Stanley picked up the cue. "Well, I'll tell you. All three of us were almost some kind of dead that night. We're moving along about thirty-five, forty. Pretty good clip, but I'm not pushing it, considering how narrow that road gets sometimes, you know, and the curves all the time. You two really out of it in the back. I'd say something to you every once in a while—had to keep myself awake. I looked back a couple of times to see if you were all right, and I'm telling you, you were really a couple of zombies with your heads bobbing around. Good thing you were jammed in with the equipment to hold you in place. What time was it—2 a.m. maybe? No traffic, hardly. I might not have had anything to drink, but I was pretty beat myself. Well, here come these headlights around a curve and then straight at me. It was right outside that village with the Moslem temple, you know the place?"

"Mosque, Stanley," said Mark, nodding yes.

"Yeah, mosque. What's the name of that place? Kiddapoor, Kiddie-car, something like that. You know where I mean?"

Roy and Mark both nodded. Roy said "Yeah."

"Well, the closer these headlights come, the more I know something's wrong. He's on my side of the road, heading right at me. I mean, I'm in this left-hand-drive American weapons carrier, driving on the side where I'm supposed to be — over on the left like the limeys and the wogs. That puts me way over by the left edge of the road. If this other guy's where he ought to be, there's no way he should seem to be aiming right for my lap. But here he comes. I can't get any farther over on my side, it's so narrow there, you remember? Just beyond that Moslem temple, with all those little huts right along the road, and the Indians huddled around their fires in front. If I went off the road I'd plow right into them. So what can I do? Even if I slam on the brakes, he'll plow right into me. And if I swerve over and pass him on the other side, on the right, he's liable to wake up and swerve over there himself at the last minute, since that's where he's supposed to be, and *wham*. You two zombies sitting on the sideboards, loose as a goose, you'd be all over the road." Stanley paused and shook his head.

Roy broke the silence. "What did you do?"

Stanley looked at him in mild triumph. "You want to know what I did? You want to know what saved your worthless hides? Well, it was your heads-up Uncle Stanley did it, like you said in the first place, Roy — with a little assist, maybe, from somewhere. I braked just enough to swerve over and go around him on the right, ready for the worst — what else could I do? But the kicker, lads, the kicker is that the other vehicle was an American jeep heading home on New Year's Eve, just like us, I suppose, or I mean like you ratbones, anyway. Feeling no pain. He tore right on past us on the wrong side of the road, shaking his fist and yelling like mad at me. I slowed down to a crawl for the next mile or so. I was shaking so much, I could hardly see. But I finally figured it out. That GI must have thrown as good a drunk as you did and just slipped back into his U.S. habits in his left-hand drive, like he was back home in Peoria, driving over on the right side. He wasn't about to change lanes. Why should he? For him *I* was the one on the wrong side of the road."

"My country, right or wrong," Mark said.

They sat in silence for a while. The boats were out of sight, searching reaches of the sea far ahead of the bow. The advance of the shadow covered nearly all the visible ocean surface by now, and the clouds that cast it had appeared overhead.

Roy stirred. He had another. "That time waitin' for the Chinese hill bandits to come down and wipe us all out—where was it?"

"Luliang," Mark said. "Yeah. The only time in the whole war I was glad they issued me sidearms. Kept that pistol on the pillow next to me all night thinking about how it would be if they did come down and break into our barracks and I'd have to use it. Kept it on safety, though; I remember that. A strange night, you know it? Really. I guess I must have slept some, but it sure doesn't seem like it now. All I remember is lying there with my mind racing and my heart pounding thinking about what they'd told us, what it would be like if they did come down from the hills, and if they did happen to pick our barracks and break in, and I did have to shoot someone after all, instead of just worrying about it, wondering what it would be like, what I'd feel like afterwards. Or maybe me getting it. Kill or be killed. All that stuff. The lectures, those training films. They come crashing in—shooting, you know—maybe through the windows instead of the doors, since we got them locked and barricaded. I kept thinking of that, trying to get ready. Maybe getting shot at the same time I'm shooting. Kill *and* be killed. You know? It happens. I kept thinking it was a false alarm, but I knew all the time it could be true and we might really have to face it, any moment, and I wasn't ready—but I had to be ready. Strange night. But exciting, I have to admit it. Was it like that for you?"

"Yeah. Pretty much," said Roy. "There we are way off and gone in the middle of China where we're supposed to entertain the troops, and suddenly we're like to get wiped out by some crazy Chinese night riders. *Chinese.* That's what got me that night. They're supposed to be on our side. The damn war is against the Japanese. But it's not goin' to do no good to try and tell that to those Chinese bandits if they decide they want what we got and feel like comin' after it. We could have been as dead from those Chinese bandits as those CIA commandos in Burma from the Japs, only we weren't askin' for it."

"Sure we were, Roy," said Stanley. "We're all in the same U.S. Army, and we're all in the same war. Like Mark said, the chances go up when you're in a war. Whatever you're doing. I mean, we didn't belong there in Luliang, China, anyway, any of us Americans, did we? Except for the war. So that's the whole story. Those Chinese people in the town are the ones that really had to worry. I don't guess any of them got killed that night, but they've got to be ready for it every night of their life, living there. It's like living on the frontier in the West a hundred years ago. No kidding. The Indians could gang up and wipe you out any time they wanted to."

He cocked his head and turned to Mark. "You know, it's funny. I never thought of it that night, but it's true. That whole deal was kind of like it must have been for the pioneers, knowing the Indians were out there somewhere—that you were in their country, but you had a right to be there. I mean it was where you were supposed to be. And yet they might wipe you out any time, if they decided to. My grandfather used to talk about that all the time. How it felt."

"Yeah," Mark said, "but then somewhere along the line it got turned around. I wonder what the Indians would have to say about it. When it turned around, about who was doing the wiping out and who was getting it."

Stanley was pensive. "You know, I was worried that night in Luliang, but I wasn't scared. It was kind of unreal, you know? Like a movie or something, even though I knew it was happening to me. I was awake awhile after we barricaded and went to bed, after we quit talking and it got quiet. I remember that. But then I went to sleep. I slept good all night. When I woke up, it was morning and daylight and there wasn't anything to worry about—kind of like there never had been."

Mark was nodding in agreement. "Yeah. The morning. That always does it when it comes. You were lucky, Stanley, you slept through it." For a moment, Mark was about to add that Stanley was lucky to have slept through the whole war, but the impulse was easily checked; Stanley would misunderstand, he might be hurt, and it wasn't, strictly speaking, true. Instead, Mark turned inward as he continued.

"The night always seems like another world. Things are just different at night. Like there's not much you can really do about them. So you just stew and think about them. That's the way it was for me that whole night in Luliang. Then I can remember when it first started to get light. I was awake and I kept looking at the window, then looking away, then looking back, trying to make it get light so that long night would be over. For a while I'd tell myself I was just imagining it, that it wasn't really any lighter, just because I wanted it to be morning so bad. Then almost at once, the way I remember it, there was no doubt. It was the beginning of the morning light for sure and the night would be over. And we weren't going to be killed and we weren't going to have to kill anybody, and it was—what? It was . . ." —Mark filled his pause with a shrug—" . . . done."

CALCUTTA AND DACCA

Roy looked up at the steadily gathering clouds. They were thickening now into an almost solid cover of gray-blue. The breeze had quickened as the clouds moved in. Their motion across the darkening sky seemed to emphasize the stillness of the *General Bliss*, holding its heading against a sea grown rather more irritated on its surface, somber in color, and opaque in its aspect. The air had cooled. It was still without chill and comfortably warm on deck, but for the first time in days the troops were without the steady, baking heat of the Pacific sun.

"You want to know when the dark got to me?" Roy asked. "When I really felt like we were goin' to get it and there was nothin' we could do about it?"

Stanley and Mark looked at him silently and waited.

"On that ride in to the docks from Kanchrapara. Closed up in the back of our truck and drivin' blind through that Indian mob."

"I'm with you," Stanley said. "That was crazy, sitting there in the dark, hearing all those Indians yelling and then those rocks or stones or whatever they were, whacking into the canvas."

"Well, I guess there weren't many rocks hit us, really, near as I could tell, but it was enough to know they weren't kiddin'." Roy thought for a moment. "It was bein' in the dark and shut up in the back of that truck, mostly. I really thought it was a riot and we might get it then. And no way to fight it. Just to sit there. Couldn't even tell what they were yellin'. Just knew they sure as hell meant it."

Stanley took it up. "Yeah. When we slowed down and then stopped. Right then. You remember? I could hear them yelling on both sides of us and getting louder. I guess it took just a minute. You could feel the driver shifting gears, racing the motor, and double-clutching like mad. That scared me, like maybe he'd kill the engine and we'd be surrounded and cut off. That was a bad moment, man, before we started moving again. That mob. Those streets in Calcutta were always full of people. I was always afraid I was going to kill someone driving through, but that was the only time I thought they were going to kill me."

"Fuckin' India," Roy said with sudden irritation. "That was really the payoff, you know it? There we were on the way to the damn ship, last chance, made it through the war, saved the damn Indians from the Japs, we're checkin' out, goom-bye, and they're like to kill us in a street riot before we can get to the docks and get out of their damn country!"

Mark joined in. "Being in the dark made it seem worse than it was, probably. But I felt the same as you did. Scared, yeah. It wasn't so dark I couldn't see everyone in the truck, though. A little bit anyway. I remember leaning forward when those rocks began to thud against the canvas. Looked around and everyone was doing the same thing. And swearing. I couldn't hear them, the yelling outside was so loud, but I could tell they were swearing. Swearing and ducking and wondering what the hell."

"That was me, ratbone," said Stanley. "I'm still wondering what the hell."

"I kept watching everybody else," Mark went on. "You know what you were doing, Roy? You had your guitar case standing up between your knees and you wrapped your arms around it and tucked your head down alongside the neck."

"All I remember," said Roy, "is thinkin' how stupid it would be to get killed with the war over, before we could even get on the damn ship. Bein' stoned by a bunch of Indians, for God's sake!"

"Hey," Stanley said abruptly in a quieted tone. "You know what it was like? Never thought of it. That was like the pioneers too." He brightened into the idea. "Never thought of it until you said 'Indians,' Roy. But it was like we were in a wagon train. You know, in a covered wagon, being attacked by Indians."

"Nice," Mark said with a smirk. "The problem was how to pull the wagons into a circle on the streets of Calcutta to do battle with the whooping savages."

Stanley conceded somewhat in his tone, but not much. "Well, it must have been something like that when the pioneers were attacked in their covered wagons. Except you had a whole lot clearer idea what our Indians were up to — why they were out for your scalps. I swear I still don't see what that mob was doing attacking us."

"That's easy, Stanley," Mark told him. "You know how the Indians were always standing around all night watching the GI movies we showed at the base? They just saw too many Westerns, that's all. Gave them ideas."

"No, really," Stanley insisted. "I know what they told us. Partition and all that Hindu and Moslem business. I understand that all right, but why were they attacking us? Why stone Americans?"

"Don't ask me," Roy said. "I couldn't figure out how an Indian thinks in a million years. You get them riled up, I know this, they'll take it out on anything. Anybody."

"The Indians don't have a monopoly on that," Mark put in. "A mob's a mob. Anywhere. They just got a lot more to be a mob about in India than most places. I kept wondering whether they were Hindus or Moslems, but that wouldn't explain much. It wouldn't make any difference. You're probably closer to the truth, Stanley. They were Indians. And they were attacking us. Cowboys. Settlers. Pioneers in our covered wagon. Cavalry. Bengal lancers. Whatever. Something like the Luliang thing you were talking about, Stanley — we didn't belong there except for the war. And the war was over. *Our* war. Not theirs, though. Not the Indians in that mob. Not their long-run war, the one they've spent their whole life in, getting ready for."

"What do you mean?" Stanley asked. "Partition? The religious war?"

"No, I mean the British. Well, British India. The British and the Americans. The whole business of who's in charge, from way back. Colonialism in the mys-te-ri-ous East. Pukka sahibs. Gunga Din. Gin-and-tonic. Rudyard Kipling. East is East and West is West." He finished, singing half-heartedly, "On the road to Man-da-lay / Where the fly-ying fishes playyy . . ."

"You mean that mob thought we were British?"

"No. Well, not exactly. It wouldn't make any difference, really. Just like it didn't make any difference to us whether they were Hindus or Moslems. British, American. We were military, Western, European, whatever we were. That's enough. We were authority. If you had to live like most of the people in Calcutta and you saw the British lording it over you and running everything all your life, and then the Americans come in and they're just the same, only worse maybe, throwing their money around, fighting a PX war, right, Roy? Well, you might feel like throwing rocks too when you got the chance. Or worse."

Roy took it up. "O.K., I know what you mean. I'm not goin' to argue with you about Calcutta. That's the bottom, man. I mean, I used to think those people in the villages around Chandranagar were pretty sad, livin' in those huts, dirt, filth, the animals right in with them, goats and those skinny cows all over the place. And that crap you'd see them eatin'—that pasty, floury stuff, scoopin' it out of those bowls with their fingers. Flies all around."

"At least they were eating," Mark said.

"Well, yeah," Roy acknowledged. "That's what I was goin' to say. Those people in the villages were pretty bad, but at least they had some room to get out and breathe, and trees, and those tanks of water they washed in, and trails through the woods, and well, like families, you know? Like the kids belonged to somebody and everybody knew where he was at. But Calcutta. Geez. People lyin' all over the place in rags starvin'. You can't tell whether they're dead or alive."

"I got to thinking the dead ones were better off," Stanley said.

"You know," Roy said after a pause, "I don't think you can tell anybody about India when you get home. There's just too much. You can't explain how it is. Like Calcutta. How are you goin' to tell anyone in Waycross, Georgia, hasn't been anywhere else, maybe a trip to Jacksonville Beach, about Calcutta?" He shook his head and shrugged. "You can't tell anybody hasn't been there."

"I tried to write about it sometimes," Mark said. "Letters to Bonnie. I wanted to try to say how it is, how it looked and smelled and the sounds and the people and how they lived, how I felt about being in India. I wanted Bonnie to know — so when I got back she'd know what I was talking about, what was on my mind, you know, if I got to thinking about it. Because I have to admit it really got to me. I hated it, but it fascinated me all the time. Still does. I don't think I'll shake it off as long as I live, the way I felt in India. The strange thing is I don't want to. I'm sick of it, and if I thought I had to turn around and go right back, I'd . . . But even so — even while I'm talking about it . . . " He trailed off and turned his head down sharply to one side, then shook it slowly.

"I couldn't do it in those letters. I don't know how you could. You can't even do it for yourself in your head. But I keep on trying. Can't help it. I think back to all that misery in Calcutta, all that subhuman existence and filth and — well, words like 'poverty' and 'suffering' and 'inhuman' just can't touch it. They're *our* words, anyway, and we don't have anything enough like India to make them mean what you want to say. And there's all the rest of Calcutta, going on all the time. Going on right now. And all of India, the whole . . . thing. Maybe the Indians could tell about it. Maybe the Indian languages would let you describe how it is."

Mark paused a moment to consider. Roy and Stanley were silent, considering with him.

"I don't think so, though. I'll bet they don't. I'll bet their words don't do it any better than ours do. Their music, maybe." Mark had blundered onto an idea, but he liked it. They all did. "You know how Indian music makes you feel? All that twanging and twisting around the melody? All kinds of different things going on and yet it's all the same. Like it's whining and singing all at the same time."

"And cryin'," Roy added. "All that wailin' and bendin' the notes. The singin', too, like there's always a tightness in their throats when they sing."

"More like their noses," Stanley said. "They all sing through their nose."

"Yeah," Roy said, "but that's part of it. I'll tell you what: it's like they're singin' through their body instead of just their voice."

"Very good, LeRoy," said Stanley. "Write that down."

Mark was still considering. "Fact is, I'll bet their language ignores all those miserable things in their lives that are so obvious to us. Or at least glosses over them. Like sex in our language. We don't have the right words. You know? Like taboos. And superstitions. Like when you're not supposed to use certain words, or name things, or say them out loud, because then they might come true, because that makes them real. You know what I'm talking about?"

"Well, you're right about the Indian music," Roy said, frowning. "It's really weird stuff, all right. They sure go for all that wailin'."

"Makes me sick to my stomach if I listen to too much of it," Stanley said. "Like everything else about India."

Roy continued. "I heard an old guy on a sitar once. In Dacca. He was sittin' in the street outside a kind of music store—a wide-open kind of place full of instruments—and he was playin' the hell out of this sitar."

"Shit-tar?" Stanley asked.

"Yeah, you know. The big string instruments they play, with the long neck and all those strings. This old white-haired guy was tryin' out the instrument, I think. Anyway, he was foolin' around for awhile—sittin' cross-legged right out there in the dirt—runnin' up and down those strings, twangin' some loud and puttin' his ear down a bit. Warmin' up, like you do. Fast. Slow. Plenty of technique.

"Well, people started to come around and I went over too, with these guys from the base I was with. I was really anxious to watch him play, but I can't say I go for the sound you get out of those things. Like a mandolin, kind of, only bigger, more sound. Thinner, but bigger, I don't know. Anyway, there was a fair-sized crowd after a while. All those Indian types—dirty ones, clean ones, old people, young people, kids, and me and these two other guys, all mixed together, crowdin' around, watchin' this old bird play his sitar."

"Did he really play?" Mark asked.

"That's what I was goin' to tell you," Roy said. "After foolin' around and warmin' up, all of a sudden he starts to play for real, with this one tone in the bass he plays all the time while he's runnin' all over the place up above it, and two- or three-note chords thrown in every once in a while. It was great. I mean I didn't like it, but he sure could play, and he was into it. That's the thing. You could feel it, just watchin' him and bein' in the crowd. I mean they didn't even pay attention to us bein' GIs, except for some of the little kids maybe, watchin' us. And you couldn't help feelin' what he was buildin', man, and every-body — there were a lot of people there — really quiet or swayin', really with it. Me too.

"Well, what I wanted to say, he's got his head down and his eyes closed and he gets to some of these places where the notes are runnin' higher and higher, like spirals or, I don't know. And then he hits these big high wails. I don't know what to call them, but they were like high notes that he held on to and bended, man, like a wail comin' out of somebody's throat. And he raised his head while he was holdin' and shakin' one of these notes, and his eyes were open, and he was *cryin'*, you could see, and I looked around at the crowd we were in and a lot of them had tears in their eyes, and I'm tellin' you, I damn near did too."

Stanley waited about a two-count before asking, "What happened then?"

Roy had clearly finished the story, an unusually full and lengthy one for him.

"I don't know," he said. "Broke up in a while. He went back inside, I think. Anyway, we left. We had to meet some other guys." He mused a bit more.

"Two other things, though, that time in Dacca. There was this crazy Indian guy in the crowd. I mean really crazy — whacko. At first I thought he was just some kind of comedian puttin' on his act. You know. He had this funny hat on and a wild outfit — a black and red vest over a dirty old white dhoti and funny glasses — goggles. A really weird character. He was gigglin' and carryin' on some sort of conver-sation with himself, babblin' like, and doing a funny dance all the time to the music. But the thing is, nobody paid any attention to him. They'd glance at him, maybe, but that's all. Like he was just someone else in the crowd. Really weirdo."

Roy fell silent again, apparently finished.

"What was the other thing?" Stanley asked him.

"Oh. Yeah. In the next block, after we left, there was this big old tree full of these huge bats hangin' upside down on the branches. Sleepin' right there in the tree, middle of the day. I mean they were great, big black bats. Some of them stretched their wings while we were watchin'. I never knew they got that big. One of the guys swore they were vampire bats, like he knew somethin' about it. We asked somebody about them, though. Fruit bats, he said they were."

AMERICAN AND INDIAN

"Water's getting kind of choppy," Stanley said. He had stood up to stretch and was facing out, hands on hips, looking over the water. His two companions remained seated on the platform.

"Where the boats at?" Roy asked him.

"Can't see them," Stanley answered. "Can't hear them either. Must be way off somewhere. Up in front. They're looking farther out, I guess."

"Those guys down there must still be watching them," Mark said, "or at least trying." He indicated a small cluster of GIs along the railing who were looking forward together and conversing unexcitedly. Now and then one would point while he spoke. There were many spaces along the fantail railing now and no one was crowding. The GIs at the rail were slack, gazing out idly, as if preoccupied. Most had moved back into the open deck areas where they were strolling about or had sat down in small groups here and there. Mark looked them over.

"Doesn't seem to be a whole lot of interest on the part of the troops at this point."

"Hard to stay interested very long in anything you can't see," Stanley said.

"Like music, Sergeant Norman?" Mark teased.

As his reply, Stanley jerked his head aslant and lowered his eyelids. It was a gesture they had picked up from the Indians, one they used often enough to become almost their own natural reflex. They understood it imperfectly as a gesture of assent or acknowledgment, or on occasions such as this, an exaggerated wink.

"Out of sight, out of mind," Roy said.

"Not so," Mark responded. "Out of sight, into mind. Memory, for instance."

Stanley was dubious. "You think those guys down there are thinking about India?"

"Why not? We are. What else? If they're not thinking about the man overboard, since nobody sees him. Everything else is either memories of what's behind us or thinking about what's ahead."

"India's the past, the U.S. is the future," Stanley said. "That what you mean? And us stuck in the middle."

"Could be," Mark agreed.

Roy was working on something. "You know, that's what it was like for me in India, bein' an American in India — like the past and the future all mixed up. And me in the middle."

Mark picked up on it. "Yeah. That's what it was like with Calcutta. The city, you know, like a regular American city in a lot of ways. The cars and trains and streetcars, airplanes. All the factories and stores, that big Army-Navy Store, and hotels — business going on, like a modern city. And then all the Indian things everywhere at the same time. The cows and the beggars. Naked kids. The people all mixed together. The whole range. You couldn't imagine it all together unless you'd seen it. Or even then. The city things and . . . the people things.

"It was funny though, sometimes," Roy said.

"Funny?"

"Yeah, funny. The way things went together. Or didn't go together. American things and Indian things."

"I know what you mean," Stanley said. He turned to Mark. "Like Govinda and his tee-shirt, huh, Mark?"

"What tee-shirt?" Roy wanted to know.

"Govinda, the bearer in our basha at Barrackpore," Stanley explained. Mark cocked his head and smiled. Stanley continued. "This Indian kid — well, you know, not a kid really. He was our bearer. You know how when you'd send your stuff out to the GI laundry, wherever they took it, you'd get back different underwear half the time. Well, once Mark got back this tee-shirt with a big picture of a factory on it all over the front. Tell him about it, Mark."

"Well, it had YOUNGSTOWN VINDICATORS printed in big letters above the picture of this building. That's a newspaper in Youngstown, Ohio, some guy told me. *The Youngstown Vindicator.* I guess some GI had this tee-shirt from his old softball team or bowling team or something. Anyway, I was disgusted with the laundry and was going to send it back and see if I could get a plain one next time — or throw it away. But Stanley had a better idea."

Stanley shrugged as he took up the story. "I saw Govinda admiring the shirt while he was folding the stuff to put in Mark's footlocker. So I told Mark why don't you see if Govinda wants it."

"Should have seen him," Mark said. "Embarrassed. You know how they are. First he thought I just wanted him to try it on, see how it would look, I guess. He put it on like he was modelling a hundred-dollar suit. When I finally got him to understand I was giving it to him, he was knocked out. Like it was the greatest thing that ever happened to him."

Stanley took over again, "He kept saying 'Certificate, Sahib. Certificate, Sahib.' Then he'd cross his wrists like this and say 'Yempee. Yempee.' We finally figured out he was afraid the M.P.'s would think he stole it. We wrote him out a note and signed it so he could get in and out of the gate without any trouble."

"Old Govinda," Mark said with a mixture of rue and amusement. "He wore that shirt every day for a month. All puffed up for the sweepers and the other bearers, grinning his betel-nut toothy grin at us all the time, strutting all over the base in his ragged shorts and his bowlegs and his bare feet and this tee-shirt, two sizes too big for him with the picture of this plant in Ohio belching smoke, and YOUNGSTOWN VINDICATORS over it."

"We used to wonder what he explained the shirt was about at home," Stanley said.

"If he had a home," Mark said, and they fell silent.

In a moment Roy grinned, ready with a story of his own. "I knew a guy up in Assam," he began, "who never let India get on top of him. Jim Gill. Captain Jim Gill. He was a pilot, but there wasn't anything he couldn't do. Wasn't anything he couldn't put together out of spare parts. Every base he flew to all over the CBI, he'd nose around for parts. He'd pick up loose stuff everywhere and bring it back to his stockpile in the hut he took over behind the officers' club. Most of the time he never knew what he was goin' to do with it. 'Might come in handy,' he'd say, and sooner or later it would. When he knew what he wanted — some item he needed when he was workin' on some project — he was the slickest man for moonlight requisitions you ever saw. The Indians around Chandranagar thought he was some kind of a magician. Or some kind of a nut. Hell, so did we. At least until he cracked up an old C47 ferryin' it down to Dum Dum. Lost one engine way out and then the other caught fire on his approach. He was pretty banged-up and burned bad, I guess. All we know for sure is they flew him right back to the States. Would have killed anyone else, but you couldn't stop Jim Gill.

"He turned his part of that little base at Chandranagar into Little America, all out of spare parts. First thing was his freezer. The guys in his bunch wanted ice in their drinks, see, so Jim whips up this ice-makin' machine, which makes lots more ice than they need, so he leases it to the officers' club for 'certain considerations.' That's what he'd always say. He was great for makin' deals, always with some joker worked into it. You could have learned a few things from Jim Gill, Stanley. Everybody did. He taught me a lot. I used to help him with some of his electrical gimmicks.

"Before he was through he had his own complete generatin' system runnin' a relay of lights and electric power and outlets all over the area. He put together an air conditionin' system for his own place, and then everyone wanted one, so he was fixin' them up one by one. Each system was different, made out of the parts he happened to have and others he'd turn up with when he'd figured out how he was goin' to do it. 'I'll gladly take care of you,' he always used to say, 'for a small consideration.' Then he'd grin like a kid.

"You know what he'd do, that crazy guy? He made himself a small hand printin' press and he printed up a batch of business cards. He'd hand them out to the Indians all the time and give them this sideshow talk like he was some kind of hotshot salesman. He printed up monthly statements for all the guys he had hooked up on his generator. They'd be full of gags. That's the way he was. He called it the Gill & Finn Consolidated Power Company, Upper Assam Division, and the charge was five bucks a year. He said that took care of his expenses, but he never really kept track. He'd wait for new guys to ask him who the 'Finn' was in the company name and he'd have a good time givin' them some crazy answer. He'd say 'Mickey Finn—you won't know what hit you.' Or 'Huckleberry Finn—that's why we're always up the creek.' It was all a kind of gag, but everybody went along with it. You couldn't help it, bein' around Jim Gill. 'Gill & Finn Consolidated Power' it said on those bills he'd send out. Under that he'd print a different motto every time. One month I remember it said 'There's Something Fishy About Our Service.' Another time it said 'Try Your Luck with Jim And Huck.' Once it just said 'Fish Or Cut Bait.' " Roy thought it over. "Old Jim Gill. Hope he made it. India didn't have any problems Jim Gill couldn't do something about."

"Never left home," Mark said, half to himself.

"What?" Roy asked.

"Nothing," Mark replied. He shifted his position. "I said he never left home, but that's not right. I'd like to have seen his rig. Some guys are like that. Young Tom Edison. Tom Sawyer. No, make that Tom Swift. I've known guys like that." He thought a moment. "They're great."

"They get things done," said Stanley. "That's what counts. Trouble with Indians, it takes forever for them to get anything done."

Roy agreed with a nod. "And then they don't take care of it. No maintenance. The Indians don't have the first idea about maintenance. Once it's done, forget about it. Let it take care of itself. Everything in India is fallin' apart. Or rottin'."

"That's partly the climate," Mark said.

"Climate, hell," Roy said. "Everybody was always moanin' about the climate. No different than Georgia or Alabama in the summer."

"Well, yeah . . . it's mostly a different sense of time they've got," Mark said, trying to explain it for himself as well as for the others. "Like reincarnation, you know, and then we'll start over again. Like, ahhh, every time is like every other time, and what you do or what you build doesn't mean as much.

"There's a guy I used to talk to at Hastings Mill when I first got to India," Mark continued. "Sinha, his name was. Pratap Narayan Sinha. He used to explain it to me about progress. How the Indians—at least the Hindus—don't think about progress, or history, the way we do. It's a different philosophy altogether. It's religion, really. How they fit themselves into everything. And just take things as they come. It's their state of mind that counts, not the things they make, you know, in the material world."

"It's the climate, too, though," Stanley insisted. "That miserable damp heat. I couldn't get up the strength to move half the time. I don't see how anybody could get much done."

"I've still got a list of things Sinha said I should read if I'd like to know more about it," Mark said.

"He sounds like a Mormon missionary in disguise," said Stanley with a grin.

"No," Mark refused the joke. "I asked him what I could read if I wanted to understand it and he made me this list. I tried one book he gave me right away, but I couldn't get through it. Too many weird Indian names and words. Stories that didn't make much sense."

"What did I tell you?" said Stanley, enjoying his game. "Sounds just like the Book of Mormon."

Mark went on ignoring him. "Well, I'm going to read everything I can find on that list when I get back," he said. There was resolve in his tone. "I ought to be able to understand it better now."

DUM DUM

"Talking about the heat," Stanley said to Roy, "did I ever tell you about my first ice cream cone in India?"

"Naw. You mean American ice cream?" Roy asked.

"Yeah. The first ice cream in the area—real stateside ice cream—at the PX. At Dum Dum Air Base. You mentioned Dum Dum before, made me think of it. Where all the big brass came in—staff officers, generals, senators, the whole lot. And that's where we got most of our special service supplies for Barrackpore, see? As soon as I heard they got this real ice cream over there, my mouth started watering and I couldn't get it out of my mind. So I got the lieutenant to requisition us some baseball equipment. Of course I volunteered to go over to Dum Dum and get it. Well, I got there first thing in the morning, drooling for that ice cream, and here was a sign at the window saying 'CLOSED,' the ice cream would be sold only once a day at 12 noon. Great. So I fool around all morning while it's getting hotter and hotter at Dum Dum."

Roy smiled. "And the idea of ice cream is gettin' better and better, right?"

"You know it. At about eleven o'clock I go over to pick up the stuff on requisition and kill another half hour getting the equipment—a catcher's mitt and a mask and some Reach baseballs. They put them in this carton and I carry them over to the PX about eleven-thirty, so I'm the first one in line at this ice-cream window outside the PX. Right out in the sun, which is something fierce by now. And humid. By five-of, I'm soaked through with sweat. But there's twenty, twenty-five guys lined up behind me, and I'm going to be the first one at that ice cream. They open the window at twelve sharp and—ta-daa—I get this super double-dip vanilla beauty. Absolutely beautiful." Stanley closed his eyes in ecstasy at the vision.

"So. I hoist the equipment under one arm and take off with the ice cream cone looking for some place to sit in the shade and eat it. Dum Dum is pretty bare around there, and the sun is right overhead, and the heat is something awful. But I see this clump of trees about a block away and I head for it.

"Well here comes this staff car towards me with a general's star, big as life, on the front of it. I'm just going to take my first real bite of ice cream—I'd only licked at it a couple of times where it had started to melt on the top—when the car goes past me and I see this one-star general in the back seat—look right at him over the ice-cream cone, and he's staring right back at me. It's the new commanding officer of the base." Stanley glanced at Mark with a grin. "The same ratbone we'd heard about. He'd just come over from the States and he'd turned everything at Dum Dum real chicken-shit—class-A uniforms, hats, ties, military 'courtesy' all over the place—the whole business. And there I am, wringing wet from that Indian heat, staring him down with my shirt hanging open, my flight cap tucked under my belt. . . . It'd been so long since I'd been in the stateside army, I didn't think anything of it.

"Well, I hear this squeal of brakes and look around, and here comes the staff car backing up until it's even with me where I'm walking along. I don't want any trouble. All I want is to get out of that Indian sun and eat my double-dip vanilla ice-cream cone. Which is starting to melt for real now, running down the sides and onto my hand. India's got no respect for ice cream. I sneak a couple quick licks just before the window rolls down and there's the C.O. staring at me, no more than six feet away. He is red in the face and he is definitely displeased.

" 'Soldier!' he yells at me, 'don't you know a staff car when you see one?'

" 'Yes, sir,' I told him. I am not so happy myself, and I just keep walking. Maybe he'll go away. I told him the truth. Out of the corner of my eye I can see the driver having a great time watching the show, holding the car in reverse, backing up to keep right along with me while I walk.

"Seems like the general didn't care for my answer, and he yells at me again, 'Don't you know enough to salute a staff car?' Before I can answer him his voice goes up about an octave, 'Stand still when I'm talking to you, Soldier! And come to attention!'

"Well, he had me there, so I stopped. But the car kept on going for a bit until the driver could shift into first and come back. Which was a good thing because it gave me a minute to figure out how I was going to come to attention. It even took me a while to realize he was talking to me with this 'Soldier' business. Like he had the wrong guy. I wasn't a soldier, you know? I'm special service in the ATC in India. P.T. Athletics. Recreation. I'm carrying baseballs, not hand grenades. Who's he calling 'Soldier'?"

Stanley was warmed up now and all the way into his story. The other two were enjoying it almost as much as he was—even Mark, although he had obviously heard it before. It got broader every time Stanley told it.

"Anyway, I drop the carton with the equipment and I take a couple of quick licks at the ice cream—slurps, really, because it's running all over by now. Then I hold it down by my side, twisting it as much as I can with my wrist and my fingers to keep it level, like this. I put my heels together and stiffen up. By this time the general is back even with me. The car stops and he gives me this long, disgusted look. Then he shakes his head and in this low, gravel voice he says, 'Come here, Soldier.'

"That means one pace forward, which is all I can take 'cause that puts me almost up against the car. He can hardly see me, I'm so close. He tries, though, putting his fingers over the bottom of the window, like Schmoe—you know, Kilroy was here—and trying to look up at me. At least I'm close enough so I don't have to look him in the eye anymore. I'm standing at something like attention and looking over the top of the staff car. Good thing he can't see the ice-cream cone in my right hand either, which is too low. But my wrist is getting tired and it's starting to tilt and the melting ice cream is running down all over my hand. All the general can see is my sweaty shirt and open collar staring him in the face. He's really frustrated and starts yelling at me again.

" 'Where's your tie, Soldier?'

"I take a big chance. My only chance.

" 'It's at Barrackpore, sir.'

" 'Barrackpore!' he yells. 'What in hell is your tie doing in Barrackpore?'

"So I tell him. 'I'm stationed at Barrackpore, sir. I'm just here to pick up this equipment.' I didn't mention the ice cream. That didn't seem to be any of his business. It was on my mind, though, because it was getting pretty sloppy, and at the angle I was holding it alongside my leg, I was worried it might fall out of the cone."

"Did it?" Roy asked.

"Never mind. Don't rush me," Stanley protested. He was enjoying the story too much now for any short cuts.

"Well, the poor general doesn't know what to say for a minute. He just sputters for a bit. Then he asks me, real gruff, who's the commanding officer at Barrackpore, and doesn't he believe in wearing ties with class-A uniform at Barrackpore?

" 'Our C.O. at Barrackpore is General McGoldrick, sir,' I told him." Stanley winked at Mark and explained to Roy, "He's really only a chicken colonel, see, but I gave him a promotion. Figured this Dum Dum C.O. wouldn't know the difference, and that would keep him from pulling rank. I kind of slurred it a bit — 'Zhe'r'l McGoldrick,' like that — half-way toward 'Colonel,' just to play safe. I didn't want to lie. 'He doesn't make us wear ties on the base,' I said, 'Zhe'r'l McGoldrick.'

"I should have let it go at that, but you know me, I thought I'd help him out, him being new. So I said 'It's too hot here in India to wear ties, sir.' He does not appreciate getting advice from me and he starts yelling again.

" 'I'll be the judge of that, Soldier!' he says. And then he yells, 'Where's your hat?' A stupid question, since it's right in front of him in my belt, and he's staring right at it.

" 'It's in my belt, sir,' I says. I always tell the truth.

" 'Well, put it on!' he yells. 'I don't know what you do at Barrackpore, but you'll wear your hat when you're on my base.' I wasn't going to argue. But the problem was how was I going to put it on with a melting double-dip ice-cream cone in my right hand. Well, I was half right about the cone. The trouble was I had to step back to have room to operate, and I did it real snappy, you know — real military, trying to impress him, I guess, and get the whole thing over with. Anyway, the ice-cream cone's still at this angle, and when I step back, there goes the second dip sliding off. I stand there looking at that beautiful American ice cream melting into the Indian dust of Dum Dum Air Base. I almost cried.

"Well, I shift the cone with what's left of the ice cream into my left hand — gently because by now it is a soggy mess — and pull my overseas cap out of my belt and somehow manage to plaster it on my head with my free hand. The C.O. looks me up and down, 'That's better,' he lies. 'Now shape up, Soldier.' And he gives this little sign to the driver, who's been sitting there trying not to break up, and they drive off.

" 'Free at last,' I tell myself. I pick up the carton and take off again for that spot of shade, licking at the soggy mess of a cone which I've transferred back to my right hand."

"Anyway," Roy said, "you've still got one dip of vanilla left, huh?"

"Are you kidding? In India? Most of it's melted onto my clothes and all over my hands by now. Well, there's some left," Stanley allowed, and he launched back into his tale. "But that poor C.O. doesn't know when to quit. I hear the brakes squeal again, and when I look, here comes the staff car backing up to me again. This time when he sticks his head out the window he is really red.

" 'Goddammit, Soldier,' he yells, 'you still don't know enough to salute a staff car!' He looks like he's going to explode, and he's sweating like a pig himself by this time, and he fumbles around in his pockets and pulls out a pen and piece of paper. 'You are the sorriest goddam excuse for a soldier I've ever seen in this man's army, and I'm going to see that General McGoldrick gets a report of this.' He gets ready to write. 'What's your name and serial number?'

"So I told him. Told him the truth. Gave him my real name and serial number, although I always wondered afterward what I did that for. I could have told him anything. He didn't know. He'd have scribbled it down. But I'd given up. Who cared? My first ice-cream cone in India had melted away. Half of it was on the ground, the rest was mush and a mess all over my hands."

Stanley paused and shook his head. But he wasn't through.

"Anyway, he scribbled it down, so mad he could hardly write. Then he looks up at me again, narrowing his eyes, trying to look fierce or something." Stanley snorted in amusement at the recollection. "Heck, he was as sorry as I was by then, sweat dripping off his nose and chin, worn down by the whole stupid business. India was taking care of him too.

"He still had to keep up his front, though, so he says, 'Now somebody must have taught you how to salute, Soldier, and when this staff car leaves I want to see you execute the snappiest salute you ever threw in your life, one you aren't going to forget.' Forget? Was he kidding? Then he rolled up his window and glared at me through it while his driver raced the motor and shifted into first. So I transferred what was left of that soggy mess of an ice-cream cone to my left hand again. I clicked my heels and brought my hand up slow and tight and a little bit cupped, you know, with my shoulder out a bit, real neat and sharp. And then I whipped it out and down just as the car was taking off, and the slosh of melted ice cream all over my hand up to the wrist went flying. It missed his window or he'd have backed up again with a court martial. But there was a solid spray of melted vanilla as a souvenir all over the dust on the trunk of that general's staff car, I'll tell you that."

Roy had been rocking with laughter through the whole tale. Now that Stanley's performance was finished at last, he drew a long breath and wagged his head back and forth slowly. "Chick-in-shit," he said, drawling out the vowels. "I wonder how long *he* lasted in India."

Mark spoke into the lapse that followed. "I never asked you, Stanley. Did you go back and get another ice-cream cone?"

"Huh! That was the worst part of it, for hell's sake," Stanley answered. The awkward oath was a Mormonism he fell into in certain moments of serious banter. "I went to the latrine to clean up the mess, and by the time I got back to the PX window they had sold out and the 'closed' sign was up—no more ice cream until noon the next day. By then, hah! I was back checking out baseballs at Barrackpore. No ice cream, but at least I'm serving my time under *General* McGoldrick."

"Deserves his promotion," Mark concluded. "Knows how to get something done as an American and still survive in India."

"Amen to that," said Stanley.

THE BEAUTIFUL MRS. RAO

Quiet fell over the aft sections of the *General Bliss*. The tense activity of the search continued, presumably, but in sectors off the bow and distant enough from the stern of the mother ship to lose any sound as well as sight of the ranging boats. The sea had increased in restlessness since the cloud cover moved in, but the ocean vista over the stern was a dull reflection of the overcast, and the flat light masked much of its movement.

Sitting on their platform, the Roy Warner Trio joined, for a while, in the largeness of the silence. Then Stanley started softly to drum a simple figure with his hands on his up-flexed knees. Roy worried idly over a callous on his middle finger. Mark, contemplative, was smiling at some inward reflection.

"This Hindu friend of mine, Sinha, at Hastings Mill, was a strange guy," Mark began. "Sometimes he wouldn't talk at all, and other times he'd just rattle on like he knew everything there was to know and didn't mind telling you. Most of the American guys didn't like him, thought he was queer or stuck-up, didn't have much to do with him. The major he worked with — Major Woodruff — never could bring himself to call Sinha by name. Called him 'you' or 'hey,' or, usually, nothing at all. When Sinha wasn't around he'd call him 'that know-it-all son-of-a-bitch' or 'that arrogant bastard.' Well, Sinha was strange, all right, but I kind of liked him. We got along fine. The fact was, he did have more brains than most of those brown-nose staff officers around the Mill, which made it worse. And of course he was Indian. They didn't go for that. He wore Indian clothes all the time and walked around splay-footed in sandals. He spoke English fine and he liked to mix in American slang words when you'd least expect it, but he had this way of making it sound Indian, and he had these little gestures with his head and his hands when he talked."

"What was he doin' there?" Roy asked.

"He was some kind of advisor or go-between. I'm not sure. Liaison, I think they called it. There were a number of Indians around Hastings Mill on the headquarters payroll. Most of them were used to working with Americans and wore Western clothes and picked up American ways. Not Sinha, though. He was a Brahmin, too, and didn't mind letting you know it. He never really fit in there, at the Mill. Were you ever there, Roy?"

"Only that mornin' I came in, when we had the briefin' for the show tour with Captain Clinton."

"Oh yeah. Well, you know what it's like then."

"No, I don't really," Roy countered. "I just saw the big open mill part where we walked through on the way to Special Service. I remember that, though, with those belts and pulleys overhead. And I knew it was ATC headquarters, of course. Lotsa brass around. Full of desks and pencil-pushers. What were you doin' there?"

Mark winced. "Playing for the big brass. Big deal. Every time they had to entertain some big shot, they'd pull me over to headquarters from Barrackpore. One time they had me on detached service at the Mill for nearly a month. I just sat around most of the time. That's when I got to know Sinha. He didn't do much either, and we'd sit around and talk. This Major Woodruff got it in his head that I was a big-time pianist in the States—a prodigy or something. So they had me play for a lot of dinners and parties. It wasn't a bad deal. Cocktail stuff, most of the time. Gershwin medleys. Rodgers and Hart. Cole Porter. All very cool. Except this one general who always wanted to hear the 'Warsaw Concerto,' so I'd have to pound that out whenever he was around. 'Rhapsody in Blue'—somebody'd always ask for that." He looked at Stanley, "Anyway, I ate good."

Stanley checked his watch. It was quarter after three. 1515 hours. There was time yet. He decided right then not to get in the chow line before it was called. With the search for the man overboard still going on, it just wouldn't seem right. Even though interest in the search among the troops had waned, the ship was still, after all, in something like a state of emergency. This time he would wait until chow call was official. Pleased with his decision, Stanley shifted his position against the bulkhead, getting as relaxed and comfortable as he could.

"Well," Mark went on, "it wasn't Sinha I was going to tell you about, although he's a part of it. It was this Indian lady who came in to consult with the staff officers—like Sinha, but not on a full-time basis. I'd seen her a few times going through the Mill on her way to meetings. Mrs. Rao, her name was. Urvashi Rao." Mark spoke it with obvious pleasure. "There was always a bunch of officers with her, trying to look official and important with their briefcases and file folders and always sneaking looks at her. You knew she was something special. She'd be walking straight ahead, cool and composed, her head up, with this little smile on her face, never looking right at any of them. You couldn't tell how old she was. I mean, she was a young woman, but you couldn't tell her age—she could have been anywhere from twenty-five to thirty-five. Forty, even. Anyway, she was absolutely beautiful. Everything went together. God, she was graceful. I've never seen anyone move like that. She just . . . went."

Mark shook his head. "No. I take that back. I've seen other Indian women move like that. It's the way they walk. Most of them, anyway. They just flow, like water. Like they don't have to think about it or make any effort especially. It's fascinating to watch. There's little bit of sway, but it's always controlled. Like a dancer—or an athlete, you know, Stanley? With everything coordinated and smooth, like it doesn't take any effort.

"Anyway, it was something special to see her walking through Hastings Mill like that, with a bunch of nervous American officers around her in their tight uniforms, all cleaned and pressed—creases so sharp you could cut yourself on them—those eager-beaver types with their crew-cuts, some of them getting bald—and Mrs. Rao just gliding along in a beautiful sari like she wasn't even touching the floor. She was the opposite of everything you felt about the place—that big ugly old mill. It was a factory, really, left over from the British—full of those staff headquarters types with their desks buried under stacks of paper and forms, everyone acting important and bucking for rank and promotion. It was hard to imagine she had anything to do with the war they were running—whatever made the whole thing necessary, and me there in the middle of it."

"Playing 'Warsaw Concerto' for the generals," Stanley put in.

"Yeah," Mark returned. "I guess I was out of place, all right, but nothing like Mrs. Rao. You never got used to seeing her there, right in the middle of all this military headquarters stuff in those soft, flowing silk saris, like none of it could ever touch her."

Mark interrupted himself with a slight frown. "Come to think of it, maybe it's partly the sari I'm thinking about. I mean the way Indian women move, inside their clothes. That gracefulness. Not just feminine, you know, but female. The saris aren't really tight, but they always fit just right, the way they drape them around, and hold them sometimes, over their arm—but you can tell just how their bodies are moving in them. I mean, there were a lot of American WACs around

Hastings Mill, some of them really good-looking. Probably some of them walked a lot better than those Indian women in their saris, but it wasn't the same at all. It was their uniforms, I guess—something like those starched officers around Mrs. Rao."

"You're crazy," Stanley said. "Some of those WACs were gorgeous. You remember Sally Andreas, that sergeant in Captain Clinton's office? Momma! I could watch her walk all day."

"Yeah," Mark agreed. "She was pretty good. But it's different. Sally walked sexy. Threw it around in that tight skirt. You could see everything she had. In a sari you have to imagine it. That's the difference, really."

Roy entered the discussion. "Maybe that's right," he said. "I like 'em both, but the Americans give you the whole show. With those short skirts, 'specially, you see most of their legs and just about everything else. And tight blouses and uplift brassieres."

"Falsies?" Stanley added.

"Well, yeah, I suppose," Roy said. "But the thing is, it's all out there on display, man. If they're fat-ass, you know it. If they wiggle, you wiggle right with 'em. But a good-lookin' Indian woman in a sari . . . "

Mark took over the lapse. "You can see her movement," he said, "but you have to imagine her body. That's what does it. You don't see any of the . . . mechanics. All you get is the suggestion of the woman's body, not the parts—not legs or hips or butt or breasts—but her whole body. You see her head and her shoulders, maybe, and that's nice, the way they hold them, straight and kind of level, while everything else below moves together. You don't really see her body at all." Mark's voice tightened and rose. "It's really an illusion, what I'm talking about. It's not what you see, it's what you think you see. That's a lot like what Sinha used to try to explain to me."

All three were quiet, considering this, each one picturing, remembering, mulling over the image of Indian women in their flowing silks and light, soft cottons.

Stanley spoke. "Anyway, they were sensible in that heat. Better than the clothes we had to wear—collars and belts. That loose, filmy material, silk or whatever it was. Couldn't see through it, the way they draped it around, but it always looked cool. I never saw a woman in an Indian sari looked like she was really hot. Except the really fat ones."

"In some ways," Mark said, taking up his story again, looking off, "Mrs. Rao was the most beautiful woman I ever saw. She had perfectly smooth skin. Flawless brown, kind of light brown. Clean and soft." He struggled for a word. "Luminous, it was—like everything about her." He turned directly to his companions. "Remember when I tried to describe her to you, Stanley? But you really had to see her. She had this beautiful face, Roy—not too Indian, if you know what I mean, a little fuller, more round than most, but everything even and just right. It was her expression, though, that got you. She was so beautiful that you didn't look at her mouth or her nose or her hair, you just looked at her face—at *her*, you know? Well, her eyes, maybe. When she looked at you, which she only did certain times, and you looked back at her. Like she was looking right into you and knew you so well and was kind and sweet, it almost made you sad, you felt so good. And . . . I know it sounds crazy, but, like she—maybe she loved you already, or would as soon as she knew you at all, as soon as you said something— said anything—to her. But she was still distant, kind of, like she was looking right through you, too, at something else—at something she could see, but no matter how hard you tried, you'd never know what it was."

Mark was savoring the image, the others with him. "This absolutely beautiful woman—you couldn't help watching her, waiting for her to look at you. Everybody did. She knew it, of course. She must have. Any woman—any beautiful woman—does. But it seemed completely natural to her. She didn't ask for it or play up to it or get cute or coy or anything. Not like you'd expect, like American women, you know, like they expect men to fall all over them, or court them, or whatever you call it. It's hard to talk about, the way she made you feel. Rich, maybe. And lucky. Because you could just look at her, and wonder about her, and admire her, and not feel embarrassed or that you had to do something about it—or that she'd ever expect you to. What could you ever do with a woman that beautiful anyway? She was so calm, you couldn't imagine her any other way, really, like if you got passionate or even rough or anything like that, she'd just be the same as she was, no matter what, like you couldn't really touch her because she already knew all about it, knew whatever you were after — " Mark raised his eyebrows and his expression lit up, " — like she already *forgave* you for whatever you felt or whatever you might do!"

"How did you get to know her?" Roy asked. "Did you get to know her?"

"It was Sinha," Mark replied. "Pratap Narayan Sinha. Sinha introduced us. He'd known her for years. Since before she was married, before she'd been to the States."

"Wait a minute," Stanley said. "You never told me she'd been to the States."

"Oh yeah," Mark affirmed. "She studied at Columbia. Had a degree from there, Sinha told me. In American History, I think. Or was it Sociology? I don't remember. You'd never know from her, anyway — except if you brought it up. You just wouldn't think of her as, you know, academic or intellectual."

"What about her husband?" Roy asked.

"I met him once. I met them both at their club in Calcutta for drinks. It was his idea. She told him I was an American concert pianist or something and I guess he thought that meant they should entertain me. He was a businessman of some sort. Indian executive type. Nervous guy. Kind of thin, tall. Not bad-looking. Little moustache. Good English. He'd studied in England and talked a lot about that. Spoke kind of British. She sounded," Mark shrugged, "American, I guess. I never really thought about it. She didn't talk much. When she did, it was very neat and precise and quiet and, you know, pleasant — like American with just that little lilt the Indians have."

"This Sinha guy have anything going with her?" Roy wanted to know.

Mark snorted in reply, "Sinha? No. Well, I don't think so. No. Did I say no one could help looking at her? Well, that's not quite true. Sinha never paid much attention to her. At first I thought maybe he was just jealous, because she got so much attention from everybody. But I don't think so. He seemed to be more just amused. He didn't dislike her. I don't think anybody could. Not just because she was so beautiful, but the way she was, too. She was nice to everybody — not just the brass, but the enlisted men around the place, too. Me, for instance. And Sinha, too. She was the same with everybody. Never raised her voice or asked for anything special. She just smiled that little smile at you and made you feel beautiful too. Always said the right thing, or else she didn't say anything at all.

"You know what? She never laughed. Like she didn't need to, she already knew what was funny. And what wasn't. When I think about her it's like she never did anything quick, anything you didn't know she'd do. Once I got to thinking about her and I realized that her eyes— that she never blinked—like she never had to blink. I watched her the next time I was with her, and it was true. She never seemed to blink. She'd just lower her eyelids slowly sometimes and then raise them again slowly and look right through you again. With that little smile.

"There was a while there when I thought about Mrs. Rao all the time. I was new in India and everything was getting to me and I was homesick and nervous about everything—just too much to get a hold of. India, you know. Calcutta especially, when I'd go in to the city. All the beggars and cripples and toothless old people. The smells. And the burning ghats down at the river. I'll never forget the first time I went down and saw them. There was a dead body ready to be burned on one of them. All wrapped up and the people around with their Hindu funeral stuff, most of them just looking around like they were embarrassed. Squinting. They always look embarrassed, like they're going to laugh. Except this one woman in a dirty black sari, an older woman, but not really old. She was wailing and talking a blue streak and waving her arms in the air. I couldn't stay around."

Mark shrugged again. "And then there was Mrs. Rao. She was India, too, and I'd never known anyone as beautiful, anyone I'd felt like that about. I was in love with her, I guess. But I was so upset and overstimulated those days I never thought about her that way. Instead, I'd just wonder about her and about her life when she wasn't there, at Hastings Mill. She was so graceful, so much at ease. Always. Anywhere. And still so Indian. I used to say her first name to myself, over and over, like it was a charm or something. 'Urvashi.' At first I didn't like it. It sounded strange. But the more I said it and pictured her, the more beautiful it became: 'Urvashi. Urvashi.'

I used to plan how I would get together with her somehow and talk with her about all the things in India that were bothering me, and have her explain them to me. She'd know what I meant. And there wouldn't be any problem—including language—between us, nothing she couldn't help me understand."

"Did you ever do it with her?" Roy asked.

"Do it?" Mark repeated. "Oh—talk to her like that? No. Not really. I did talk with her a number of times. Just us. Never for very long. She always had to get someplace. I don't even know what we talked about. Nothing like that. It was always fascinating, though, talking to her. Like there was something deep hidden in everything she said."

Mark clasped his hands behind his head, elbows out. He stretched, lowered his arms, and relaxed again.

"No. I talked about all that stuff with Sinha instead. We'd talk for hours. Like I told you, sometimes he'd go on and on and giggle and wave his arms and I'd just listen. Other times, he'd be real cagey and say very little and just look kind of amused—this is what put everybody off, you know. He'd be kind of smug. And then I'd have to ask him a lot of questions. I always felt free to do that with Sinha, that's one thing—and he'd give me those short answers and let it go at that. Sometimes they weren't answers at all, but it would just set me up for another question.

"Well, the last time Sinha and I got together, before they took me off detached service at Hastings Mill, I got to talking to him about Mrs. Rao. Sinha and I got pretty close, and I let it all out, how I felt about her. I told him how beautiful I thought she was—and how mysterious. I talked about how her beauty seemed ageless and timeless to me—like she was, oh, the embodiment of all the things I yearned for and couldn't hope to attain. That kind of talk. It sounds silly now, but it sure wasn't then. We used to get into all that sort of thing anyway, Sinha and I, so it wasn't so unusual. It was just all connected this time with the beauty of Mrs. Urvashi Rao. And I meant it. There was so much about her and my feelings about her that I couldn't understand, and I hoped that talking with Sinha would help. He'd known her a long time, and he knew pretty much how I felt about India, and he was my friend—a pretty strange one, I'll admit, but my friend—the only one I really had around there.

"I told him that I'd never known anyone as full of grace as she was, as complete and peaceful, whatever she was doing, as if she had solved all the contradictions that made the rest of us unhappy and unfulfilled. I talked about her smile and the secrets that seemed to be hiding just behind that bewitching, forgiving little smile. All the while, Sinha was listening and nodding slowly as I raved on, tilting his head and looking half-lidded.

"I talked about her eyes, and how she seemed to see so deeply into my real feelings, no matter how trivial or commonplace our conversation might be — how I fancied she could see right on through my words to some spiritual reality that held us both, beyond us both.

"Sinha started nodding more rapidly at this and muttered something about 'that look of hers,' " Mark added. "I must have paused to catch my breath, and Sinha went on in his small voice, his Indian lilt going along with his nodding head. 'One of Mrs. Rao's little vanities,' he was saying; 'quite nearsighted, you know,' and his head quit going up and down and started to wag sideways. 'She just won't wear her glasses.' I went right ahead. My steam was up. The taunting vision of the beautiful Mrs. Urvashi Rao, who seemed somehow capable of assuring a man's transport to Nirvana, was full upon me. . . . "

Mark grew eloquent and expansive, warming to the climax of his story as he sat erect there on the battleship-gray deck platform. The troopship USS *General Bliss* was still dead in the water, but Sgt. Mark Reiter had his steam up. Stanley Norman and LeRoy Warner were right with him as his reminiscence built to its coda.

" 'Can you explain it to me, Sinha, my friend?' I pleaded." Mark raised his chin and extended one arm out toward the darkening Pacific horizon as he spoke. " 'There is something about her I'm afraid I'll never know, something so close to my deepest feeling and yet so far from what I am able to understand. When I look in her face it seems so close. It's the mystery at the center of her beauty, so comforting because I can sense it — and yet so frustrating because I'm afraid it will always be just beyond my reach. Can you tell me? Can you help me understand, Sinha, somehow, *what it is* about Mrs. Urvashi Rao!' "

Mark lowered his eyes and his voice as he continued. "Pratap Narayan Sinha went on nodding" — Mark imitated the motion — "first up and down, then wagging slowly sideways. 'It is after all quite simple, my friend,' Sinha said to me in his Indian lilt, smiling his giddy smile, quite smug as he lifted up his forefinger vaguely, then pointed it directly at his temple. 'She is dumb.' "

CHAPTER FIVE

The world below the brine,
. . .

Different colors, pale gray and green, purple, white, and gold,
  the play of light through the water,
. . .

Sluggish existences grazing there suspended, or slowly crawling
  close to the bottom,
Passions there, wars, pursuits, tribes, sight in those ocean
  depths, breathing that thick-breathing air, as so many
  do. . . .

— Walt Whitman

THE SHIP

During the era of World War II, the technical capabilities of communication underwent a startling revolution. Sensitive electronic instruments broke through our human physical limitations and gave unprecedented scope and precision to what could be seen, heard, and detected — by radio telemetry systems, radar, sonar, electronic bombsights, and an array of navigation and tracking devices.

The USS *General Bliss* reflected this new world of communication. Adjacent to the bridge, the Combat Information Center collected and coordinated the information sensed by such devices. The ship's interior communication systems were also efficient and effective. The bridge had direct communication with all stations and lookouts, backed up by a second, sound-powered system to be used in case of electrical power failure. The general announcement system linked everyone instantaneously, the sound from its overlapping speakers probing even the most remote sections of the vessel. *"Man Overboard!"* the disembodied voice from these speakers had cried, and it was heard simultaneously by every soul on the ship, each in his own place, absorbing this startling communication at once into the current of his own life and thought.

During the search and rescue operation, however, military communications on the *General Bliss* followed a peculiar regression to techniques of an earlier time. While the lines from the lookout stations to the bridge stayed open, they soon were merely standing by and grew dormant, having nothing of consequence to communicate. It was as if the situation were too basic — in a sense too simple — for the sophisticated technology of World War II.

Directing operations from the bridge, the Captain had chosen the old line-of-sight visual methods of communication at sea. First this had been by semaphore, with the signalmen whipping their red-and-white flags from position to position like fluttering extensions of their clockwork arms, while the receiving signalman on the other end read their spelled-out messages and passed along the reconstructed word.

Before long, however, the Captain switched over to signal lights. For one thing, the two boats were moving farther out in the orbit of their search, and the signal lights carried over greater distances than semaphore. For another, as the day darkened under the advancing cloud cover, the visibility of the lights increased. Instead of semaphore flags, the men in the boats aimed their hand-held lights back at the hulking troopship, where the signalman on the bridge, with the OOD at his elbow, answered with the large signal light mounted in a directional swivel base.

To those close by, the signal light made a reassuring clatter as the shutter was flipped rapidly up and down, open and shut, interrupting its beam in the irregular rhythms of its coded communication. For the troops on the forward decks who were in position to watch as the boats ranged far out over the bow, however, it was a peculiarly mute exchange. Only the light punctuated the silence, flashing back at them from far out over the darkening waters—far enough at times so that the boat itself was a wee dot below the horizon and its signal light a disproportionately large, nervous blinking eye, transmitting messages to its communicant partner on the bridge across great intervening stretches of sea.

While this dialogue by eye went on between the mother ship and her roving boats, the bodiless authority of the voice over the speakers had fallen silent.

It was a peculiarly democratic interlude for the GIs deployed over the decks of the *General Bliss*, drifting dead in the water, with the attention of its crew and its command turned entirely aside from the routine of its mission as a troop transport and concentrated instead on the salvation of a single life. The long break in communication from any designated authority temporarily set the society of the ship apart from both of the worlds which its journey bridged—the military world of wartime behind them and the postwar civil world yet ahead. For the troops it was a curiously static, yet free, time when neither their thoughts nor their activities seemed monitored.

If indeed the lapse in communication from troopship authority had contributed to this state, the first signal that the strange interlude was ending occurred at 1530 hours, when the speakers throughout the *General Bliss* came suddenly back to life with the split-tone whistle of the bo'sun's pipe. It was followed once again by the manner and language which brought to the troops all the announcements in their regular daily schedule:

"*Now hear this. Now hear this. Evening chow lines form on the main deck, port and starboard sides.*"

Whether in peacetime or in war, there are some routines, like the biological imperatives in which our lives persist, that have small tolerance for interruption and delay. The needs of the body must be served.

Again, the voice from the speakers, seeming even more familiar as it repeated:

"*Evening chow lines form on the main deck, port and starboard sides.*"

STANLEY NORMAN

Stanley was surprised to find his chow line relatively short when he joined it and moving rather more steadily than usual. In practically no time he was at the bulkhead door at the top of the first set of steps leading down. Halfway on that first flight, which was narrow and steep like all the stairways, more like ladders, really, the forward progress of the chow line abruptly stopped. Evidently the initial slack in the human chain of GIs had been taken up. The line was now tight from the narrow hatchway entry into the mess hall far down and ahead, back up to the end of the line behind and above Stanley on the main deck. The line would move slowly now, inching along as, one by one, the GIs at the front picked up their trays and moved mechanically past the cramped serving line into the small, hot, stand-up mess hall. As each one stepped through the doorway to confront the KPs dishing up the food, a short wave of motion — a kind of slow peristaltic ripple, the width of one man's position — passed back through the entire length of the snaking chow line, back up around corners and up stairwells, through hundreds of fatigue-clad bodies, until the last man up on the deck shuffled a step forward to await the next impulse that would advance him again.

There was always a lot of time to think in the chow line. Or not to think. Generally, the talk grew thin as the GIs passed through the doorway off the main deck and started their descent into the bowels of the ship. Once the opening of that entry, with its patch of Pacific sky, was out of sight behind them, talk seemed alien, and each man fell into the web of his private thought, or — as was more often the case through the long, boring course of standing, moving up, waiting, standing, leaning, moving up, waiting — of conscious thoughtlessness. This was an ability most GIs acquired early in their service when so much of their time, both on duty and off, consisted of enforced idleness, endless delays, and laggard, sluggish lines. Caught in the irony of inactive readiness, GIs throughout the military services had a common sardonic response to their situation. "Hurry up," they said with a smirk, "and wait."

Ordinarily, Stanley Norman would have fallen into that customary empty lethargy of the line, but on this occasion his mind was alert, his thoughts alive and restless. Actually, he was always somewhat nervous below decks. He would grow vaguely apprehensive as soon as he funnelled from the fresh air and open sky of the deck into the constricted chutes and scaled-down passageways below. Some degree of claustrophobia was inevitable for anyone not accustomed to them. Stanley's case was only somewhat abated after two weeks on the ship. He was larger than most of the men and therefore had to stoop and bend and weave his way through with more sense of misfit than some. But it was the pathway to food twice each day. All in a good cause, he could customarily console himself.

This time, however, he was more than usually uncomfortable about leaving the main deck and plunging into the comparatively airless confines below. His eyesight was slow in accommodating to the light of the bulbs protected in their wire cages overhead and at strategic locations on the walls. It seemed more dim and yellow than he remembered.

Stanley had the sensation of moving through tunnels. Except for the uncompromising cleanliness of the painted metal surfaces everywhere, there was more than a suggestion of passing through sewers. The prevalence of pipes and tubes of various sizes running along the ceilings and wall cornerings helped the impression. Stanley had always felt himself moving underground as he descended through the layers and stairwells, but for the first time he was conscious of descending toward the waterline. At what level, he wondered each time the slowly advancing line brought him to another ladderway, would they reach the surface of the sea? At what point would they pass underwater? The preoccupation added to his uneasiness in the descent.

The stimulation of the afternoon's events was still with him, too. Despite his waiting until the chow lines were called, he carried with him a lingering sense of inappropriateness, almost embarrassment, about standing in a chow line while an all-out search continued for the man overboard.

All these factors contributed to a rather tentative feeling Stanley began to experience in his stomach. It was a vague, shifting kind of uneasiness, aided by the slight roll of the vessel, well short of nausea, yet enough to take the edge off his appetite. He tried to ignore it, but it was no use. On the open deck with the horizon in sight, he might have disregarded the feeling or talked himself out of it, but not here in the close air and constricted space he was committed to.

The trouble was that it brought to mind rather too vividly a bout he had experienced in India with amoebic dysentery. It was a severe enough case so that he had suffered considerably through the siege in what the ATC medics at Barrackpore called "sick bay." He had even supposed from time to time in his misery that he might not pull through. And in one instance, his fears almost came true. In fact, it occurred to Stanley that if his amoebic dysentery had come to mind during the earlier conversation by the Trio about times when they could have been killed, his experience in the infirmary would have been a notable addition. In spite of himself, his thoughts went back over that ordeal, still vivid in his entrails as in his memory, for he had been told the amoebae might not be totally eradicated and he could well have recurrences later.

It was a dinner at an Indian restaurant which catered to the military near the Barrackpore base that did it. The ABC Cafe it was called—for American, British, Chinese. The place had been off limits from time to time, for obvious reasons, but the food was delicious, especially the fried prawns, which is what Stanley ordered. They were huge, succulent, meaty river prawns, fried in the Chinese style. The dysentery had not erased Stanley's craving, and his saliva quickened at the thought of them in spite of his wayward stomach as he shuffled ahead, preoccupied, in the chow line.

Curry was another matter. Oddly, it was Indian curry that he associated with the dysentery. Ever since his illness he could not abide either the taste or the smell of curry. Of course it was not necessarily the prawns that had brought about the infiltration of amoebae into his system. It could have been anything at the ABC Cafe, the silverware or plates as well as the food.

Whatever the cause, Stanley already had a stomachache and rumblings when he went to bed that evening. Later—he never was sure of the hours through that harrowing night—he awoke with sharp pains in his abdomen which came in great waves and doubled him over as they mounted. During periods when they would subside somewhat, he was able to drift off into troubled bouts of sleep, only to wake up again as they returned. In time, as the pain grew more constant and severe, sleep was out of the question. He moved from pain to more pain and began to feel some desperation in his plight. Appendicitis, he kept thinking, as the pain would hit, but he knew something about that from his P.E. training, and he suspected this pain was too high and too generalized. Even so, he should get to a doctor as soon as possible. That was not always easily done in the service. The infirmary in this case was a half mile away, at the other end of the base, and sick call—the only way he knew to see an Army doctor—was from six to eight a.m. Still, he'd better get over there and wait while he could still manage.

When he got up from his charpoy, though, he could barely maintain his balance. He was weak, and his head was spinning, and, worst of all, the pain in his middle was so constricting that it doubled him up. It was impossible to stand up straight. Swaying in an agonized crouch, he fumbled his way into his clothes, then sat down, breathing heavily through the waves of agony in his gut. *Should I wake someone else in the basha to take care of me?* he wondered. *No. No sense in that.* He didn't want to depend on anyone else. What could they do? Couldn't get anyone to look at him until sick call anyway. It was getting on to five already. He might as well get over there himself and wait. He could make it.

The stumbling, pain-racked trip to the infirmary through the predawn dark was the most difficult thing Stanley had ever done. Indeed, he wondered many times along the way if he could make it. The pain grew searing at its peak, as if it might cut him in half. More than once he fell to his knees, not a long fall since he was moving in a full crouch, his arms cradling his midsection, and his forward motion was more a process of falling and recovering his balance through momentum than walking in any normal manner. Afterward he could remember only this pitching and falling through the night, and one interlude when he tripped, fell prone, and crawled for some yards in a paroxysm of agony, unable for a spell to face the additional pain of straightening enough to rise again to his feet.

What he remembered of his thoughts at that moment was odd, amusing, and a bit embarrassing. He had never told anyone, but he recollected it well. It was an occasion of vainglorious self-dramatization. Grimacing and crawling in excruciating pain, he dug his fingers into the Indian earth in the dark, half-way between his basha and the infirmary with the rest of the base slumbering away the early morning hour, and pulled his slithering, doubled-up body a few inches closer to salvation. He continued this craven crawling longer than was in any way reasonable, enjoying in the melodramatic process a heroic image of himself and his struggle—alone, all grit, sweat, pain, and intractable determination, moving inches by sheer will, keeping going at all odds, perhaps to die in the attempt, but not to give way to the pain short of unconsciousness, not to yield short of oblivion. After a few moments of this groveling in feverish dramatic glory, he was again on his feet, shoulders down, clutching his middle, plunging ahead on his way.

At the infirmary, a medical orderly was fortunately on duty, awake, and alert enough to catch Stanley's loud arrival. No stranger to the symptoms of amoebic dysentery, he had his patient in an infirmary gown, in bed, and sedated within five minutes, ready for the doctor's formal diagnosis and treatment on his sick call rounds an hour or so later.

Shuffling along in the chow line through the bowels of the *General Bliss*, Stanley recalled the incredible weakness he had felt through the early days of his recovery. It was an immense physical effort to rise and stagger out the screen door and down the path to the outdoor latrine of the infirmary, a feat he performed at very frequent intervals, for the urge was upon him almost incessantly and he had only tenuous and tentative control over it. Bedpans were out after the first few rounds. Once his treatment had begun he was expected to look after himself. It hadn't seemed fair, since he was so debilitated and felt so helpless. It was a threatening experience for Stanley, whose physical training regularly kept him feeling muscular and strong, to be so woefully weak and drained of energy, all of it going to the involuntary activity of his churning viscera. But Stanley was not one to ask favors or seek pity. He did what was expected of him, assured that the pain and discomfort gradually would diminish day by day. He took his medicine like a man. Yet that had nearly been his undoing.

Now, isolated in the troopship chow line, the queasiness in his stomach continued to challenge his appetite as he replayed the memories of his dysentery. The glum, quiet chow line suddenly struck him as a line of prisoners, without visible chains but shuffling to their piti-ful meal in a kind of lockstep, without alternative and without the freedom or inclination to break the pattern. They must be somewhere near the waterline now. It was unsettling to suppose they were pass-ing together in this fashion to levels below the surface of the sea, that the KPs on the serving line were going through their mindless rou-tines under water. It had been the routines of treatment at the ATC sick bay to which Stanley, with his small pride, had submitted him-self, that might well have been his end. Somehow, moving ahead in the expanding–contracting spasms of the submerged chow line while recalling his misadventures at the infirmary, Sgt. Stanley Norman felt for the first time the full irony of those events.

The treatment for amoebic dysentery in the CBI at that time was a carefully regulated daily dose of an arsenic compound and bismuth, presumably toxic enough to kill off the majority of the rampant amoe-bae without doing in the host patient in the bargain. During his sec-ond day of treatment, Stanley had routinely, if inadvertently, been given two full doses of the prescribed medication within ten minutes of each other. One orderly had done his duty before going off, but had neglected to note it on the right line of the military form on his clip-board chart. His successor then had done similar duty, supposing righ-teously that he was covering his buddy's oversight. Stanley, who had dutifully been taking his medicine without much knowledge of what was going on and without the strength at that point to care, sensed infirmly only that something was different, not that anything was wrong. Luckily, by the slender grace of his own good will, he had managed a weak pleasantry as, returning to bed after his next feeble trip to the latrine, he passed the second dutiful orderly at his station. "Boy, that double dose sure cleaned me out this trip," he whispered, angling at his bed. "What double dose?" the orderly wanted to know.

The next twenty-four hours, he learned later, had been crucial, with constant concern, ministration, and monitoring of the patient. It was the most attention Sgt. Norman had received in his whole mili-tary career. He had been made sick, adding the disease of his stomach to that of his alimentary canal, for they had induced vomiting and taken further precautions against his ingestion of the full double-dose of arsenic and bismuth.

The doctor in charge had been furious at first. Deep in the lethargy of his misery, Stanley had been grateful and felt partially redeemed in that. But as he now recalled (the hatchway leading into the serving line and mess hall was just ahead, around the next corner, and he could sense the oppressive heat and smell the confusion of odors from the steamed food) the doctor had been strictly routine with him thereafter—if anything, more harsh and unforgiving than with the other patients, as if Stanley were somehow accountable for the error that had caused him the extra trouble. . . .

Stanley suddenly found himself at the hatch, through the opening, and opposite the stack of mess trays. It was always sudden and unexpected, this confrontation with the serving line itself after the long, lax, self-absorbed wait in line, calling for quick responses before one was ready. Reflex actions took over. Without purging the drift of his mind back over his memories of dysentery, he snatched up a tray and side-stepped along to hold it in front of the first KP, moving into the ratchet-like geared rhythms on both sides of the steamy serving line. On the other side, the sweating, tee-shirted KP dipped his long-handled serving ladle into the tub before him and emptied it, splat, into a compartment of Stanley's tray—something like porridge, vaguely off-white, compacted and grainy, neither liquid nor solid. Dehydrated potatoes, Stanley supposed, or dehydrated something. His stomach disapproved, but he advanced another notch as the ratchet moved him along. The next serving spoon dipped and rose. In the poised instant before it lowered to clank against the edge of his tray and dislodge its contents into the second compartment, Stanley saw the yellowish sauce of its lumpy, mustardy burden. The odors in the heat of the mess hall were mixed and indistinguishable. It was not so much his nose and eyes as his stomach that warned him. Curry! In a counter-reflex he pulled his tray back at the last instant. The spoon descended through empty air. The shank hit the edge of the serving table with no tray in its appointed place, and the lumpy yellowish contents went splat, down the front of the table and onto the floor. By the time the poor KP, his vital rhythm broken, looked up from the mess, Stanley, in the inexorable flux of the line, had moved on, and the next GI—or was it the same one? the KP's astonished expression seemed to ask—had thrust a tray before him.

Sheepish and meek, Stanley continued dutifully through the rest of the line, his shoulders hunched, stooping somewhat, trying to make himself less conspicuous, perhaps in response partly to the increased promptings of his wayward stomach. He hurried to a space at the stand-up tables, dabbed at the glutinous porridgelike substance, ate a few overcooked mushy peas, turned to the pineapple slice in the dessert compartment and managed to finish that off before he emptied the rest in the slop can, rinsed his tray in the series of three cans of boiling water next to it, surrendered it gratefully at the end of the line, and headed out for the blessed deck and fresh air.

LEROY WARNER

Roy begged off when Stanley asked if he wanted to go along to chow. Roy rarely got in the chow line early anyway, preferring to wait, as did Mark, until near the end of the chow period, after all the chow-hounds had been through and the lines were shorter and more relaxed. Besides not being ready to eat when Stanley left, LeRoy had other things on his mind.

From their platform, Roy and Mark watched Stanley climb down the ladder and saunter along the deck toward the chow line amidships. He walked on the balls of his feet with a kind of controlled lilt, agile for his size — an athlete's gait.

"Stanley the manly," Roy said with an affectionate smile.

Mark agreed with a shake of his head. "Norman the Foreman," he said, "going to organize a little troopship food."

With Stanley gone, Roy and Mark sat back, relaxed, and were quiet. They seldom talked much as a pair, although they were perfectly at ease together, accepting each other with comfort and a secure, tacit affection.

For a time, each was complete in his own musing, until, at length, Mark spoke.

"I may not eat at all tonight," he said. "No appetite at all."

Roy shifted his position, was unsatisfied with it, shifted again, then sighed and stood up. He brushed off the seat of his pants. It was more gesture than need, for the deck, however hard and unyielding to sit on, was clean and dustless.

"Well," he said, continuing to slap idly at the back of his pants legs, down to the inside of the knees, "I sure got no eyes for that mess-hall C-rations stuff." He put his hands on his hips, dipped his knees once, twice, took a deep breath, and looked out over the water.

"I got to move around, though. Gettin' stiff. Think I'll wander down to the galley. See if I can talk them out of some real food. Somethin' worth eatin'." He looked over at Mark. "See you back here in, like, an hour, O.K.? Half-hour, maybe. Before Stanley, anyway."

"Sure," Mark said. "I don't want to eat. Not now, anyway. I might wander a bit, too. See you back here."

Roy, already edging toward the ladder, nodded in agreement and was on his way. He ducked into the first open hatchway he came to and started down. He had visited the ship's galley often and was familiar with a number of routes which would lead him there from various parts of the ship. This current route had the advantage of avoiding any portion of the chow lines which were weaving their way to the transient mess halls and the evening meal.

As an extension of his friendship with one of the chief petty officers there, Roy was on good terms with all the Navy crewmen in the galley. Following a show the Roy Warner Trio had played for the crew, this CPO, who "played a little gui-tar himself," had sought out Roy with unqualified admiration, eager to talk about his playing and to look over his instrument. Roy was seldom indulgent with effusive fans. With the least sign of encouragement, they were too likely to want to try a few licks on his guitar and mishandle the equipment. But he was willing to be more considerate on this occasion, since they were playing for Navy rather than Army — for their hosts, so to speak. Fortunately, the CPO was genuinely impressed by Roy's playing and respectful in his approach. When they discovered they were fellow Georgians, the association was clinched. The CPO insisted that Roy come down to his domain in the galley the next day, where he introduced him around to all his staff and took him on a tour of the facilities with enthusiasm fit for a visiting admiral.

The advantage for Roy, of course, was that as a special friend of the CPO he had access, right along with the galley crew itself, to the ship's food supplies—not just the C-rations destined for the troops' mess halls, but the more varied and tasty fare meant for the officers and the ship's crew. This included fresh, cold storage, and refrigerated foods of the highest quality. The galley crew were pleased to show off their bounty and to share their privileges with Roy. His easy Southern ways and congeniality, along with his celebrity as a guitar-player certified by the admiration and sponsorship of their CPO, made him a welcome visitor. Whenever he showed up in the galley, he could expect to be offered the best of whatever was in preparation.

Roy was wise enough, though, to keep alive their good will and the privilege of his situation by conscientiously not taking advantage of it. He never accepted all the food they urged on him. Often, he refused it altogether, or merely sampled, to confirm their recommendation of this or that as really special, indicating that he'd come down just to visit (to "sit in," as he put it) because he was bored hanging around up on deck and enjoyed their company. The prevailing tone and atmosphere throughout the galley was set by the CPO. As a fellow Georgian of similar demeanor and inclination, Roy had no trouble blending in.

For LeRoy Warner, though, acceptance by the galley crew and access to the food stores of the *General Bliss* offered a distinct advantage beyond Navy friends and galley food. His initial tour of the facilities with the CPO had revealed in the enormous stores section shelves loaded with spices and exotic condiments, one of which in particular caught his eye.

"Nutmegs."

He said it to himself, almost unconsciously, but it was loud enough for his attentive guide to hear.

"Yeah. Plenty of nutmeg. We loaded up on a lot of spices in Calcutta this trip. That's where they come from. The Indian Ocean. The Spice Islands, they call 'em. Use a lot of ground nutmeg for desserts—applesauce, custard, rice pudding. Gives it flavor. Vegetables too. Green beans. We get the whole nutmegs. Grind 'em as we need 'em." The CPO indicated the nutmeg grater on a shelf below the spice containers. "Stays fresher that way. More flavor."

On his way through the ship's interior, down toward the galley, it was not food LeRoy had on his mind. It was nutmeg.

The prospect of the nutmeg brought to mind Floyd Washburn, an old-time reed man LeRoy had fallen in with in Waycross. Old Floyd had introduced LeRoy to musicians' drugs back before the war when the two were thrown together in small pick-up groups playing around south Georgia bars and roadhouses. They smoked marijuana pretty regularly on the job. "Mary Jane," or "tea," or "weed," they called it. Old Floyd grew it in the backyard of his ramshackle house on the outskirts of town, along with patches of melons and collard greens. He used to subsist for months at a time — except for occasional candy-bar treats — on nothing but boiled peanuts, collard greens, whiskey, and weed.

The marijuana used to slow him down intolerably on the job, so that before the night was over he'd be honking whole tenor sax choruses of medium or up-tempo tunes on just two or three ludicrously sustained notes. But that was better than the nights he was able to cadge enough whiskey from the customers to get really drunk. He had a repertoire of three acts he would perform for drinks. One was careening around with his long arms dangling in his gorilla imitation, a second was declaiming the "quality of mercy" speech from *The Merchant of Venice* (he'd win bets on this one), and the third was bending his double-jointed fingers back until the women would scream and hide their eyes.

Roy winced, remembering nights when Floyd would ham it up so outrageously that he was embarrassed for him. With the crowd egging him on, he would bound from table to table between sets with his pitiful begging antics, crooning "Whiskey, ah luuuv whiskey. . . . "

When Floyd really got drunk his playing would fall completely apart. He'd lag and then he'd jump tempo or meter. His embouchure, never very dependable, would go completely slack, and his reeds — particularly on alto or clarinet — would squeak and squawk. He'd forget tunes halfway through, or take off on the wrong bridges, and generally make a shambles of the music. If anyone expressed anger or disgust about his condition, he grew tearful and maudlin over his lot. If he was really drunk and his fellow musicians got on him about it, he would be moved to abject slobbering about his worthlessness and to promissory threats of self-destruction so they "wouldn't have old Floyd to ruin things for them anymore."

Roy was thinking about those times with old Floyd Washburn as he wended his way down and through the aft passageways of the *General Bliss* toward the galley. Twice he had got high with old Floyd on nutmeg. When Floyd first mentioned it, Roy thought he was kidding. Floyd was always kidding and full of awful jokes when he was high on weed. Like that tired routine he pulled on waitresses, every time. "Watsa matter, honey, you gotta cold?" he'd ask, and when she'd answer "No" he'd grin his lopsided, miserable grin and say "Well, how come your chest is all swoll up?" He loved those awful jokes. But Floyd meant it about the nutmeg. The first time was at his place, a special treat he offered Roy as amends for the bad drunk he'd thrown the night before. That time Floyd had put on an elaborate, solemn act over the selection of the whole nutmeg and the process of grating it and warming some milk to just the right temperature to help it down, as if he were passing along to an acolyte the sacred keys to pagan rites. It was early afternoon and neither of them had eaten since the job the night before. Floyd had grated a spoonful for each, which, Roy was surprised to learn, produced, on an empty stomach, a considerable high, rather dizzying, with a kind of ringing in his ears, but not unpleasant. He was also surprised, supposing the nutmeg to have minimal aftereffects, like marijuana, when the next morning he awoke with something like a hangover, aching joints, and weak muscles.

The second time was Roy's idea, before a job. He stopped in a grocery and bought a small, square can of ground nutmeg on his way to pick up Floyd for the job that evening, and they killed it in the car outside the roadhouse before going in. Old Floyd was grateful but a trifle contemptuous of the store-bought ground kind, Roy thought. He'd hoped that a nutmeg high going into the job might help prevent Floyd from starting in on the whiskey too early — which maybe it did, since Floyd behaved pretty well that night, only falling into his lumbering gorilla antics a couple of times near the end of the job, and then for the entertainment and approbation of a couple of giddy young women rather than for payment in drinks. Roy himself recalled no effects that second time, either during the job or on the morning after.

Roy did remember, though, the long talk he and Floyd had the next day. It was probably the only time, Roy realized, thinking back to it, that he had ever heard old Floyd talk seriously out of his own experience, when he really knew what he was talking about, not like when he would try to show off by talking big about music or, even worse, when he was on a serious drunk and wanted to talk about Shakespeare or philosophy or some other high-toned subject. That was always pitiful.

This time, though, Floyd began talking about the difference between whiskey and weed, between getting drunk on alcohol and getting high on marijuana. "Ah luuuuv whiskey," Roy could almost hear him saying it, "but Old Lady Whiskey, she don't love me. Ain't nice to me like Mary Jane. Mary Jane's mah sweetheart. Never gives me no trouble, just makes me feel fine. Whiskey don't know when to quit. Feels so good goin' down, then it ain't nothin' but trouble from there on. . . . ."

Roy had often thought about it on his own since, as he did now on his way to the galley of the *General Bliss*, and to its store of nutmeg.

Everybody drank in the service. Almost everybody. There was Stanley, and there were a few others he could think of who didn't drink. Very few. Generally, it was beer in the PX or the NCO clubs or off the base. Whiskey and mixed drinks in the officers' clubs. At Chandranagar, what else was there to do? He drank too, as much as most, less than some. The difference, he thought, was that he never got really drunk, not mean drunk, like so many guys.

Like that limey officer at the New Year's dance they'd been talking about. Or, better yet, Roy thought sharply, his Chandranagar buddy, Richie Wickham. That time after the Fourth of July party. There was a case where too much liquor just about ruined everybody. Talk about a mean drunk! Roy thought he knew Richie pretty well before that night, knew him the way you get to know a buddy in the service, working together on the flight line, bunking next to each other, talking early and late, sweating out the war together.

Richie came from a small town in South Carolina, had worked in filling stations after high school and played semipro baseball summers before he was drafted. They'd sent him to airplane mechanics school in the States and then shipped him right over to the CBI. He wasn't the world's greatest mechanic, wasn't quick like some of the guys on the line; but he was persistent and serious about his work. When they weren't in a hurry, the flight crews liked to have Richie working on their planes. He always stayed with a job until it was done right, or, if he finally decided he couldn't handle it, he'd turn it over to someone who could. Richie was a fairly quiet guy, always ready to be in on a laugh or joke but never at the center of things.

But he did like to drink. And when he drank, he got louder, and he'd start to talk about big-time sports and brag about how slick he was as a ball player—a great glove man, not big but quick and wiry, who could hit for the averages. If he hadn't been drafted, he'd always get around to bragging, he could have had a shot at the majors. Three teams in the Piedmont League had scouted him, he'd say, if anybody began to scoff. Athletes and musicians, Roy thought. Funny how alcohol gets to athletes and musicians.

It sure got to Richie that night at the Fourth of July blowout— enough so that he would have killed Lt. Manning. Roy believed that. He really would have killed him with that knife. It still made Roy nervous to think about it. They'd all had a lot to drink. And it was Lt. Manning who had thrown the party for the squadron, had got the booze and arranged for the mess hall, the whole thing. That's part of what made it so weird, like a bad dream with everything going all wrong.

Maybe Lt. Manning was a fairy, like Richie said, and maybe Richie ought to know, from what he once told Roy about his queer old bachelor uncle who had raised him, but so what? Manning was a good enough guy—for a second lieutenant especially. Never bothered anybody, so what if he was a homosexual, which he could have been, Roy supposed, the way he popped his eyes when he talked and moved around kind of swish sometimes. But he was one of the best officers they had around. If you really needed something he'd always go to bat for you. So what if he didn't know how to throw a baseball? Anyway, the party was his idea. It was a good bet most of the liquor came out of his own ration, and probably the rest out of his own pocket.

Roy had done his share of drinking, too. One of the things that stuck in his memory—he revived it now, thinking back to the effect of the alcohol on him that night—was trying desperately, once he discovered what was going on, to cut through his own drunken haze, struggling for the kind of mental clarity and physical control the frantic situation demanded of him.

It was after midnight when he first missed Richie. The party was at that point where some of the guys were starting to pull out and the real drinkers were settling in. Lt. Manning had been looking after everybody. Earlier, Richie had passed a few of his snide remarks about Manning to Roy. His usual. Nothing too bad. But when Roy asked around and one of the guys said he'd seen Richie head out toward their basha, Roy felt an uneasiness—a presentiment, almost, as if his own alcoholic state gave him powers in exchange for those it took away. Richie could have just bottomed out and headed for the sack, as he often did, but Roy felt the need to check. He shuffled out into the dark, muggy Indian night and headed toward their basha. He remembered vaguely looking for Richie along the way, in case he had passed out and needed to be roused and put to bed.

The next memory was the jolt: just short of the basha, feeling reassured and ready to drop on his own sack and call it a night—then Richie plunging out of the doorway, colliding with him, and the two of them spinning and going down in a muddle. Richie, then, up on his knees, staggering back to his feet, and that big knife, the GI jungle knife he kept in his footlocker, out of its sheath, clutched in his fist.

"Outa my way, LeRoy," Richie's words were thick and hard to make out, but there was no question of their intent: " . . . kill that fuckin' fairy . . . goddam queer son-a-bitch . . . cut his friggin' heart out . . . homo bastard . . . " Richie in a drunken rage, lunging, staggering, falling, muttering a string of oaths, up on his feet again, the mess hall and Lt. Manning, innocent and unsuspecting, a mere fifty yards or so ahead.

Roy tried to remember what he had said, what he had done to try to stop Richie from accomplishing his murderous intent, but most of the details were lost back there in the alcoholic confusion of the event itself, now almost comic as he reviewed it from such a distance, the two of them moving along together in erratic bursts of energy, then tumbling and rolling headlong, Richie cursing and Roy aware at one level that the naked, waving knife was a deadly threat to him as they would tumble together and fall apart, and that at any moment Richie's semicoherent wrath—and the blade—could turn on him. Strange, Roy mused, recalling how he had used their drunken ineptness to detain them by blundering into Richie again and again and hugging him as they floundered and went down, then rolling with him on the ground as they grunted and parted like lovers, all the time urging, imploring, explaining, cajoling, trying to win Richie back to his senses somewhere short of the blind homicidal deed he and his knife were intent on.

What had he babbled about in his own drunken medley of strategies? He could remember only snatches: Richie's wife and small daughter, whom they rarely talked about—something about their photos back in the footlocker lid: "Rosie's picture, Richie, le's go back and see Rosie's picture, huh?" Self-preservation: "Hey, boy, you goin' hurt yourself you don't look out wi' that knife." Whirling commentary, jokes: "Whooo, look a' that sky. Hol' still sky. C'mon, Rich, le's jus' stay here and wait till the sky slows down." Straight-out: "You don' wanna kill nobody, Rich, baby. C'mon now, ain' no use to kill somebody, you know that." And all the time Richie spending his drunken energy in the struggles and his bursts of inchoate outrage and hate.

Finally, in a development Roy could recall clearly out of the fitful nightmare of their advance toward the mess hall, Richie broke free and surged forward at a loping run. Plunging in pursuit, Roy brought him down neatly with a clean flying tackle around the ankles, and they lay there panting for the moment, both of them, in a strange conjunction of agony and pleasure at the intensity of their contact.

"Touchdown, Notre Dame!" Roy had blurted out with a kind of wild glee between the heaves of his breathing. "Six points for Ol' Richie Wickham!"

And then he was laughing uncontrollably and everything was reeling, and when he looked hard at Richie and could finally focus on him he saw that Richie was looking right back at him and beginning to laugh too. The two of them lay there and hung on to each other and laughed and sobbed and wagged their whirling heads and grovelled until, exhausted, they rolled away onto their backs. Roy pictured the two of them there flat on the ground outside the mess hall, eyes shut, mouths open and gasping, arms flung out in an attempt to steady themselves against the tilting earth, under the wildly spinning night sky of Chandranagar. Assam. India!

Roy had no trouble remembering what he finally said when, having at last grown quiet enough to hear the low noise from the tailenders at the party inside, he fought against his own stupor to rise to his knees, struggle to his feet, and then turn to help Richie do likewise.

"C'mon, buddy," he said before they stumbled arm in arm back through the dark to their basha, "you can kill somebody tomorrow when you can stand up better."

Alcohol, Roy thought. "Booze . . . " he said, half aloud, as he turned down the last passageway leading to the galley stores section. Ol' Floyd Washburn had it right. Not that it did him any good. Floyd couldn't stay away from whiskey, never knew when to quit. Who did? Roy wondered, once they really got going with it. The weed, that was different. Marijuana never would have got them into that Fourth of July fix. Old Floyd's sweetheart. "Mary Jane," he liked to call it, like it really was his girl. LeRoy always preferred "tea," which sounded casual and harmless, like the tune that sang or played or tap-danced in his head so often, before he was aware of it—"Tea for two, and two for tea. . . . " He'd heard of guys that had gone off or got spooked on weed, and he supposed that could happen—too many reefers, just like too much of anything. But he'd never had anything but a mellow high himself, nor had he ever seen anyone else turn mean from tea, like, sooner or later, everyone seemed to do on booze. Now, nutmeg. . .

Roy opened the hatchway into the stores area. Ah. No one there, and the other doors, into the galley section and back into the other storage sections, both closed. Everyone probably tied up with the meal for the transient mess halls, as he'd figured. He preferred privacy while grating the nutmeg, of course, but under the circumstances, he'd rehearsed his act in case any of his galley friends came in. He would just be grating some nutmeg like the CPO told him they had to do every once in a while—helping out, doing his bit. And if they didn't buy that, he'd simply laugh off his own bluff and tell them the truth. Everyone knows jazz musicians need a little lift now and then. They were always urging him to help himself to food down there. No big deal, no problem, over a spoonful of nutmeg, right?

Roy selected a couple of medium-size whole nutmegs from the container. That ought to be about right, he thought. A spoonful. Maybe a bit more. Like everything else, he told himself. You don't want to overdo it. Got to know when to quit. Since he'd be eating this on an empty stomach, a spoonful ought to be plenty. Didn't want to get too high or he might be weird when he got back up on deck with Mark and Stanley.

Up on deck . . . Roy had hardly been conscious of his descent through the interior of the *General Bliss*, preoccupied all the way. He was suddenly aware of the heavy metal bulkheads on all sides, of the honeycombed passageways and layered weight of the enormous ship above him. Was he still above the waterline at this level, he wondered, or had he passed below? Was he, in effect, submerged as he stood there, aware of the slight tilt and roll of the ship, grating his nutmeg? The thought was oppressive and he felt momentarily trapped. *Great,* he told himself in an effort to dispel the feeling with good humor, *I have to come this low down if I'm going to get high.* The thought of the man overboard intruded. It was a dark, vague, underwater form-in-suspension thought. *Man overboard!* he voiced to himself. *More like a man underboard down here.*

With an uneasy, grim kind of excitement, Roy hastily finished with the grating and emptied the ground nutmeg into the palm of his hand. Looks O.K., he thought. That's about right. He felt confident in his judgment. *Never too much,* he assured himself. *That's the trick. You must get to know when it's enough, when to quit. Just a matter of who's in charge.* He felt a kind of pride in his sense of control, in the whole business, a pride not retrospective, as with most accomplishments, but anticipatory, as in his music when he'd take off into an ad lib solo, confident that the notes would all be there, would fall in place just right, would in the end all add up exactly to the way he felt.

MARK REITER

Left to himself on the platform overlooking the fantail, Mark became more acutely aware of the stillness of the ship. The numbers of GIs on the deck below him had thinned out. Many, like Stanley, had joined the chow lines. Others, Mark reasoned, had probably sought more likely locations forward where they would have a better view of the boats still searching out over the bow. Mark had seen groups moving forward while he and his companions were engaged in their conversations, but he hadn't thought about it.

Now, as he watched another group of GIs break from their position at the rail and head forward, he thought of the shifting dispersal of men all over the huge vessel. Four thousand bodies confined on this ship at sea, yet relatively free to dispose themselves all over its decks and surfaces, and — at least through the passageways that led to their quarters, to their meals, and to the head — below decks as well. Four thousand men. An enormous number, difficult to comprehend, except in its gross aspects. Yet Mark felt able to grasp that aggregate total of four thousand — to surround it somehow — because of the strict limits of the ship that held them. Everything beyond the ship's sleek metal sides cutting their "V" deep into the supporting sea and its tiers of decks and superstructure above, was either ocean or sky. Everything, Mark reminded himself, but one of those four thousand men. He had now been overboard for an hour and a half or more. He had become a part of that other sea world beyond the human community of the ship all that time — and perhaps forever.

That sobering thought was superimposed on Mark's last sight of the group of GIs as they passed from his view, cut off by the solid bulkhead. He recalled the figures of Stanley Norman and Roy Warner as each had passed that same spot moments earlier and disappeared, Stanley with his lilt, Roy in his casual slouch, hands in his pockets.

In that instant, as the image of the disappearing GIs coincided with that of his friends, Mark suddenly, surprisingly, felt himself able — if only for the moment — to conceive and understand each of the four thousand individual human lives compressed on the troopship with him. He knew each one to be separate, distinct, isolate among the rest, each seeking to be whole as he himself sought to be, as perhaps that one they searched for, the unseen one overboard, had become — prematurely whole, tossing inert and lifeless below the surface, rocked in the cradle of the deep.

The intrusion of the musical cliché in his thought dispelled the instant. Mark sang it inwardly, as if indulging a bad joke: Rocked in the cra-dle (then, with the descending whole notes in *basso profundo*) of . . . the . . . deeeeep.

He got up. He was stiff. He thought of Roy getting up a few minutes earlier and doing knee bends. He pictured Roy below decks, passing through the artificial light on his way to the galley. He thought of Stanley below decks in the slow shuffle of the chow line. He thought of the GIs moving forward on the decks and the circulation of bodies around the ship, like ants in an anthill, cells through the bloodstream.

Standing and stretching, he felt his own potential mobility. He noted how really few GIs were still there below him on the fantail. He pictured the bow and the whole forward deck area swarming with GIs who had moved there from other parts of the ship. Perhaps the man overboard was being rescued at that very moment and the word was passing around, and everyone (except him — how would he know?) would move up to watch, to be in on the dramatic finale. Would the shifting weight of the four thousand GI bodies to the front make the *General Bliss* dip? Would that be dangerous?

If everyone shifted to one side, Mark thought seriously, everyone suddenly to port or to starboard, maybe that could capsize the ship. (Had he ever heard of that happening? It seemed so. In the Chicago River. Photographs of the ship on its side. An excursion ship. The *Eastman*? . . . *Eastland*.) He recalled the voice of the Captain over the troopship's speakers instructing all transient personnel to stay where they were. At the time he'd thought: to keep us out of the Navy crew's rescue operations. Now he thought: to keep the ship level, maybe to prevent a shift in weight that could tip and capsize it.

Mark looked down to the railing and pictured the drop of the ship's side beyond it, falling steeply away under the broad main deck until it cut into the water. The breadth of the whole ship was narrower there than above, narrower still as it continued under water. What held it up? he wondered, that gigantic mass of welded steel with its added passenger weight of four thousand human bodies? How did it stay upright with so much weight balanced on the narrow thrust of that submerged "V" and its hollow hull? Maybe it wouldn't take much to tip it. He imagined the *General Bliss*, with its engines stilled, no longer pushing its way through the ocean, tired of maintaining its peculiar balance, tired of it all, just letting go and turning over on its side to lie down in the sea.

The thought gave him a strange unsettled moment. A sense of threat and danger centered in his groin and abdomen as his legs adjusted consciously to the slight, easy roll of the ship. Was the uneasiness in his bowels? He considered for a moment. Very likely. He hadn't been to the head all day. Probably he should go now, but he didn't want to. Instead, he leaned back against the solid bulkhead and tried to relax.

In an elementary way Mark knew the answers to his questions about the ship. His college physics course had touched all the bases. He even rehearsed Archimedes' principle, more as ritual than as reassurance: " . . . buoyed up by a force equal to the weight of the fluid displaced." Even so, it was hard to suppose that the water displaced could equal the enormous weight of the ship. The same principle, he thought, worked for the man overboard. Or maybe worked against him. Like wood, floating until it's waterlogged; then it sinks. The body, taking water into its lungs instead of buoyant air.

Mark didn't like the train of thought, but it was hard to stop. His mind would not let go of that unnerving sense of the tremendous weight of the vessel and the miracle of balance that kept it upright and afloat. It's almost a matter of trust, of faith, he thought. It floats and keeps us out of the ocean because we believe it will. Archimedes said so. It's all an enormous confidence game. A game of chance. Four thousand of us (minus one?) taking it on trust, trusting ourselves to the ship, to whoever is over us, to the whole military order of command, trusting the whole complex of our lives to others, to principles, to the ideas and the decisions of others. No choice, really. (What will it be like, he wondered, on a sudden tangent, to be a civilian again, to have that choice back again, to have yourself to trust—to have to trust yourself!) The ship, though: trusting the ship to float simply because it does, even though *I don't really know why*. With all this incredible weight it ought to sink right down like a rock. It would sink, he thought, if it were thrown or dropped, as by some gigantic hand. If it had not been eased into its position of precarious floating balance at the beginning when it was launched, with the weight distributed gently and properly, it would have sunk at once.

From far back in his mind came a snatch of languorous music and the words " . . . like a rock cast in the sea." What blues was that from? He couldn't recollect. What was the rest of the lyric, then? "My baby's . . . " No. "My man's." Yeah: "My man's got a heart, like a rock cast in the sea." Was that it? He thought so. Billie Holliday, if he was right. He could hear the line being sung in that bent, cracked precision of her voice, lagging just behind the beat. The authentic ambivalence of the blues.

The paradox of blue: Blue skies, smilin' at me. The bluebird of happiness. My blue heaven. But then, the blues. Saint Louie blues, blue as I can be. I get the blues when it rains.

The paradoxes of being human. Body and soul. Desire and restraint. The emotions, pulling away from the intellect. The friction of fancy against fact, and the perpetual quest for balance. The need to stay afloat amid the rocking and swaying of our moods.

So many paradoxes, he thought. Four thousand men, for instance, on the way back to their own lives and freedom in the democratic society of the U.S. Yet in the process confined more severely than ever, crowded into the limited space of this troopship—all body and bodies, and no soul. Or the soul somehow held in abeyance, somewhere ahead, out there. One soul really out there, he thought, separated from the body of the ship—the counterpart for each of them cast out there into the limitless sea, with their innermost feelings searching for its palpable form.

Like a rock cast in the sea. In the mold of his own blue mood, Mark mulled over more paradoxes. The sensuality of the body and senselessness of the soul. The immateriality of music. Musical notation written on the page unlike the music in his ears, in his beating heart, in his unthinking hands! He remembered a story about Wingy Manone, the one-armed jazz trumpet player—what he said when someone put a sheet of music in front of him: "Man, that's just a bunch of grapes to me." He considered the marvelous duplicity of Billie Holliday singing the blues, the thin, controlled tightness in her throat easing her despair into musical plaint and pure ear. When your music really worked: "Man, you really wail," the jazz musicians said. The highest praise.

"I ain't got no-body and no-body cares for me"—until you sing it and someone else hears, Mark thought. Another tune floated by, with another twist: "My body lies over the ocean, my body lies over the sea. . . . " The echoes of this one pulled him part way out of his reverie, but not out of his blue mood. He smiled, but ruefully, quite to himself, and was again aware of the ship, the unyielding bulkhead against which he leaned.

The USS *General Simon P. Bliss.* The "P," he realized, must be for *Peter. Upon this Rock* . . . He looked at the metal under his feet. Battleship gray, they called it, but it really was blue, a dull shade of blue. The "blues" is plural, he thought. One of those singular-plural things. Like "student body," back in school, like back when he was writing for the student paper in college.

His musing was interrupted by another twinge, a turning or quickening, in his lower abdomen. No question, no duplicity about that. And no sense ignoring it any longer. Time to go to the head. It was time for him to move about anyway, but there were places he'd rather go than down to the head. In his current state of mind, everything kept turning into paradoxes. The "head." What an idiotic term for it anyway. Where did it originate? Some ancient Navy humor, he supposed.

Mark broke his inaction at last, climbed down the ladder, and moved along the deck, but his mood remained pensive and blue. "Like a rock cast in the sea," his mind played over again. He walked over closer to the railing and, slowing down, looked slantwise into the ocean. It was opaque and dark under the overcast, without the dancing facets of reflected sunlight he'd been accustomed to see for two weeks aboard the *General Bliss.* He thought of the ocean's pull on him, the urge he'd confessed to the others to jump from the lower deck into the pulsing surges of blue-green-and-white water levelling out into the endless smooth blue promise of peace beyond. Little of that now. The sea was ominous in its current aspect. The agitation of its surface was nervous rather than playful.

Mark considered again his intuition that the man had jumped overboard rather than falling or being pushed. He lingered a moment by the rail, almost stopping; but an internal nudge from his bowels kept him on his way. He crossed the deck to the hatchway opening which would lead him down to the head. He passed through it and into the artificial light of the ship's interior, still considering the motives of self-destruction, feeling for the kinds of weight, stress, and circumstance that could come together to make suicide reasonable in the face of reason, desirable and even proper in the face of propriety.

Mark Reiter had experienced one clearly suicidal episode himself, an interval that took him well beyond the intellectual question-

ings and the emotional depressions which he—and he supposed everyone—occasionally went through. Now, as he picked his way down
the ladders and through the passageways leading to the head, the memory of that episode came back to him strongly.

He was alone at night at the time, in the transient barracks at the
Kermitola Air Base in Assam. It had rained steadily all day. After four
or five beers by himself at the base PX, he had grown increasingly
depressed and retired to the empty barracks. He undressed with the
incessant Indian rain drumming on the sagging canvas roof. He began
a letter to Bonnie, but it was going nowhere and stalled after a few
preliminaries. It sounded like all the other letters he had written from
India, trying to mask his desperation and convert it into concern and
hope. He quit and tore it up.

He sank back on his bunk, hoping to avoid self-pity in the sur-
cease of sleep. Instead, his persistent mind dropped him into a widening pit of empty, confused dejection. As he lay there prostrate, waves
of vaporous, melancholy emotions assailed his will. By degrees he gave
up his vital sense of self. General depression devolved gradually into
hollow dispiritedness, then into descending circles of despondency,
finally into a monumental sense of purposelessness, from which he
grew silently, unarguably suicidal, ready—and able—to end his own
life.

The circumstances which had brought him to Kermitola were
peculiar enough. It was during his period of detached service at
Hastings Mill. Major Woodruff, the officer he was assigned to, had
some business at Tezgaon, an ATC base in the Brahmaputra Valley of
Assam, and suggested that Sgt. Reiter, who had no ostensible duties
at the Mill, accompany him. Major Woodruff's suggestions usually
carried the weight of orders, so Mark went.

The plan was to fly up in the morning and back that same evening,
but the paper work and red tape involved in the Major's business held
them up at Tezgaon, and they had to stay over for a second day. Then
the Indian weather closed in, the airstrip was shut down, and they had
to stay throughout the second idle day, over a second night, and into a
third day before it lifted enough for them to fly out.

Ordinarily, Mark might have relaxed and enjoyed this unexpected
vacation. He did, to some extent, on the day they arrived, while he

waited through the initial delays for the Major's paper work to clear the Tezgaon channels. He strolled along the flight line and wandered freely around the base, fascinated by the island of American military equipment and activity planted so oddly in the middle of what seemed to him the timeless landscape and ancient culture of India.

But when it became clear they would have to stay over, trouble arose regarding his enlisted man's billeting. There was no difficulty about Major Woodruff moving at once into officers' quarters, but Mark was told bluntly that there were no beds available at the transient EM barracks. After an hour of badgering and waiting, it was finally arranged for him to stay at nearby Kermitola, the sister base of Tezgaon, where he was assured there would be room. Weary and discouraged, Mark ate a hasty dinner of scrambled eggs, toast, and black coffee at the Tezgaon flight-line mess before catching the military shuttle bus over to Kermitola.

Once there, feeling worn, isolated, and irritable, he went through the lengthy ritual of checking in as an unscheduled and unexpected enlisted man. He drew his bedding from an off-duty supply sergeant who had to be summoned specially by the after-hours CQ in the Orderly Room. They were both as irritable as Mark during the procedure. By the time he finally got set up in the canvas-top, tent-style barracks, empty but for himself and the effects of two others at the far end, both absent, Mark simply stripped to his GI underwear, hit the sack, and, feeling exhausted and alien, fell quickly asleep.

It was his second night there, after the day-long curtain of straight-down Indian rain had kept him cut off from the rest of the world, that his mood had turned suicidal.

Mark took a certain perverse enjoyment in his current dark mood as he plodded through the descending levels and passageways of the troopship, indulging the memory.

It was already drizzling when he woke up that second day in Kermitola, but it didn't turn into intermittent downpour until after he had found the mess hall, eaten a solitary, soggy breakfast—eggs, toast, and coffee again—turned in his bedding, and slogged through the mud to the Orderly Room to finish checking out of the transient quarters.

"Oh. You're Sergeant Reiter," the CQ said, shuffling through the forms and notes on his desk. "Just got a call about you from Tezgaon. Everything's grounded. Nobody's flying anywhere until this lifts. Here it is." He'd found the note. "Major Woodruff says to stick close and he'll call you as soon as he gets clearance."

Mark had waited in the Orderly Room all day, watching the rain, leaving only to trudge miserably through it, slogging in the sea of mud underfoot, to the mess hall for lunch and to the latrine as necessary. It was late afternoon before the call came with the word that they would have to stay over a second night. Numbed from the boredom and uselessness of the long idle day sealed in by the rain, Mark again signed in, drew his bedding, and moved back into the empty barracks. By this time, like everything in Kermitola, he was soaked. The wooden walls and floor of the barracks oozed, the bedding was wet, his clothes were soaked through and clung heavily to him when he moved, his GI shoes sloshed when he walked, his hair was matted and rank. Warm rivulets of water ran down the sides of his face and dripped off the tip of his nose as he sat, head down in dejection, on the edge of his transient's bunk.

He rose at length to trudge again to the mess hall, where he picked at a supper of lukewarm C-rations. Then he crossed to the base PX and, with minimal conversation, handed over chits for beer, given him earlier by the CQ, who had requested permission to issue them when he learned Mark would be staying a second night. It was the only show of concern from anyone in two days.

How much of his depression could be attributed to the four or five beers he drank, Mark could never decide. The fact was that he couldn't remember afterwards just how many he had stretched over the two hours or so while he sat alone drinking in the PX, but it indicated that his mood was well along before he returned to his barracks for the night.

The course of his suicidal state as he lay on his bunk in Kermitola, sealed off by the unrelenting monsoon of India, seemed both vivid and vague. He remembered the enveloping sound of the steady rain on the slanting canvas overhead and the expectation that it would collapse and expose him, defenseless, to the elements. He remembered feeling the threat in this, but being unable to care. He was defenseless in any event. He remembered the hot, swampy atmosphere of the barracks and sweating so profusely that he had the sensation of floating in total moisture, his own indistinguishable from that in the supersaturated air. He remembered in the midst of that oppressive wetness feeling a series of chills and wondering if he should put his clothes back on, and not caring whether he did or not.

Above all, he remembered the desolation and finally the utter totality and perfect uselessness of self in his misery, feeling wretched beyond meaning or consequence. He remembered then, out of the suspension of that awful negation, realizing slowly but with gathering clarity that there was one act still possible, one thing he could do, one inevitable way. He could actually negate himself: he could take his own life. He could destroy himself—not to oppose or deny the overwhelming purposelessness that racked and swamped his being, *but to affirm it*. And with that realization he knew the dimensions of the vortex in which his tortured consciousness spun, knew that somehow he had reached its nadir and passed beyond. That he would kill himself, then, became the only basis he could imagine for affirmation, for the reconstitution of purpose itself.

The paradoxes! Mark thought as he descended the last ladder down to the level of the head, stimulated by the intensity of his recollections and amused by the irony in the turn of events which had resolved them on that strange night in Kermitola.

For as his will to self-destruction overcame the profound lethargy of his despair that night, he had risen slowly, trancelike and possessed, to seek through the thick blackness of the barracks for the instrument of his only possible affirmation, the service pistol drawn for him (against his own inclinations) by Major Woodruff, who never flew anywhere in the CBI without side arms. As Mark stood up, however, and before he could move to the foot of his bed to locate the lethal weapon in the sodden heap of his clothes, he felt a great fullness and pressure in his bladder and the overpowering need to urinate. The PX beer had completed the cycle of its influence. The next thing Mark could remember, he was standing barefoot in the warm mud, drenched by the unsullied pouring rain, feeling deliciously relieved and affirmative as he arched his long steady yellow stream into the saturated air and soil of Kermitola, India.

Inside the transient barracks again, he had dropped back on his bunk feeling emotionally worn out but bodily restored, and had fallen asleep almost at once.

Now, as he entered the ship's head, Mark paused to take in the bizarre scene before him. It was one that always surprised and amazed him. Far below decks, the large ship's hold that served as latrine for the troops was dark and cavernous. The few well-spaced overhead bulbs which were its only source of illumination were hardly enough to light the center of the hold, much less to penetrate into the murky shadows along the bulkhead walls and corners. The air hung heavy and dank, without apparent circulation, a malodorous mixture of metallic and fetid fecal smells, stale urine, and acrid cigarette smoke.

Along one side was a series of open salt-water shower stalls, some with naked GIs seen indistinctly gyrating their bodies under the cold salt-water spray released by a pull cord to one side. Mark had used these showers only twice and would not do so again. The first time he had learned the hard way not to use soap, which would not rinse off in the salt water but congealed instead into a gummy layer that took days to wear off. The second time was a token ritual to cleanliness. He got sticky wet rather than clean and then towelled the stickiness in. For the rest of the voyage, Mark, like most of the troops, would make do at the battery of lavatory sinks against the adjoining wall.

Along the remaining wall, toward which Mark now moved, was a row of toilets and a line of urinals. Sometimes when he had come down to the head these would all be in use, with disgruntled GIs standing by, waiting their turn. It was during chow time now, though. More than half were empty, and Mark did not have to wait.

But it was the activity that took up the open central floor space of the head, which he now passed by, that most fascinated him and drew his attention. For there, on their knees in a dreamlike underworld tableau of artificial light dimmed by a thick pall of cigarette smoke, were a number of intent, sweating GIs, some of them stripped to the waist, surrounded by shifting ranks of rapt spectators and hangers-on, all clustered around a GI blanket on which, to the accompaniment of the chanted litanies and ritual supplications of the players, a pair of dice were thrown and retrieved, thrown and retrieved, thrown and retrieved endlessly in the hypnotic divinations of a deadly serious crap game.

Money passed back and forth swiftly and silently at the bidding of each throw. Piles of bills grew and diminished, some pocketed, some stuffed between the fingers of the players' hands, folded lengthwise and waved in the thick air over the perimeter of the olive-drab GI blanket that commanded the obsessive attention of all eyes. Mark had heard from common scuttlebutt throughout the ship that this was a continuous game; that it had started before the *General Bliss* had even left Calcutta and would cease only when the ship emptied at the Port of San Francisco, or, more likely, simply move on from there; that some of the players had yet to see the Pacific Ocean and the light of day on any weather deck, being absorbed completely in the crap game, with flunkies bringing them their food, and taking naps only as needed right there in the head or in adjacent areas far below decks. It was said that enormous sums, fortunes by any reckoning, were being won and lost, that the winners at the conclusion of the voyage would be set financially for life. Mark could believe it, reflecting, from where he now sat along the far wall, on the intensity within the rhythms and steady pace of the game.

As Mark relieved himself physically, he felt freed partially from the burden of his dark mood as well. He was looking out again, observing. The head was as far down as he had been in the ship. Below must be only the hollow compartments of the submerged hull and beyond that only the dark underworld sink of the sea.

It all goes together, Mark thought, like the cosmology of Dante, the psychic scheme of Freud, here in this submerged head, this *id* hidden in the depths of the ship, from which nothing of the clear daylight drama of life, nothing of the natural orientation of the human world's surface activity can be seen except indistinctly, by subconscious reflection, and from below.

He looked around at the human shapes in this public private purgatory: naked figures antic and askew in the dark showers, half-naked bodies bent over the sinks or staring into the metal mirrors above them, men standing lax except for the slight thrust of their hips at the urinals, or, like himself, sitting abjectly on the toilets, pants crumpled around their ankles, and no one speaking, no one apparently even noticing anyone else. Except, of course, for himself and those crowded and concentrated around the crap game blanket, muttering in the peculiar argot of their money-and-numbers game — speaking in tongues, Mark thought — and even these talking not to one another so much as to the insensible rolling dice. The scene was surrealistic. A primordial cave in which the soul was cramped and in perpetual danger of being plunged into darkness. Out of time, yet strangely complete, with no direct, immediate, rational connection with any world but its own. The odd half-light and its peculiarly soft play of shadows. The heavy air with its effluvium of sulphurous smells. The slightly echoing, muffled sounds. The salt-water showers from which one could never emerge clean.

Strangest of all, he thought, was that eternal crap game on the GI blanket in the midst of the infernal concourse, enveloped in its blue haze of cigarette smoke hour after hour, day after day, heedless of the diurnal cycles of the world above and beyond. The piles of paper money and the flow of United States bills struck him as an entirely displaced presence at the center of the scene. There was nothing for sale on the *General Bliss*. The money could buy nothing. Its value on the ship was purely make-believe, imaginary, taken on faith, an anachronism, at best either a memory or an anticipation of some distant reality.

Mark finished and prepared to leave. He flushed the toilet and heard its hollow sucking sound as at a distance. The plumbing in the bowels of the ship, he thought, and the plumbing of the alimentary canal.

He became one of the anonymous shapes moving to and from the doorway. Like sleepwalkers, it occurred to him. The sensation of perpetual night. Motion and time in the underworld of the head grew anti-realistic. He was conscious of the very slight roll of the ship, but there was no ostensible reason for it, nothing in it to apprehend, anticipate, or properly adjust to. There was no issue there but the passage of human waste.

He stopped at the door in momentary defiance of his growing urge toward the fresh air of the deck and his need for the sky over his head, for the consoling companionship of his friends. He looked back around the head and through the yellow light at the fervid activity at its center that continued completely oblivious to its grotesque, repellent surroundings. He listened to the players, down on their knees muttering their devotions, paying homage to chance.

Human waste, human greed, human hope, he thought. Fantastic. It all goes together. The floating crap game in the head, forever grim, brazen, feverish, demoniacal, absurd, down there in the bowels of the *General Bliss.*

THE CAPTAIN

Throughout the first full run of expanding squares by the searching boats, the atmosphere on the bridge of the *General Bliss* remained tense, alert, expectant. Along with the sense of urgency imparted by the Captain, each member of the bridge crew felt his own complicity in the drama. Each scoured the sea in all directions, eager to be the agent of the first valid sighting of the man overboard. They all watched the boats with exhilaration equalling that of the troops on the decks, enhanced by a clearer understanding of their movements and an unrestricted view from the bridge.

The signalmen kept their eyes trained on each other, ready to receive or transmit at any moment. If anything, their attention intensified as the boats, gradually enlarging their squares, moved farther and farther from the ship. True to the Captain's instructions, every suggestion of a foreign body in the water, no matter how momentary or dubious its appearance, was reported and checked out. Seven times during the first hour a boat was called out of its expanding pattern to investigate an area where a possible sighting had been announced. Each of these occasioned a flurry of activity, with the signalmen and the boat crews responding as rapidly as possible to directions from the bridge. All of these reports, however, were, from their inception, highly tentative. While they did raise some suspense and small hope from time to time, their failure to raise the man overboard himself was not altogether discouraging, since they served to the crew as a kind of

confirmation that, disappointment notwithstanding, they were following every lead and doing everything they could to recover the lost
man.

Eventually, though, when the boats completed their first full run
and were recalled from their far perimeter to begin again, there was a
drop in both spirits and expectations. By then the two boats had been
searching systematically in their overlapping patterns for nearly an hour
and had covered an area of almost three miles square. If the man was
out there and still afloat, their activity, together with the vigilant scan-
ning from the bridge and all lookout posts, should have raised him.

The Captain gave the order for the boats to begin again, this time
with new coordinates at points well off the bow which the wind and
drift made more likely. His manner reflected the same firm intent he
had shown all along; if his tone displayed less emotion than before, it
carried no less determination.

The Captain knew well enough, of course, that the chances of
recovery had dwindled drastically. It would be a fluke if they found
the man now. But that did not mean they could lessen the intensity of
the search or their dedication to it. He was no longer inclined to press
his men in the matter, but neither would he allow them to relax their
effort.

He, himself, was thinking ahead carefully. The cloud cover which
had moved in during the first hour had affected the search in a number
of ways. The second run of the boats would be different. The light
was now indirect, and the contrast was gone. This reduced what could
be picked up by the naked eye, but by the same token it increased the
definition and reliability of what could be seen through binoculars. In
addition, the wind had freshened as the clouds came on, and now,
under a full cloud cover, there was a steady and considerable breeze.
The sea had been relatively calm at the beginning of the search, with
smooth wavelets, gentle crests, and a rolling, glassy appearance. As
the winds increased, the sea responded with at first slight, then moderate disturbance.

The Captain, as a matter of course, had studied the changes in
surface conditions. Initially, the small wavelets had grown larger and
their crests began to break gently into glassy foam. Now, with the
wind moderate at a steady 13 to 15 knots, the wavelets had length-

ened into small waves with a mean height of perhaps five feet and a scattering of white caps at their tips. Visibility from the boats had become hampered accordingly. While they were not yet in any particular danger from these moderate seas, their maneuverability was reduced somewhat, and navigation through their square patterns became rather more demanding.

There were other considerations which the Captain began to weigh when the first hour of concerted effort failed to raise the man overboard. His emotional dilemma in dealing with the situation was tied in somehow, he had come to suspect, with the transitions involved in this Pacific crossing, transitions which were as much his as they were, more obviously, those of the troops he was transporting.

The Captain had struggled to keep the same image of his GI passengers with which he began the voyage, when he had accepted them proudly as comrades in arms. The Captain now realized that he had seized on the image of the man overboard as a kind of last vestige of that sense of comradeship. Knowing nothing of him but his complete dependence upon the U.S. Navy procedures and the skill of the *General Bliss* crew in following those procedures successfully, he had clung to the man's identity as a comrade in the war.

But the war is over, the Captain had to keep reminding himself, almost bitterly. The man was no longer, in this view, a soldier with whom the Captain faced a common sworn enemy. The war which had been their peculiar bond was over. That man was virtually a free citizen at this point rather than a soldier. More precisely, he was a veteran of the finished war. The Captain honored that fact, for he felt he could understand what a true veteran had been through. But along with the war itself, the man's military service to his country, quite unlike the Captain's, was finished.

A chance bit of military service phrasing, as much as anything else, helped the Captain overcome his unsettling emotional identification with the unknown man overboard. The common term for the process of discharge was "separation from the military." Once delivered to the Army authorities at the Port of San Francisco, the troops would be sent to appropriate centers to be separated formally from the military. The Captain chided himself for the ease with which he appropriated this term when it entered his considerations; but it worked on him all the same. In going overboard from his troopship, the man had simply short-circuited the system. He had already separated. He had done it himself. And here they all were, frantically trying to recover him and bring him back under the protection of the military, so he could be separated their way later on. It was a bad joke, he knew, a twisted notion, an irresponsible pun at best, not even a proper irony; but in its subversive way it contributed to the Captain's private rationalizations as rescue of the man overboard grew more and more unlikely.

Thus, as the search moved into its second hour, the Captain began to weigh the factors in the whole episode differently. The alternative he now had to think about was failure. Clearly, if they were unable to raise the man overboard, the command decision at some point would have to be to abandon the search and set the *General Bliss* once again on its course to San Francisco. The Captain certainly did not like the idea of failure, but he disliked even more the paralysis of indecision.

He had explained away his emotional confusion regarding the man overboard, but a human life was still at issue. That remained the prime fact and demanded unflagging diligence as long as the search was continued. The problem would become how long, in the face of failure, it should continue.

No one else on the bridge supposed that the Captain was concerned about anything other than the successful termination of the search. While he had not been particularly active on the bridge himself, his attention to the situation and to the activity of the others had been intent and unwavering. He spoke little, affecting the proceedings more by his presence and air of expectation than by direct involvement. However, before the boats advanced very far into the patterns of their second run, the Captain's mind was working actively on the factors pushing him toward the decision to end the search. Under the circumstances, he had concluded that a two-hour outside limit would be reasonable. The weather, although not yet a serious deterrent, grew less favorable all the time, and the light of the short February day, now occluded by the cloud cover, was beginning to fade. In another half hour or so, visibility would be lowering toward the murkiness of early dusk under the overcast. Fuel in the boats was another factor. Sometime around the two-hour mark, they would have to come in to refuel in any event.

There was a question of morale as well. His crew showed signs of slackening vitality in the search effort. The questionable sightings which had been announced and followed out with some frequency at the outset had diminished with time. There had been none at all since the boats began their second run. The Captain understood the reason for this. The eagerness with which the searchers sang out at any hint of a body out there at the beginning, following his own specific instructions, changed into a natural reluctance to be wrong again. No doubt the men in the boats were also reacting to the frustration of their fruitless activity over the first hour.

The morale of the thousands of GI troops aboard, a matter more difficult for him to evaluate, was also a factor. He had been encouraged by their obvious interest in the deployment of the boats, although he had misinterpreted the cheers and shouts from the crowded decks, missing entirely the atmosphere of a competitive sporting event which contributed much to their reactions. Later, though, he began to notice that they were more casual and restive, milling about in their usual shiftless fashion as time went on and the force of his early directive to them over the speakers eroded. He was aware that their mood, their welfare, and even their opinion, if he could sense it, had a bearing on his decision.

But the most compelling factor of all in bringing about the Captain's decision to halt the search before the two-hour limit he had proposed to himself, came not from the factual circumstances he could observe, but from the haunting uncertainty at the heart of the matter. It was the insubstantial nature of the man overboard himself and the material question that went unanswered at the center of the whole episode: *Was there really a man overboard?* Had there ever been, in fact, a man overboard?

The only basic fact, as the Captain appraised the situation, was that they had acted upon an unsubstantiated report from a source which he was unable to consult or properly evaluate. The GIs who reportedly saw the man go over could not be located, at least not in time to be of any use in the search effort. That could mean that they chose not to volunteer themselves, not to become involved. It could also mean that the whole business was a hoax perpetrated by anonymous GIs who, out of boredom, or on a bet, or for whatever reason, yelled out "Man overboard!" and then withdrew to see what would happen.

Considering these possibilities threatened to swell the Captain's mounting resentment toward the troops. But in his present state of mind he was able to see that dealing with them was no longer his responsibility, if it ever had been. He would simply leave that and the identity of the man overboard to the Army chain of command to track down—if there were such a man. The Navy had done its duty. The Captain had called for a muster of all Naval personnel and could account for all his men. But that had been a simple and routine affair. He could appreciate the difficulty of mustering the four thousand troops aboard. It would be a while before he could expect the Army to come up with the results of that.

Even so, the uncertainty plagued the Captain's considerations. Had there ever been a man overboard? It would not do, of course, to give the question voice or to transmit his nagging doubt in any way to his crew. Most of them were probably asking themselves the same question by now. He couldn't prevent that. But as long as the Captain gave no indication of doubt that the man was out there, able to be seen and recovered, the search would go on unabated.

For his own part, though, the longer the fruitless search went on, the more dubious he became regarding its validity at the source. It irritated him that the sailor who first passed the word—the lookout, Haines—could not provide clear testimony of the man's body in the water. Yet he was inclined to credit his account as accurate. It would have been easier, he reasoned, for Haines simply to report the GIs outcry or to corroborate it by saying yes, he saw the man in the water too. What led the Captain to believe the lookout's account was the sailor's doubt, his unwillingness to say with certainty that it was a man he saw.

The Captain speculated on scenarios to allow for this, featuring items that might be taken for a man going overboard instead of the man himself. A duffle bag, perhaps, the large, cylindrical canvas ones that held all a soldier's belongings. That would be roughly the size and shape of a man. Or even more plausibly, a set of Army fatigues in the water. There could be a number of explanations for this. He imagined GIs (against orders, of course) sunbathing on the decks and their nearby fatigues whisked overboard by a quick gust of wind. Or tossing a balled-up set of fatigues around, playing catch or keep-away in some kind of teasing horseplay, and over it goes. Or most reasonable of all, an enterprising GI, having washed out his fatigues in the head, tying them too insecurely on the railing to dry in the breeze past the bow.

Any of these could conceivably account for the guarded description by Haines of what he saw in the water. Indeed, such scenarios could even exonerate the group of GIs who may also have honestly supposed they saw a man overboard and legitimately issued the cry. The Captain's private conjecture went on to allow that it could have been the technique of their hoax as well.

When at length and on balance it seemed that to continue the search was no longer reasonable, the command decision was made more logical by two matters of shipboard schedule. One was the intrusion of the evening meal for transient personnel and the announcement to form chow lines. That struck the Captain as fortunate timing: a distraction for the troops that would serve as a natural transition from the search back to regular troopship routine. The other was the changing of the watch at 1600 hours. If the search were discontinued in time to recall and secure the boats and get the ship under way again before the routine change of watch, that could return the crew members to their normal schedule as well.

The Captain, however, did not intend his command decision under these peculiar circumstances to appear willful, sudden, or ill-considered. The technique he chose was to air some of the deliberations before the bridge crew by pointed dialogue with his Officer of the Deck.

"Lieutenant," he began in a casual but concerned tone, "The light's getting pretty flat and dark out there. See what they have to say about current visibility from the motor whaleboat."

"Yes, sir," the OOD replied. He relayed the query through his signalman and stood by while the response flashed back. "Visibility poor and closing in."

"How much longer would you judge we'll have enough real day-light to do the job?" the Captain asked.

"Hard to say, sir," the OOD responded. He was looking at the Captain rather than out to sea. "The clouds have been getting heavier all along. Maybe a half-hour at the most. Probably less."

Pretty good, the Captain thought. *He knows what I'm up to. All right. We'll just let him play it on out then.*

"What's the total elapsed time now, since you started — since the word was passed?"

The OOD consulted his notes and his watch. "I make it an hour and . . . forty-two, forty-three minutes, sir."

The Captain shook his head. "Should have raised him. Should have raised him," he muttered. "If that man's out there, we should have raised him."

The OOD said nothing but continued to look, rather blankly, at the Captain.

"Lieutenant, I'm concerned about the men in that motor whaleboat. It's no picnic to handle one of those in rough seas. Even conditions like these can be dangerous." He squinted out toward the distant boat. "And they've been out there," he turned his gaze back to the OOD, "going on two hours?"

"Yes, sir," the OOD said.

The Captain looked away again and let a moment of silence go by. The members of the bridge crew within earshot were still at their business, but listening. His manner shifted suddenly. The tone of his next question as he turned back to the Lieutenant abruptly was busi-nesslike, earnest, intent.

"Lieutenant, how would you judge our chances of raising that man from this point on?"

The OOD, not so much surprised as cautious, considered his reply carefully.

"About like the visibility out there, sir — poor," he looked at the Captain directly, "and closing in."

"Exactly," the Captain said. His tone was reflective again, his words measured, "and we haven't had a single confirmed sighting of him yet."

The Captain sighed. His eyes were still on the OOD but their expression had grown compassionate, almost fatherly. When he spoke next his voice was matter-of-fact, quiet, almost confidential.

"It may be a man's life, Lieutenant," he said, "but when you're in charge, you've got to know when it's enough, when to quit. That's the trick. You make your judgment according to the total situation. And then you trust it."

The Lieutenant had no reply. There was none called for. When the Captain spoke again, he resumed his usual tone.

"Check your watch, Lieutenant. We'll give it five minutes more, then signal the boats to cease search and return to ship. In the meantime, I want you to draft the proper message to inform Fleet Command of our decision."

"Aye-aye, sir," the OOD said. He added to it the formality and the finality of a salute.

CHAPTER SIX

I usually look for a certain kind of character . . .
a likeable guy, a happy sort of guy as well as a
nice musician. . . . And I like to keep adding things
to the book all the time. It inspires the men, I
think, to have new arrangements to work out.

— *William "Count" Basie*

THE PLATFORM

Mark Reiter was the first of the trio to emerge from the interior of the ship into the expansive open air of the deck. He thought it cooler than before but still comfortable rather than cold. He breathed deeply and felt his physical wholeness spread to his limbs. Nothing seemed to have changed on deck except his attitude toward it. The search for the man overboard apparently was still going on, but it would be hard to confirm it as he headed aft to the platform. The GIs scattered along the rail were relaxed and undemonstrative, as were all the others moving casually, like himself, about the deck.

Mark studied the sky. It had darkened some while he was below decks, but that did not bother him. It was natural enough with the clouds taking over and evening coming on. It seemed right. So did the ocean, similarly darkened but not ominous as it had appeared to him earlier on his way to the head. The surface was rather more active in response to the wind which had arisen, but it was no threat. The deck he walked on and the whole ship under his feet felt no less stable and steady than before—and somehow more reasonable. It all went together naturally enough, and he felt curiously akin to it. All the elements, with the ship in their midst, were quite acceptable in relation to one another, just as the parts of his body, fanning out from the bellows of his lungs, made a complementary whole. He walked calmly, inhaling into his system the freshening, salt-tinged Pacific air. He felt in his movement, as in the movement of the ocean beyond, a continuity, a kind of active ease. He rounded the bulkhead onto the fantail, crossed to the ladder, ducked under the barrier, and mounted to the platform, all without special effort, without breaking the rhythm of his movement. Once on the platform, he set his stance, folded his arms, and gazed out equably over the rounded stern of the troopship.

He didn't know why he felt so good. He thought about going to the piano, wondering what he might be able to improvise in his current state. There were two times, generally speaking, when Mark felt the need for a piano: when his spirits were low and when, as now, he was unaccountably elated. It wouldn't do, though. He'd told Roy he'd meet him there on the platform.

And before long Roy Warner appeared, pulled himself up the ladder, and joined him. Roy didn't speak but dipped his eyes and compressed his lips sharply, as if to say "there, I made it." Then he cocked his head to one side with a synchronized closing of the eyes in the Indian gesture.

"Salaam, Sahib," he said, his face easing into a grin.

"Salaam yourself," Mark returned. "That was pretty quick. Did you eat good?"

"Sure did. Just what I needed. Not much, really. Just a few bites. You goin' to chow?"

"No. Not yet, anyway. I'll wait till Stanley gets back. See what he says. Let the chow line run down some more."

They stood together in companionable silence. Roy folded his arms and assumed Mark's stance with rather elaborate mimicry, his body facing out but his eyes turned sideways at Mark.

"See anything out there, Sahib?" he asked, still smiling.

Mark studied Roy for a moment before responding. Then, suddenly antic, he began to sing. "I joined the Nay-veee to see the world . . ."

Roy took up the next line, " . . . And what did I see?" They joined in the answer together:

" . . . I saw the sea!"

They were both smiling broadly now.

"Ready to sit down again," Roy announced. As he backed up to the bulkhead he sang out in the elaborate manner of the army order of preparation, "Readeeeeeee . . . " followed by the crisp order of execution, "Sit!" And he sat.

Mark moved over to lean against the bulkhead beside him.

"Won't be long before you don't have to do things by the numbers any more, Roy. Nobody giving you orders any more when you get back home."

"Damn right," Roy said. "Anybody tries to tell me what to do . . . I'll just tell 'em what they can do."

"Tell 'em to go jump in the lake, huh, Roy?"

"Spit in the ocean," Roy said. It didn't make much sense, but they both laughed at the spontaneity.

"Still looking for the man overboard, I guess," Mark said after a bit.

"They'll never find him," Roy said. "You know what? I'm gettin' used to them not findin' him."

Mark caught his companion's tone, and kept it. "Part of the deal," he said. "They're not supposed to find him. I say he's the Unknown Soldier of World War II. Now, how can he be the unknown soldier if they find him and pull him out and check his dog tags?"

"That's right," Roy agreed. "And that's goin' to be me too, man. Soon as I hit Georgia and get that discharge. I'm goin' to take these dog tags and throw 'em into the Okefenokee and just be me. No name, no rank, no serial number, and nobody to give me no orders."

"What are you going to do, Roy?" Mark asked, half-amused, half-serious.

"I'm goin' to play my guitar," Roy answered, "and I'm goin' to screw around, and . . ." —he lifted his chin and his smile broadened into a grin— "I'll just do whatever I decide I'm goin' to do."

Mark smiled back. Tilting his head to one side, eyes closed, and then rocking it back, he returned the wagging Indian gesture Roy had greeted him with earlier. "Lots of luck, Sahib," he said.

Roy shifted his gaze out over the ocean and scanned it from side to side.

"What direction we headed in, anyway?" he said. "Can't tell any more. Which way's San Francisco?"

"Not headed anywhere," Mark said. "Still drifting." He looked to both sides, overhead, and then straight out. "I think east is over there," he said, nodding to his right. "It is hard to tell, though. Can't tell where the sun is any more. At least from here. Have to wait until we start up again."

Neither spoke for some time. Then it was Mark who picked up his own lapsed thought.

"Wonder how much longer they'll go on looking for him."

"I was thinkin' the same thing," Roy said. "I suppose they've got regulations, how long you're supposed to look for a man overboard before you give up. Got regulations for everything."

"Yeah," Mark agreed. "Military regulations. If you go by the book they can't blame you for anything that goes wrong."

"I'll bet it's different for this, though." Roy reconsidered. "Maybe there's a minimum time, but it can't be all by regulation. Too many variables. Somebody's got to figure them out and make the decision."

"Well, it must be the Captain of the ship who gives the order. It'll be up to him, won't it?"

"I don't know. Sometimes it's the second in command has to do the dirty work. Like in our company it was the adjutant ran the show, gave all the orders. The Old Man just stood around and checked him out."

Mark shook his head. "Well, whoever has to decide this one, I don't envy him. If the man's still out there, how do you know when to quit, when to head out again and leave him behind?"

"Don't give him too much credit, man," Roy said good-naturedly. "He's got his regulations to go by, whoever he is. Hell, he's got to think about his ship. What's one little old GI to him when he's got the whole troopship to think about?"

Mark looked down at the deck. "One sad sack, huh? Only one out of four thousand." He squinted. "But he's still one, Roy."

Roy shook his head. "Good thing you weren't in the real war, ol' buddy. You'd have made one godawful soldier. You know it? We'd have lost the damn war."

"No argument," Mark replied at once. But then he thought about it.

"I don't know about that." He shrugged and sat down abruptly beside Roy. He put his hands on his up-thrust knees. "How can you tell what you'd do if you really had to? I don't think you can figure it out ahead of time." He turned and looked hard at Roy. "That's the way it is with anything that's really important. And, you know, I'm glad that's the way it is. No matter what you think ahead of time, you can only find out when you have to—when you . . ." —he shook his head—" . . . when you have no choice but to choose!"

Roy frowned at him. He was used to Mark's abstract conversational gambits. Usually he just indulged or ignored them. But this turn caught him, and he was surprised by the immediacy of his understanding. "Yeah," he said slowly, "when you've got to choose"—he smiled—"and the situation does most of the choosing for you."

They were silent again, sitting motionless. At length Mark stirred. "Well, I'll probably never know."

"Not if you're as lucky as you were in this war," Roy added.

Mark stared ahead absently for a while. Then, abruptly, he spoke in the small voice of a child, "W'a'd you do in the Big War, Daddy?" He turned to Roy and answered in his own light-hearted, mocking tone, "Me? I played the Pee-ano. All over China, Burma, and India."

Roy laughed and clapped him on the shoulder. "That'll be a stopper, man."

They heard someone shuffling up the ladder, and Stanley Norman mounted to the platform, nonchalantly joining the conversation almost at once. "What'll be a stopper?" he wanted to know.

"Sergeant Norman, Sahib," Roy spread his arms and bowed in greeting. "Tellin' everybody how we won the war in Asia," he explained to the newcomer, "playin' jazz music, handin' out softballs, runnin' ping-pong tournaments for the troops."

"Keeping our boys occupied with wholesome activities in their spare time," Mark threw in. "Idle hands . . . "

" . . . off the nasty streets of Calcutta," said Roy.

" . . . out of the opium dens and whorehouses of Greater Chungking," said Mark.

"Entertainin' our fightin' ATC troops over the whole goddamn C, B 'n' I," said Roy.

Stanley moaned. "Come on, what are you guys raving about?"

Mark and Roy, prolonging the tease, smiled knowingly at Stanley and were silent.

"How was chow?" Mark asked him at length.

"Miserable, as always," Stanley replied, happy to have the other business dropped. "Don't bother going down — unless you can't make it till morning."

Mark gave Stanley a long look, then relented. "We were talking about how far we were from the war in the CBI," he explained.

Stanley grimaced. "You guys. There you go again. So we were in India instead of Europe or the Pacific. Big deal. Just because we didn't get the headlines . . . "

"That's the truth," Roy said.

"That's the point, Stanley," said Mark, right on his heels. "Nobody back home knows anything about the CBI. All they know is the big battles in Africa and Europe and the war in the Pacific. The war in China? The war in India? What war you talking about? they'll ask you."

"Like the generals," Roy went on. "There's Ike Eisenhower and General Mark Clark, and Old Blood-and-Guts Patton, and Omar Bradley, and General MacArthur and the marines wadin' ashore on all those Pacific islands . . . "

Mark finished the list in ringing tones, " . . . and General William Tunner, Commanding General of the Hump. Ta-daa!"

Roy grinned. "Yeah. Old General Tonnage. Get those crates in the air, boys. China needs those crates! Never mind what's in 'em. We've got to beat last month's tonnage!"

Mark took it up. By this time Stanley was their willing audience.

"Now, Chiang Kai-shek, sitting in pomp and splendor on the other side of the Hump in his headquarters outside Chungking, that's another story. Folks will know about him."

"Yes sir," Roy said. "The ol' Generalissimo. Nothing too good for ol' Chiang. The hell with the weather. Fuck the Himalayas. Just get those crates over there for ol' Chancre Jack!"

"The fighting Air Transport Command," Mark went on. "Who ever heard of the ATC?"

"I know, I know," Stanley finally broke in. He had heard this one before. "It ought to be called the ETC. And so on and so forth . . . "

That stopped them, at least long enough for Stanley to follow up his advantage.

"All right. You ratbones finished? You never know when to quit, do you? How come you're always putting everything down?" He shook his head. "Nothing wrong with the ATC. In fact, I always felt pretty good about it. And the CBI too"— Stanley smiled easily at this point— "at least now that I'm out of it. Feel pretty good about getting all that stuff to China, too. They'd never have made it without us. I don't care if anybody else knows it was important. I know it. So do you finks. Why don't you admit it? The more I think about it, now that I'm getting out of it, the better I feel about the whole thing—the CBI, the ATC, Special Service. Nothing wrong with any of it. It's all the same war. And we won it, lads. All of us. None of it was easy. I can tell you this, when I get out I'm going to feel just as good about being a real live veteran as any guy who was in Europe or the Pacific."

Mark applauded with his hands against his thighs. "Bravo, bravo. Strike up the band."

"More, more," Roy was saying. He added to the applause, hitting the platform with the flat of his hand. "Sergeant Norman for Veteran of the Year. Go, man."

Mark struck an attitude he supposed looked like Franklin D. Roosevelt. "Sergeant Stanley Norman," he said grandly, "for President!"

Stanley lifted up his chin to match. "*Ex*-Sergeant Norman," he intoned just as grandly, and all three broke into laughter.

"I'll tell you what," Mark Reiter said. "Anybody who never heard of the CBI, we can tell them the truth—that we put in our time sweating it out in the Pacific." He gestured out toward the darkening sea.

"Under the command of General Bliss," Stanley Norman added.

"Right," said Roy Warner. "No need to tell 'em the war is over. . . . "

. . . Suddenly, the ship's speakers come alive with the piercing *whoo-eeeeee-ahh* of the bo'sun's whistle, a startling event that calls them back to the present reality and the sobriety of their scene. The broken, rising-and-falling pattern of the piping is longer and more drawn-out than they have heard it before. The effect is melancholy as well as arresting. They sit motionless and listen, their eyes lowered, through the silent pause that follows, a long moment during which the entire ship seems to fall into mute benediction.

The voice that speaks into that silence is incisive, firm, deliberate, and clear. It is also personal in its modulations and unexpectedly human:

"This is the Captain speaking. I am sorry to say that all our efforts to recover the man overboard have been unsuccessful. We have been unable to find or even sight him. Any likelihood of rescue has now passed. We are therefore terminating the search. I have recalled the boats. As soon as they are secured we will resume our course and make up the time lost in our schedule."

The announcement has been articulated smoothly and without interruption to this point, but the Captain's voice hesitates for an instant before continuing.

"I wish to thank and commend the members of the crew for their professionalism during the search. You did your best. And all transient personnel for their cooperation."

The speakers cut out and are silent once again.

TRIO

STANLEY: That does it, lads.

ROY: You were right, Mark. Captain's decision.

MARK: You were probably right, too. Regulations.

ROY: That wasn't regulations I just heard. That was the Captain.

MARK: Well, it's done.

STANLEY (mimicking): "This is . . . the Captain . . . speaking . . . ."

ROY: Captain Who, I wonder. The Captain. The Captain. Hasn't he got a name?

MARK: When you get to be the Captain you don't need a name. Don't even want one. It'd make you just like everyone else.

STANLEY: He's the Skipper. The Old Man.

ROY: He's the Man Upstairs. The Man with No Name.

MARK: He's got a name all right. But it's beside the point. It's that poor GI he's leaving behind in the ocean who hasn't got a name.

ROY: The Unknown Soldier.

STANLEY: Into the Great Unknown.

MARK: "His name is writ on water."

ROY: What?

MARK: That's somebody's epitaph. Some musician or writer. I forget who.

STANLEY: Well, it's over. Too bad. The Unknown Soldier, huh?

ROY: They'll find out who he is, sooner or later.

STANLEY: I suppose so. We'll probably have a roll call of all the troops. See who's missing.

MARK: I wonder. I wonder if they'll ever find out about him—even that way.

ROY: Sure they will. Check the troops, check the records. Maybe they know all about him already. We're the ones they'll never find out about. The rest of us. We'll be the unknown soldiers.

MARK: Now you're talking. CBI? ATC? What war were you guys in?

STANLEY: Here we go again.

MARK: No. I mean it. We're practically anonymous. We can blend right in when we get home. Nobody will notice us. Part of the scenery.

ROY: Now *you're* talkin'. That's what I'm after.

STANLEY: Not me. I got plans.

MARK: Fine. Doesn't make any difference. It's even better that way.

ROY: You're goin' to make a name for yourself, huh, Stanley?

STANLEY: Nothing wrong with the name I got now. I just intend to let people know it.

MARK: Exactly right, Stanislaus. Here we go again. Carry on. You're perfectly right.

STANLEY: Did I miss something? What are you talking about?

MARK: I don't know. Hard to explain. The search for the man overboard is done and we're on our way home again. And everything seems all right to me. You're right. The Captain's right. Roy's right. Everybody's right. Even the poor GI out in the middle of the Pacific Ocean, where we're leaving him so the rest of us can get on our way again. So we're a part of whatever happens.

ROY: You been drinkin', Mark? Where'd you get the booze?

MARK: I don't know. The fresh air did it, I guess. I went down to the head while you guys were gone, and when I came up, I . . . just felt good.

STANLEY: That explains it.

MARK: No, it's more than that. It's like . . . well, look. Lots of things go wrong. O.K. Things aren't always the way you want them. O.K. But it's all right because things go wrong. You see what I mean? Things can always go wrong. That's the only reason you can really feel good. The only way you can know when everything is all right.

STANLEY: And two plus two equals five. You want to run that past me again?

MARK: No. Forget it. . . . It's just that you've got to know it can go either way if you're ever going to feel really good. Like I do now. Or like I did before I started talking about it.

ROY: Goin' wrong on you, huh, man?

MARK: In fact, sometimes it's because of something that went wrong that you feel good about things later.

ROY: Like what?

STANLEY: Yeah, name three.

MARK: All right. What about the Roy Warner Trio? The three of us?

ROY: What about us?

MARK: One of the best things that ever happened to me, being with you guys, where we've been, playing together. The way it works sometimes in the music when we're playing together, too.

STANLEY: Yeah . . .

MARK: Well, it took World War II and all of us getting shipped to the CBI, and the ATC, and all that misery in India to do it.

STANLEY: What's the misery in India got to do with it?

MARK: Maybe nothing. Maybe everything. I don't care. It's part of it, isn't it? I know it'll be part of everything for me from now on. Just like you and Roy'll be, even if I never see you again.

ROY: And the Captain We-Don't-Know-His-Name, huh? And the man overboard.

STANLEY: . . . who shall be nameless.

MARK: Well, yeah. The whole picture. Not just the part you want — or think you want . . .

ROY: . . . but whatever happens, huh? Maybe I dig what you're sayin', man.

STANLEY: Well, maybe I do and maybe I don't. You want to try it on me again?

ROY: O.K. Let me try, Mark. Think of it like music when you're playin'. Like jazz music, anyway. You hit a note, see? You don't know ahead of time what it was goin' to be. Or even if you thought you did, it might turn out to be somethin' else when you play it. That'd be like the wrong note, see?

MARK: Right. But you don't quit just because it isn't what you — or anyone else — expected.

ROY: No. You just see where that note fits in, where it takes you, 'cause it sets up the next notes you're goin' to play.

MARK: In fact, that's when it can start to get really good. Because it went wrong.

ROY: Yeah, 'cause it has to fit in different than you thought it was goin' to. Or nothin' much happens.

MARK: But it still has to work. You've got to take what happens and work it out.

STANLEY: Or work it in?

MARK: O.K. Anyway, that's what makes it interesting, when it gets dangerous, even.

STANLEY: Yeah, I know. Sometimes I hear you play something wrong — or really different, anyway — just to see what happens. To break it up.

MARK: Sure. Part of the deal. You can't always go by the book.

ROY: Another thing. It happens best when you're there, Stanley. With the rhythm. So we always know it's there. It all depends on the rhythm too.

MARK: That's right. You've got to depend on the rhythm, no matter what happens.

STANLEY: I know. I can feel when it's going right.

ROY: Like sometimes when we're talkin'.

MARK: Like lots of times. If you just think hard about one of those times — you can see how maybe everything's really all right.

ROY: It's right because it can go wrong, huh? Man, that's wild.

STANLEY: Like being in India, you mean? Those times we were talking about?

MARK: Maybe. Yeah.

ROY: Well . . . not always right while they're happenin', Mark. You got to turn it into music later. Not the same thing.

MARK: I don't know. Why not?

ROY: 'Cause music is more like rememberin'. Like rememberin' afterwards the way you felt.

MARK: Maybe some kinds of music, Roy. Like you been there before. But not when it's really good. That kind of music has to happen right while you're playing it.

ROY: Well, maybe. Sometimes, man, it just goes so good you can't understand it. You don't even want to think about it. You just feel it and go with it, and everything works and everything fits.

MARK: Now you're talking. Even if you're playing some low-down blues, right?

ROY: Especially playin' the blues. And it just moves.

MARK: How about up-tempo? How about fast blues?

ROY: Well, yeah. It works both ways. You can play the blues slow and tired—full of everything that ever went wrong, full of gloom and misery—and it can make you feel so good, feel so much like yourself . . .

MARK: . . . and then you can play those same blues up-tempo—the same chords, same changes—and they turn bright and happy.

ROY: And you feel good but in a different way. Yeah.

STANLEY: And the people listening feel it with you. They start saying yeah, like you just did, Roy.

ROY: Well, they know what you're feelin'.

MARK: Anyway, whether you play it slow or fast, the music's got to be happening right then. And it's got to have some sense of the harmonies behind what's developing.

ROY: The chords, yeah. But the melody, too. The melody line that takes you along.

STANLEY: And the rhythm, lads. Lest we forget. The rhythm, too.

MARK: There are times in your life that go like that. When you're in tune.

ROY: And everything that happens is right. You don't even think about it, it feels so good.

STANLEY: I know what you mean. When it all goes together. Yeah.

—STANLEY'S SOLO—

"*. . . when it all goes together. Yeah.*"

. . . that's when it's best. When I just try to lay back. Hold it all steady. Go with it. Sometimes it works. But it's harder than they think. Got to go with that steady rhythm. No matter what. Hold the beat. Never try anything really different. I know. Let them try something different. Play around. Play something "wrong." Well, they're right, of course. They need me to hold the tempo steady. O.K. I do my best. Sometimes I find the groove and it just goes. They're right. It feels real good. Hard work, though, most of the time. Hard to hold Mark back sometimes. He rushes the tempo when he takes off. He knows it sometimes. Part of what he's doing. But not always. Hard work keeping steady when he takes off. Not much problem with Roy. Never rushed a beat in his life. Roy likes to lag, though, sometimes. But that's not as hard. Easy to lead someone with the tempo. Harder to try to hold them back.

Best when it all goes together, all right. It's like floating when it happens. When nothing forces the tempo. Like time out on the desert . . .

Can't wait to get back to Nevada. Back to the desert again. Into the mountains. Do some fishing, hunting. Get me a horse and just ride out into those canyons. The rhythm of the horse's hooves under me. Swaying in the saddle. Time out in the desert. No clocks. Nevada doesn't want clocks. No clocks to tell you when to start, when to quit. Just the sun. And shadows. Everything taking its own time. Everything according to the sun. And the moon at night. And the wind. And the stars. The stars! . . .

. . . the stars that summer with Uncle Lyman's sheepherders in the Ruby Mountains up north. Just a kid, but I felt like one of them. And the millions of stars at night. I could hardly sleep. Lying on my back, looking up into that incredible sky. Thinking about the stars and all that space. So full of stars on moonless nights. Feeling so small, my thoughts so big . . .

In the daytime, moving with the sheep. The sun so bright and hot. The air so clear at six thousand, seven thousand feet. Everything in its own time. The sheepherder's old wagon. The fires on cool nights. The stove. The old Basque camp-tender, Juan, and his suppers at sundown. Twilight time. The cooking smells while I watched. I never ate so much. Never tasted anything so good, after the long day. Roast lamb, potatoes, hot bread. More lamb, more potatoes, more bread. Drinking coffee for the first time in my life. One time, a swig of their wine, even. Uncle Lyman saying go ahead, he wouldn't tell my bishop. Part of the life. Part of the whole thing. Like everything else out there. The sheepherders and their sheep. The lambs. Like the Bible stories I used to like to hear. But I knew it was different. It never really seemed like the Bible. Not like those shepherds. It just wasn't the same. Not with Uncle Lyman there, telling his own stories. When he was a boy. Homesteading and ranching. And the Basques. Old Juan, anyway. Drinking and singing their Basque songs by the fire. Juan keeping the rhythm, playing the spoons. Teaching me how to do it. And their sheep dog, smart as any of us. Shoo-mee, they called him. Deserts and mountains and sheep. Like the Bible stories, I know, but never the same. It was Nevada, after all. It was my desert and my mountains. And Uncle Lyman's sheep. And the long summer days. The peace. While we worked. While we rested. Even me, just a little kid. And the stars.

What we did. Where it all happened. Each day. Each night. Everything. Heyyy! . . .

. . . that day in Sylhet! No wonder! How come I never thought of it? Why I felt so great. Everything so right. Of course! That whole long beautiful hot clear day. Outside of Sylhet after coming down from the rest camp at Shillong. Like one of those days on the slopes of the Rubys. In the morning, waiting for our plane in the field, by the dirt airstrip. The dry meadows and the Khasi foothills beyond. The sun hotter and hotter into the day. Only that sheet metal shack for shade. No bigger than a sheepherder's wagon. And the plane that didn't come. Never came that whole day. The other guys all miserable. Sweating and griping about the heat. About the plane. Like Mark said. Moaning how everything was going wrong. And me, letting them moan, feeling like everything was great. Like we were lucky the plane didn't come. Lucky to be there with such a day. Spreading out. Loving it. Letting it happen . . .

. . . If the plane had come that morning, it wouldn't have happened. We'd have been right onto the C47 and whisked away. On somebody else's schedule. Bucket seats back to Calcutta. Back on the clock and the calendar. Instead we had that whole day to ourselves. Those dummies just hung around that shack all day. And moaned. Sweating and cursing the luck. Playing cards. Cussing each other out. Trying to sleep. And me feeling great. I didn't care about the plane. It was my kind of heat. I remember how I just took off about noon. By myself. Just walked right off. Across the field and over the rise . . .

. . . I hadn't felt that good for months. Years, maybe. Like it was all strange, but like I belonged. Walking easy in that baking heat. Across that open land. Not as dry as Nevada, maybe. That's why I didn't think of the connection, probably. And it was India. But drier and better than anywhere else I'd been in India. Stripped down to my khaki shorts. Good solid heat. Just kept going. Forgot the plane. Forgot the Army and the war. Over the rise and out of sight. Another world. Into the rolling dusty fields, with the foothills beyond. Nothing much growing there. End of the dry season. Then that low line of brushwood I headed for. Maybe water, I thought. That was before I heard anything. It pulls me again, thinking of it. The first thing that happened, because otherwise it was so quiet out there . . .

. . . the sound. That small, reedy sound. So thin and distant at first. The heat shimmering, like the desert, when I looked ahead, trying to locate it. Then the faint tinkling bell of the lead goat. Couldn't mistake that. Finally, the Indian herdsman himself. And that reed flute I'd heard, even before I could see him. And the little kid with him. By the stream bed. Just a trickle in it when I got up to it. And the herd of goats spread over the hillside. Grazing, looking up. Grazing and looking up. The dry smells of the dry land. Perfect!

Everything perfect there, that time. Everything that happened. Me too, in the middle of it. How come I kept right on, walking? How come? Right up to them. I knew it was all right. That Indian herdsman wasn't worried. Not embarrassed or self-important like most of the Indians in the cities. When he stopped playing his flute he just smiled. Just watched me come and smiled. Bobbed his head at me when I got close. Just smiled and started talking. Not even a formal greeting, I don't think. And the little boy. His big brown wild eyes. Wearing only those shorts, way too big for him. Bare feet. Cocky, curious, happy. full of energy, full of mischief. When I bowed and spoke back to the man, the boy so tickled he almost danced.

One of those times. That whole thing. It all fit. Everything that happened. And me too, the way I felt all through it. The beating sun. The open land. The clear air. That baking heat and a brightness over everything. It made me expand. I felt so full of everything. All the brightness in me, too.

The way we couldn't understand what we said, but how we talked anyway. The way he just started to play his flute again. How I drummed along the rhythm for him on my knees. How his eyes smiled at me over the flute. How the boy showed off by chasing a goat, as if it were a stray. Yelling, waving his stick. How I chased another one, clowning, acting awkward. How he laughed and jabbered at me. Everything so warm, so open. In the heat of that day, stranded outside Sylhet. Somewhere in India. The middle of Asia. The middle of World War II. The other side of the world. Yet I never felt so much a part of things. Never more right, more glad to be alive . . .

. . . unless it was that time with the sheepherders in the Rubys. Much the same. But I was just a kid then. Was I a kid again that time in Sylhet? Was it like being a kid again, with the Indian goatherd? No,

I don't think so. There was the Indian kid. I was just who I was. They were who they were. We were just what we were then, together. Doing what we were doing. Right where we were. That was the thing. There was no other time, right then, but right then. Everything happened just the way it happened. It all went together.

How it stayed with me afterwards. When I got back to the strip and the guys. How I didn't tell them. I knew they wouldn't really care. It didn't matter. I still had it with me. How we finally gave up on the plane that day. Walking back in to the outskirts of Sylhet. How they moaned and griped all the way. Going into the British Army Compound. Putting our shirts back on. How I talked us into dinner and overnight.

Even the next morning, still with me. Out to the strip again, and the plane on time that day. The last glimpse I got of the scene, taking off. Through the Plexiglas windows. Their scratches, their dirt, their distortion, between me and the scene below. Falling back below. Then behind as we turned. Still perfect. The way it all happened. The way it all moved from one thing to the next. Still being everything, all the while. Will I feel like that again? Back in Nevada, sure. There'll be time. Without clocks. But I won't be a kid there, anymore . . .

. . . and the place'll be different. The place is changing. Can't waste much time when I go back. So much I ought to do. Got to figure what to do. Get busy. The Church, too. All that LDS stuff. Can I get back into that? Sure. Why not? Got to get along. Good for business, too. Las Vegas, watch it grow. I guess he's right, Brother Catmull. It can't miss. Got to get in on the ground floor, now the war's over. There's the dam and Boulder City, and the new lake. I could do something there, maybe. Strange to think of that lake—all that water—there in the desert. Filling up all those canyons. Never see those canyons again. Well, a lot'll change, like they say. Nevada. The gambling and the casinos. The ranch lands. Real estate. They'll need lawyers. Maybe I should go to law school, be a lawyer. Would that take too long? Boulder Dam and the electrical power and the new lake. Boats and recreation. Tourists, too. It'll all change. The rhythms. The way things go together . . .

. . . or the way they might pull apart. You've got to keep the rhythm steady. Whether the beat is slow and easy or fast-tempo. They need the beat, the rhythm steady behind them. They're right about that. I'm not a musician. O.K., but I know something about music . . .

. . . What'll I be like back there? In Las Vegas, Nevada, USA? McCarran Field and lots of Air Force guys there during the war. Flyboys. Some of them'll want to come back. No clocks, maybe, but we'll be on the map. The mountains, the desert. The electricity and power, the town, the gambling places. Two different beats. Got to keep it steady anyway. If I do it right, maybe no problem. Maybe lay back a while, take it easy. No need to go overboard. Watch and see what happens. Still, be a part of it. Got to concentrate. How to make it all go together, play it right.

—ROY'S SOLO—

"The chords, yeah. But the melody too. The melody line that takes you along."

. . . Well, there are times like that when you forget about how things can go wrong. Everything just takes you along and whatever happens you know is goin' to be right. Somethin' like I feel now, but maybe it's the nutmeg, anyway it's usually different when you're on a jag like I guess I am now, but I sure don't feel much. Funny I can't always tell the difference, like now, but that's best of all, when you don't even think about it but just go with it, I mean you're with it, you're in it, so there's no reason to think about whether things are right, they just are. When you're playin' music, of course, that's when you want to turn off everything else and put it all on the line, what you're feelin'. You don't want to think about it too much or you can lose it, lose the way it wants to go. Concentrate, I guess that's the word, except it always sounds like you're just sittin' and thinkin' about one thing when what I mean is that you're wide open to everything but it all goes right into what you're doin', you don't have to stop and figure it out especially. Later maybe you can think about it . . .

. . . like just then, I took a deep breath and rubbed my nose with my fingers—with my left hand—I know I did, I mean I'm payin' attention to all those things, Mark and Stanley too, what they say, and those little bumps, the rough places in the metal on the bulkhead and the deck, and the color of the sky, and the waves out there, the bigger ones — there — with the white caps, and everything, 'cause I'm really aware of all those things, all at the same time, but I can single them out too, when that's what I do, focusin' on somethin', sharp, and then movin' on to somethin' else. Sharp, that's what I mean, but without any edges, everything workin' together. Like other times, you don't need any nutmeg or weed or anything else and it happens, in fact it's probably even better then because it's the way it really is, everything mixin' together, and not just because you're on a jag and feelin' high. That one time in the booth, for instance — I don't know why I always keep thinkin' back to it, should have been ordinary but . . .

. . . that night at the base when I subbed for Cowboy Miles in the projection booth at the outdoor movie, I don't know why I felt so good or why it was so special but anyway it was great and maybe that's what I mean about sometimes when everything that happens is right, 'cause it sure was then. I felt so good about that whole deal, it was such a lift but I don't know why, and I guess I don't really care, 'cause I sure didn't worry about it then while it was happenin', and even though I think about it sometimes, I'm sure not goin' to worry about it now.

. . . Except I remember everything so sharp, all the parts that night, even though the way I felt was like it all went together just right, I guess somethin' like music, but like I tried to tell Mark it's not the same until you remember it — until you remember it, it's just what it was . . .

. . . that India sundown light was part of it and the air startin' to cool off after the heat all day. I know all the colors were changin' while the sun was goin' down and the way the light was kind of soft when I got there and stepped into that homemade booth I'd helped the Cowboy to put together, I can see all the slats and the rickety floorboards and lookin' out at the movie screen over those plain wooden benches, and it started gettin' darker with guys comin' in from all over the base and sittin' and wisin' off, just like before every movie we had there, but this was different 'cause the Cowboy was on pass and I was takin' over in the booth sittin' next to that old 16mm Bell and Howell I'd worked on so often I knew it inside out and it was oiled and tuned and runnin' smooth and ready to go, me too . . .

. . . takin' over the whole show that night. First playin' V-discs through the projector sound system I'd hooked up for the Cowboy, the record I remember best, I guess because it was such good corn and everybody imitated it, was Vaughn Monroe singing "Racin' with the Moon," and that crazy pfc from the motor pool would always stand up on a bench in front and sing along holdin' his nose. That whole deal that night, everything so sharp and movin' right along as natural as the sun goin' down and the dark comin' on, and the guys all wanderin' in and relaxed, the day over and everything turnin' cool. Me perched on the stool next to the old B and H watchin' 'em straggle in, maybe a hundred, a hundred-fifty officers and men together there finally, sittin', talkin', smokin', laughin', yellin' across that outdoor theatre we'd made, yellin' at their friends, yellin' at me to start the damn movie—like they'd yell at the umpire at a ball game back home—everyone coolin' off together in the first stir of a breeze we'd had all day. And there in the background all the time, sometimes drownin' out the music over the p.a. with a sudden roar, the C46's and C47's out on the ramp warmin' up. A part of me listenin' close to them too, listenin' for a miss, for the knock or the hard-edge whine that says somethin' might go wrong over the Hump, that we better break down that engine again and find the trouble, listenin' without even thinkin' about it, knowin' when those engines too were in tune, that easy hum and purr when they're warm and everything's working fine . . .

. . . then it's dark enough to start the show so I put on the first reel and cut the sound over from the phonograph to the projector and we're ready to go, what a good feelin', we're all ready to go and I'm the one runnin' the show and I know just what I'm doin', I know the whole thing. Cheers and hoots and then they're all quiet, just lookin', it's Paramount News with all that heavy music and I've got the volume up enough to cover the background noise from the airstrip, there's a section with a fashion show, those wild, crazy hats on the gorgeous models smilin' their perfect empty smiles and turnin' this way and that, and each one gets a chorus of hoots and whistles and groans from the guys, it's great. All the time the rest of the base goin' right ahead, whatever they're doin', the activity out there with the planes on the flight line, the KPs still cleanin' up from dinner over at the mess hall, the night CQ at his desk in the Orderly Room with the rest of it dark . . . back off to one side of the theatre that low-built plaster latrine building, the washroom end toward me, the lights on inside, it's dark enough now so I see in it clearly, lookin' back past the projector whirrin' and clickin' beside me, I can see two guys stripped to the waist standin' at the washbowls, one shavin', the other combin' his hair, each one bendin' down to see himself in a small pocket mirror propped on the shelf runnin' clear across over the faucets — in the sky over the latrine while I'm watchin', the beacon from the operations tower sweeps its beam over our heads . . . a motorcycle and then a jeep buzz past on the road that turns on the left and runs parallel to the theater, their head-lights flare over the audience and then hit the screen as they pass and wipe out the picture on the screen for a minute with their brightness, but no one notices especially, it's just one of the parts of how it all goes together, everything that's happenin' there, I always think about how everything fit together that night with me bein' the film jockey there in the booth, right in the middle of it . . .

. . . near the end of the reel the "GI Movie" comes on and there's Walter O'Keefe singin' "The Daring Young Man on the Flyin' Trapeze," we're supposed to sing along with the words printed in syl-lables and the bouncin' ball on the second chorus and all the guys in the audience watchin' it but nobody singin' until this one guy comes in with a loud falsetto "and my love he has stol-en a-way," and he gets cheers and applause from the crowd. The whole thing, I remember everything in that whole show just sittin' there in the booth with every-thing goin' on and me makin' it go . . .

. . . end of the first reel, sound down, lamp switch off, let it run through, pop the reel off and into the box, second reel on, thread it just so, sound loop just right over the sound drum, back to the take-up, good, power switch on, all goin' right, projector lamp back on, sound volume up to:

a Grantland Rice Sportlight (everybody cheers) about roller skat-ing (boos, groans), Ted Husing and the groans are drowned out by the awful roar of a big C54 revvin' up and changin' prop pitch, and every other sound disappears into the roar. Cheers again when the feature comes on, Columbia Pictures presents Richard Dix in *Mark of the Whistler*, title frames over a dark figure in the background and a queer little weird melody with strange intervals that somebody's whistlin'. A tech sergeant comes in bangin' the screen door, hands me a message, I turn the volume down — good thing it's still just the titles — and stick my head out and yell "Lieutenant Baxter report to Operations," which nobody pays any attention to, except Lieutenant Baxter I hope, since this happens a dozen times every movie. It was all so sharp that night though, I don't really know why I felt so good there runnin' that show, the Bell and Howell oiled and purrin' beside me, all the base hummin' and me in the shack feelin' like it's all mine but I'm really just a part of it like everything else, doin' my part there in the middle of it in the booth, was that it? nobody really payin' attention to me, couldn't even see me there in the dark booth, didn't even know it was me instead of Cowboy Miles, or even if they did, who cares, as long as everything goes along, it's not their business, as long as everyone's doin' whatever they're doin' they got nothin' to worry about sittin' there in the outdoor theatre off-duty, everything bein' taken care of . . .

. . . just like here on the troopship, here on the *General Bliss*? Well, somethin' like it, just sittin' and watchin', someone else runnin' the show and everything else that's still goin' on at the same time all over the ship — all over the world, if you want to think about it . . .

. . . then, later in the movie every time when the plot gets tense and it's supposed to be scary, it's O.K., I mean it's part of what's goin' on all over the base that night, and we're all there at the movie, so when it looks like somebody's goin' to get it and the shadowed figure in the background starts whistlin' that little eerie melody, well, each time more and more everybody in that GI audience whistles it right along with him and laughs a little, me too there in the booth right along with 'em. I don't know all those guys, maybe only a dozen out there I really know, some more I've seen around and we recognize each other, but most of them like guys I've never seen before, probably never see again, but we're all doin' it together before the show's over, whistlin' that little strange melody whenever the shadow comes on . . .

. . . maybe the man overboard, I wonder, it could be, one of those guys in the audience that night when everything seemed so right, or even some other night when the Cowboy was runnin' it, doesn't make any difference, he could have been in the audience watchin' the show, wherever he was stationed he probably saw *Mark of the Whistler* anyway, those movies circulated to bases all over the CBI Theatre — funny they call it a *theatre*, the CBI Theatre — and he probably saw it, the man who went overboard, and whistled that weird little melody with all the rest of us when we saw the shadow in the background, just like we did, hell, he could have been whistlin' there in my audience that same night . . .

. . . that whole night I felt so good I didn't even think about it, all the way to the end of the show when everybody got up and stretched and started talkin' and makin' jokes and slappin' at each other and I watched them from the projection booth movin' out, walkin' off in bunches and pairs and some by themselves to their barracks and bashas for the night — feelin' great all the way to the end and after the show, rewinding the reels over the top, listenin' to the motor of the B and H sing and the film makin' that tinny sound against the spinnin' reel while I braked the take-up feed with my fingers to keep it steady and tight like a governor while it rewound — just me finally, the whole theatre empty except for me, and quiet when I flipped off the switch on the projector, quiet so that the night sounds came on and the noises from the airstrip seemed closer, and just me now, finishin' up with the light on inside the booth and the night darkness all around, with the moths and other flyin' insects bangin' into the screens, that sound too while I packed up the film ready to ship to the next base on its itinerary the next morning, took one more look around the projection booth and out over the empty darkened theatre, then turned off the power and walked off into the darkness myself.

. . . Why was it such a lift that night? I didn't even talk to anybody but I felt right with them, everybody watchin' that dumb movie and the others workin' on the night shift out on the flight line, those guys in the latrine, everybody — 'cause it did all go together, somethin' like playin', 'cause I was there in the middle makin' it happen, but nobody knew it especially or paid any attention, that's one reason it felt so good—I was puttin' on the show but it wasn't me. I wasn't the show, it was all of us . . .

. . . It was me and the equipment too, now I think of it, that old Bell and Howell wouldn't have been runnin' so sweet if I hadn't worked it over every couple weeks, I knew every screw and sprocket in that old workhorse, and the whole sound system too, that was mine—well, me and the Cowboy and that tech. sergeant from across the base, what was his name? and Lieutenant Manning requisitioning all the stuff we needed—but it was my system really, that night anyway, everything workin' fine. Nothin' I like better than gettin' electrical equipment set up, the more complicated the better, like my guitar amp—when I get back home I'm goin' to look into a new outfit, maybe put together my own, get me a bigger speaker, maybe two of 'em to get that binaural sound I want. I'll have to read up on it, take a course maybe, you can do that by mail and study up . . .

. . . I really ought to get more schoolin', I know that, all kinds of things I could do with electrical stuff, speakers, amps, whole systems, I bet, hell, I already know more about tubes and circuits than anybody else I know. What I'd like is to learn some other things too, though, things like Mark knows, well, not so I'd be like him, but I would like to know more words and talk better, I can never find the right words like he does, you get that from bein' in college and readin' a lot of different kinds of books, not just music and electrical manuals. I'd like to do that. Nancy does that. Nancy Hamilton ever since I've known her, readin' books, always talkin' so good, I mean sayin' just what she means and not showin' off, always just the right words, no big deal, not like Mark sometimes when he goes off and like he's talkin' to himself . . .

. . . why don't I go to college myself, maybe in a year or two? No reason why I shouldn't, nothin' else I've got to do. Go up to Georgia Tech maybe, and take some engineering, that'd be tougher than studyin' by mail, I suppose, but they've got the latest equipment at a place like that and they'd know what's goin' on, all the new stuff in electronics, there's a lot happenin' from the war and they'll need guys who know somethin' about it. I don't want to quit playin' guitar, but I don't have to do that, I can play anyway and make enough at night maybe while I go to college in the daytime, I wouldn't mind that if the two things would fit together. Hah, think of my old man if he knew I was thinkin' about goin' to college, but Ma she'd sure like it if she knew. I think I'll talk to Nancy Hamilton about it, she knows what it's like in college and I can trust her, if she doesn't think I should do it she'll tell me. Maybe it could all work out even though I don't want to count on it too much, somethin' always goes wrong, but it sure would be nice if it all could work together, with Nancy Hamilton too, though if that doesn't work out when I see her there are plenty of other chicks, as long as I keep playin' music anyhow, but I guess I ought to quit foolin' around some time and figure out what I ought to do. I'll think about it when I get home.

—MARK'S SOLO—

" . . . *some sense of the harmonies behind what's developing . . . times in your life that go like that, too. When you're in tune*"
. . . In tune, in June, it rhymes with moon and croon and spoon and we'll be cuddlin' soon—those simple-minded lyrics, which is why I seldom pay attention to the words, or even, after a while, the melody. The tune, they call it. Well, I guess that's close enough. The tune is what you sing.
. . . but then you got to sing *in tune* and that's the other kind of meaning, more like the mathematics and physics behind it all. The music of the spheres. It's all a matter of vibrations, oscillations, frequencies. Overtones and undertones. The complications, to say nothing of the implications, of the diatonic scale: going up from middle C on the keyboard with the majors and the minors intermixed—white key, black key, white key, black key, white key, white key, black key, white key . . .
. . . how that used to fascinate me at first, when I was a kid fooling around with the keyboard, back before I even picked out chords and taught myself to play. I'd just go up the scale in C and down again, and then I'd find the matching intervals in other keys. I'd always get tricked up by those two odd pairs of white notes right together—

E and F, and B and C. Why didn't they simply alternate the blacks and whites over the whole length of the keyboard, top to bottom? I thought that would be simpler then, to play a keyboard alternating all the way, with no surprises in the pairs you had to watch for . . .

. . . But then there's got to be surprise, or things won't fall in place. That's what I meant about those times when everything is right. Still, Roy may be right that music's like remembering . . .

. . . I always think of those experiences I had the summer I was ten. They both were mystical—the word I didn't want to use before because they'd think I meant "mysterious" or something else besides that sense of perfect wholeness, everything together in its place and movement, like a trance. Both times that summer at the lake. First time just sitting by the willow at the shore, transfixed by light and color, shadow, sky, the rippling water, trees and leaves, flowering weeds and lily pads, and then—that turtle dry and motionless there on his island-rock just off the shore, and then—the darting-poised-and-darting dragonfly that in a sudden blink of perfect motion settled on the turtle's shell and stopped my breath. The world and my eyes went blank and whole that instant in a kind of godlike recognition first of time and then at once of timelessness. It was a universe in which my presence was the key and yet the slightest element of all—of *all*—that self-fulfilling, selfless moment when that child I was the summer I was ten exulted in the whole. The sense of harmony!

Another day, the second time, back in the shaded woods alone one afternoon, entranced by my repeated motions throwing objects in the murky pond left from heavy rain the night before. The rocks and stones, the twigs and parts of broken branches, wood and clods of earth I lifted from their forest bedding, hardly looking. Then I'd rise and cock my arm in one continuous perfect motion, graceful, slow, unbending, then the half-step forward and the cunning action of the wrist to launch the missile easy on its arc into the waiting mud and water—arc and plop!—the cue to lift the next and link the moves with exultation through a body sequence I alone could cause and feel the grace of, fusing time with motion . . .

Yet I wonder if the mystic sense in these events is just as much the product of remembering—of all the times since I was ten that I've recalled the easy glory of those episodes. By now they have no meaning but their own, no context to intrude upon their wholeness, just my current need to have them there, complete and absolute in memory . . .

. . . I remember more directly my delight the first time that I played both ends against the middle all the way, starting at both the top and bottom of the keyboard. I was hardly big enough to reach both ends at once, sitting at the old upright piano in the living room with nobody around, walking my fingers up from the bottom and down from the top at the same time, watching and hearing the combinations of black and white keys fall together till they finally ran smack into that half-step dissonance of the white keys E and F, right there in the middle of everything, after all those two-part harmonies I'd listened to, working inward toward those last two white notes smack against each other . . .

. . . at first I used to think there ought to be another note right there in the middle, right in the crack between that clash of E and F, the whole progression of those pairs resolving into one, at last. I'd try to hear that final tone exactly in the middle, but I never could. It seems to me that even then, I didn't really want to. Somehow if I did, it would be over. And I'd be done. That's strange. As if I didn't want the two-part harmonies themselves resolved. Although I tried, the keyboard wouldn't let me bring it all together in a final note. Suppose it had, back then. Or any time while I was learning. Would I have quit?

Well, how about it now? The war is over. Where do I go from here? Up and down the scales again? Two lines playing out together, seeking harmonies? Everything has changed; yet nothing much has changed. After that collision in the middle of the keyboard stopped me short of any final note, I used to backtrack—just reverse direction, right hand walking up, left hand backing down, note by note in neat chromatic pairs. Those simple two-part harmonies that closed down to that collision at the white keys E and F would simply open up again, wider now and wider yet, until they're back where they began, back to where the keyboard ends, the bottom A, the top at C, a fitting combination—a minor third, in fact—but so spread out, so open and so far apart their frequencies don't really mix. The backtrack trip would turn their tones percussive, back where it all had started—animal growls down at the bottom, toy wooden plinks up at the top. The rest of my life was waiting to be played out in between . . .

. . . the riches that were waiting for me in between! More hours at the keyboard than I can ever calculate, discovering how the tones congeal and mix, how each mute key is secretly in league with every other, how harmonies evolve and fall in place the way they do—like butterflies. It's still a challenge, though, like drifting into counterpoint before deciding which melodic line will gain the upper hand and take me where it knows the music wants to go, the tune . . .

. . . the tune. I'm back to that. The trouble is, I know (Roy knows it too), sometimes I think too much about my music, work so hard for nuances, climbing toward my climaxes, that I forget to sing. But then, I think like the piano. All the range is there with endless combinations waiting to be found and sounded, endless possibilities waiting for me to find out how to surprise them into song, to strike a chord . . .

. . . the grand piano that I play is part of my trouble. The instrument itself. The hinges, pins, and hammers hidden by the keys, the pads and dampers, sounding board and pegs—the strings themselves, bass notes wrapped for resonance, the rest high-strung and tense, enormous pressures pulling at them all the while the whole piano seems to stand at ease. Two strings are strung for every treble tone—ah! that's a secret only the piano knows—the tension of those double wires drawn tight to resonate, when struck, precisely at the designated pitch, the stroke and sound together in a twine of tone so richly singular it's truer than the number *one*. And that is that. As long as it's *in tune*. Pianos simply have to be in tune. There's no alternative. Unless, of course, you choose to turn the whole thing into a cartoon or comedy. Or irony. Or honky-tonk burlesque, like that effect you get by putting newsprint through the strings, like Western barroom scenes and "tickling the ivories"—or like the "professor" in a whorehouse down in New Orleans . . .

. . . that's funny, Roy called me "professor" back before we'd worked together. He knew I'd been through college and thought I only played the kind of highbrow stuff he wouldn't understand. Oh well, he dropped it soon enough. He could have picked it up again, the way I sounded on those beat-up old pianos I ran into on the tour.

Around Calcutta wasn't bad, but on those bases in Assam and China it was murder—keys and hammers missing, pedals broken, dampers ineffective so the notes would ring on endlessly like chimes. But what could you expect, in Asia, in the middle of the war? I'm really proud to say I blundered through and learned not to complain. I kept myself in tune regardless of the kind of instrument I had to play. Good thing that I could think the music clear enough to disregard the sounds those clunkers made—or failed to make. And after I got smart and got the tools and taught myself to tune the strings that worked before I had to play, it wasn't quite so bad. I learned a lot . . .

. . . I learned it for myself, what I'd been told about the tempered scale, how only the human ear, attuned to nuances, could coax the quality of certain notes by the slightest nudge of the tuning hammer just beyond mere mathematical precision into cones of brighter sound and sympathetic tones unknown to mere numerical relationships. What did I learn in World War II? I learned at least to bring my own piano into tune . . .

. . . this whole routine concerning tunes and tuning—well, I can't ignore it, since I play the dumb piano. Which means, of course, I only play the keyboard. The piano plays the notes. Alas, I cannot play the cracks between the keys. I'm not the instrument, although I'm instrumental. How can I hope to sing? The piano is my instrument, to which I'm accidental. I have to think about the music while I'm playing. It happens here, as well, within my mind—the melody, harmonic patterns, rhythms, all that matters. You think my playing ought to loosen up, to entertain? O.K. But doesn't it help to entertain a thought . . . ?

All right, LeRoy. All right then, Stanley. I'll work it out. Ol' Mark comes down to earth in time. He circles back around the tune and darts on by—a dragonfly? More like a loon in flight than twiggy songbirds singing in the sun. The loon flies underwater too, as well as whistling through the air . . .

. . . I really want to play Satie, Debussy, and Ravel. Oh well. Right now I'm only a pianist in the pit, although this pit feels like a stage . . .

. . . We're back to staging, boys—not back to Kanchrapara, where this all began, but back to back and heading east again. Three loons /

We rhyme with tunes. I want it known it's more than the piano that I play.

—ENSEMBLE—

We're movin'. We're really movin' now.

Cal-i-forn-ya, here we come . . .

Great to see that ol' wake behind us again.

Hah! Wake up, everybody!

Yeah. Churnin' up that ocean. That beautiful white water down there.

Hey, look-a-there, ain't she pretty!

Yeah. Churn, baby, churn.

Look down, look down, that lone-some ro-oad . . .

Get that steam up, Mon Capitaine. Let's get out-a here.

Beautiful stea-mer, wake un-to me . . .

Hey! Look how far we've come already. You can see where we started from back there.

Yeah. Go. Right back where we started from . . .

You mean back where our wake starts.

Our wake? Or his?

What's the use of worryin'?

It ne-ver was worth while . . .

Don't blame me. I'm just glad it's over.

Just one of those things . . .

N.R.A. We did our part.

Hot diggity. It feels so good to be movin' again.

Geor-giaaa, Geor-giaaa . . .

Go-ing home. Go-ing home . . .

Come on with the come-on, you ratbones. What say we get down off this platform?

Ready to hit the deck for a while?

New deck for us to shuffle when we get home.

There'll be some changes made . . .

Fine and dandy. Just play them cards the way they're dealt.

Let's go somewhere we can move around, loosen up.

Good idea. Gettin' tired of lookin' backwards from up here.

Let's try it up front. Like to see where we're headed for a change.

You go to my head . . .

Let's do it . . .

Well, it's all right with me.

Good-night, la-dies;
    Good-night, la-dies;
        Good-night, la-dies;
We're going to leave you now,
Merrily we roll a-long,
    roll a-long,
    roll a-long;
Merrily we roll a-long . . .
. . . o'er the deep
    blue
    sea

(final chord, unresolved, tremolo . . .)

THE LIEUTENANT

When the Captain announced that he was retiring to his cabin, the Lieutenant thought it odd. Granted that the search for the man overboard was over and done. Granted also that as Officer of the Deck the Lieutenant was fully competent to get the huge ship once again under way and back on course. Still, it seemed premature, perhaps even callous, for the Captain to leave the bridge at this point for the privacy of his quarters.

It was poor timing, an anticlimax, the Lieutenant felt. They should all be together for a while longer, the whole bridge crew who had worked so intensely and well together throughout the search. The failure of that search to find the man overboard made it seem all the more necessary to stay on as a unit for a while, perhaps to talk over the whole episode together, to consider its implications, its ironies. The Lieutenant knew the notion was foolish, but that didn't prevent him from feeling an abruptness in the Captain's departure. It broke up the team and the rewarding sense of common effort the Lieutenant had discovered and enjoyed during the emergency.

He had been a bit miffed when the Captain held on to his command through the whole process of raising and securing the boats.

He might have trusted that operation to his OOD. Yet the Old Man had been congenial rather than imperious during the procedures, talking freely with the Lieutenant, commenting on the differences between the recovery operation on a low-slung destroyer and a General-class troopship like the *Bliss* with its awkwardly high freeboard, almost as if he were admitting, with some candor, that he was not altogether sure of himself under the circumstances and wanted the practice.

A more customary reaction to the Captain's departure from the bridge soon followed, however. Once the business of getting under way was completed, the bridge crew, the Officer of the Deck included, settled back into their routine roles. Everyone relaxed. Relaxed on the surface, at least, and with one another. They'd done their job. The Old Man himself had said so.

For the Lieutenant, the absence of the Captain was also a release, and he gradually felt himself becoming a person again rather than a function. Still, his thoughts lingered on the search and its object. It was unfinished business with tantalizing unasked and unanswered questions, some of which could only be asked of oneself, others which needed airing.

"Mordecai . . . " the Lieutenant said, tentatively, as if musing aloud.

"Yes, sir?"

"What kind of man is this Haines?"

Mordecai hung back momentarily.

"I mean, how reliable is he? Do you think his report was dependable?"

"Yes, sir," Mordecai replied, but he could tell the Lieutenant wanted more. "Well, I mean he wouldn't want to kid about something like that—a man overboard. He told us everything he could."

"Yeahh," the Lieutenant sighed. "I wonder, though. . . . " He shifted his position and looked across the bridge. "Well, you can't help wondering. . . . " He looked back at his talker, narrowed his eyes, shook his head slightly and was silent.

"Yes, sir," Mordecai said to ease the silence.

It wouldn't do, the Lieutenant realized. He couldn't talk about it with the men under him any more than he could with the Captain. It was stupid, but that's the way it was. Whether it was up the chain of command or down, you just couldn't talk about anything that was personally important to you, couldn't admit to even having personal thoughts or doubts. Rank has its privileges, the saying went. It also has its handicaps, the Lieutenant reminded himself.

He moved casually over to the bay of windows, folded his arms, and leaned bodily forward against the sill. The night was coming on now, no longer dusk under the heavy skies so much as a gathering darkness. The sea was a mass of indistinct motion, whitecaps showing faint and gray here and there against the vague shapes of the waves. It would be a dark night, and the *General Bliss* would continue to plow steadily through those restless seas, farther and farther into the deepening blackness ahead and away from the location where they had drifted for nearly two hours, away from the isolated, abandoned body they had sought so intently, so hopefully, to rescue—if in fact there was a body overboard, the Lieutenant thought.

The image of that body returned to him again, only now it was not the figure of the man he had envisioned throughout the search, bobbing at the surface, struggling to keep up the minimal motion which would sustain him afloat until the ship could find and restore him. Now it was the inert, sodden shell of that man submerged in the dark ocean, the green fatigues turned black in the water, now clinging, now billowing as the sea flowed through them, the man's form almost indistinguishable from the shadowy currents that had taken it over with endless, mindless motion.

And the Captain, coolly returning to his quarters, the Lieutenant mused, probably calling his steward and ordering his dinner. Military stoicism. Business as usual.

Maybe not, though. There had been some moments during the emergency, moments during which the Captain had not so much let down his guard as he had projected his own personal dedication and had led the others to enlist their own in kind. Leadership. Maybe that's what it was. The Lieutenant wondered in the privacy of his thought whether he would himself ever convey that quality. It could be that the Captain was feeling the weight of their failure in the search and the loss of the man overboard more than those who stayed on the bridge. Maybe he had retired to prevent the others from seeing the effects on him.

Maybe, but not likely. The Old Man's dedication was too military, too much the impersonal, autocratic, dictatorial, ordered dedication of the professional military officer. It was necessary in war. No question about that, the Lieutenant acknowledged. But the war was over. What now? What manner of leadership was called for in the years to follow?

The Lieutenant had never been clear in his own mind about whether his commission in the Navy was to be his temporary accommodation to a world at war or a lifetime career. In recent weeks, particularly since his assignment to the *General Bliss*, he had begun to consider returning to civilian life as soon as his service commitment would permit. He would remain a reserve officer, of course. He liked to think the Navy needed him. For one thing, he was genuinely eager to command, not for his own sake, although pride was a factor, but rather out of a confidence in his own competence. Beyond this, he held the belief that he could humanize the military experience for the men and women serving under him.

The conviction was growing, however, that he did not need the Navy. The world was already turning again to civilian needs and civilian leadership. His assignments as a naval officer had provided experience in both shipboard and shore duty. He felt equally at home on the bridge or behind a desk, and he took some pride in his adaptability. He could make the transition from his military assignments to executive positions in the postwar civilian world smoothly and without loss of career ground, if he decided that was the way to go.

A letter from his wife, delivered to him in Calcutta while the *General Bliss* was loading there, had made clear her hope that the years ahead would have fewer and fewer separations like the current one. He had read over that letter often during the days at sea. His wife was proud of his advancement in the service, and it was unusual for her to raise such matters, at least as directly as she had done in this letter. The implications of her wish grew stronger at every reading. He always missed her and longed for her when he was at sea, sometimes with a desperation he was reluctant to admit even to himself.

"You know I'm here," she had written at the end of the letter. Then her customary: "Love, my dearest, all there is, Barbara." How complete that litany of her love made him. He almost winced as her words and the quiet intensity of her voice echoed in his thoughts. How incomplete, unfinished he felt without her. How they would fill in each other's lives with their candid, honest talk, as eagerly and wholly as they would fill each other's arms with their bodies. It seemed he had never talked freely as himself, never shared, never really been with anybody since he had last been with her. She was waiting. She would be in San Francisco. He could see her — her hair with its curl framing her lovely animated face, her wide eyes with their sensitive range of expression, her mouth, her . . . precious mouth. His own mouth almost involuntarily framed her name at the thought, "Barbara, Barbara, Barbara." He felt a quickening, a sudden warming throughout his whole being as her image took over his mind.

The Lieutenant's thought shifted to the Captain, now comfortably ensconced in his quarters. The Captain, too, had a wife. He had mentioned her once or twice, in passing. The Lieutenant had no idea whether she would be there at dockside to meet him. Such a meeting was hard to picture. What would she look like, the woman he would be married to? Would there be any show of affection? Not on his part, the Lieutenant decided, and therefore little, if any, on hers. At least in public. Maybe afterward as well. This turn of his thought struck him as odd. The Captain was certainly manly enough, even attractive in his controlled, masculine way; yet his masculinity seemed to have nothing to do with women. Picturing him with a woman, even with his wife, he imagined the Old Man as forbearing but ill-at-ease, decorous but properly distant. *Preoccupied* was the word he settled on.

The Lieutenant snuffled inwardly at the presumption of his own thoughts. What did he really know of the man? How much could he ever know of such a man beyond the character of his command, his conduct as an officer, the facade of his military bearing? Then again, was it a facade, or had it become the man himself over the years of service, the normal expression of the skills, the regulations, the duties which had turned into not only a career but eventually a life?

That was the trouble, the Lieutenant thought. And, for himself, perhaps, the danger. He had watched the Captain conduct an intensive search for a man overboard without let-up for nearly two hours, an unstinting effort to save a single man lost out of the welter of thousands aboard. The Lieutenant had spent those two hours at the

Captain's side caught up in the man's controlled passion and dedication to their common duty. He had shared that passion throughout the unrelenting search until, when their duty had been faithfully discharged, the Captain had turned to him, his Officer of the Deck, with a skillful cue for assistance in releasing the crew from the emotional strain of the unsuccessful search effort. The cue had been calculated in the Captain's demeanor as much as it had been expressed in his words, shrewdly and admirably done, as the whole performance had been.

Yet — and here was the nub as the Lieutenant reconsidered it — he could not honestly say that in the Captain's passion for an all-out search to recover the man lost overboard there was any sign of compassion for the man himself. It had been an admirable performance, to be sure, but in retrospect it became the performance of a military duty rather than an act of human responsibility.

This was true also of the shrewd shift in his manner at the end, with the orderly transfer of responsibility for his decision to quit — away from his personal will and into the circumstantial evidence at hand, away from his sole commanding presence and back into the regular procedures of the deck officer and crew. That, too, was admirable, perhaps, but it was not done in deference to the real feelings of the crew. Even less was it intended to recognize the role of the Officer of the Deck and give him his due. Instead it was the means best calculated to dispel the emotional zeal he had induced and maintained during the search and to return the ship to the safe, orderly routine of its prescribed mission as quickly and efficiently as possible.

Or so it seemed as the Lieutenant now considered it, staring out over the bow of the ship at the darkening Pacific. The horizon as they headed east was now dissolving into the coming night. The distinct agitation of the ocean in the foreground faded to distant darkness where the sea merged into the black, starless sky.

It was all admirable, he had to admit. And effective. The Old Man had settled the crew down and absolved them neatly of any self-recrimination which might affect their proper performance over the days and nights ahead before they arrived in San Francisco.

What about the troops, though? What about those thousands of duty-less GIs roaming the ship through the rest of the voyage with little to occupy them but the play of their own thoughts, their hopes and no doubt their apprehensions over the untried days ahead? The Old Man had let them off with only that perfunctory remark about "their cooperation." A patronizing remark at best, as it struck the Lieutenant now. The troops had contributed nothing to the search, except as an unwelcome complication during the operation. After all, it was one of their number who was the cause of the whole thing, or more than one if, just possibly, it was a stupid trick, a hoax, a false alarm in the first place. Under the circumstances, the Old Man's half-hearted thanks for their "cooperation" could have been taken as Navy sarcasm. There could even be repercussions from the idle troops over the stretch of shipboard time yet ahead . . .

Two weeks, and then San Francisco. He'd have time then to think seriously about his plans, about the years ahead. The crossing was half-completed. From now on it would be less and less a matter of leaving the Asian ports farther behind and more and more a matter of closing the distance to the United States. Odd that the man overboard incident had stopped their progress so nearly in the middle of things. It was a pivotal point for them, the fulcrum of the voyage, like the point of balance at the center of a teeter-totter, and they had now passed to the other side where their weight would gradually bring about their descent back to earth.

The Lieutenant grew wholly contemplative, lost in his speculations. Somehow the past seemed so irrevocably past, the future ahead so inevitable, yet so open and uncertain, so full of both opportunity and threat. One thing was sure. It would be a different world they were heading into. What he was feeling now he had never felt before. The atom bomb and the awesome power of its destructiveness now in human hands had seen to that. There was something in the elemental nature of its force that the world had never had to reckon with before, something which invoked in the Lieutenant's searching thoughts both monumental hope and inexpressible dread. Where was humankind bound with such prodigies as the military demands of war had produced? Where would his own fate lead him in such a world?

Where were all of them, all the thousands of men homeward bound, heading — beyond the night that was swallowing up the ocean and sky surrounding them in midpassage, beyond the light of the day they would wake to in the morning, and the days at sea still ahead, beyond San Francisco and the separation centers and their long-awaited transition from military uniform to the individual, personally selected dress they would wear as civilians? All, that is, but one of them, if there was that one still back there, futureless, one joined forever with the inexorable movements of the sea.

There or not! It no longer mattered! The Lieutenant realized in a sudden surge of illumination and fellow-feeling that the man overboard was a part of all of them, a part of all their lives, now and in the days yet to come, a legacy of war and chance and human irrationality, a compound of their common subjection and the tantalizing dream of freedom.

The Lieutenant felt himself very much alone for the moment. Then impulsively gregarious, he turned back into the soft light of the bridge interior where the crew members were settled calmly at their stations.

"Mordecai," he said, and he ambled over toward the talker. "The transients on this ship are going to have bad dreams about that man overboard business. I've been thinking about what it's like for them. It really could be upsetting, you know? I mean, if you weren't used to the sea and living on ship. It's no picnic for them. The Navy does all the work, but it's no picnic for them."

Where did he get that phrase? It wasn't his. He probably shouldn't be talking like this. He paused and searched Mordecai's expression for encouragement. The talker was silent, but his clear attention was a kind of assent. The Lieutenant went on.

"They're going to need attention, activities, entertainment, things to occupy them, things to look forward to. More than ever. What do you think?"

"I don't know, sir," Mordecai ventured. "What kind of things do you mean?"

"I'm not sure," the Lieutenant admitted. "Trying to keep four thousand men occupied doesn't give you much leeway. Maybe we can set up some sort of recreation every day, something besides calisthenics and chow lines."

"There's too many of them, sir. Doesn't the Army do anything for them like that?"

"I suppose so," the Lieutenant said, "but they could use more. Something for large groups. Maybe something that would include our men too, right with them. Make for better feelings on both sides. Some kind of entertainment. Shows, maybe."

Ensign Martin had wandered over and was listening to the conversation. "How about that jazz trio on board, Lieutenant?" he asked. "Have you heard them?"

"No, I haven't," the Lieutenant said, looking up. He was pleased to have the dialogue with his talker enlarged. "What about them?"

"Jazz trio," Martin repeated. "Piano, electric guitar, and bass. They're really good. Part of the troops. They play all kinds of stuff. I've heard them a couple times. They were playing in the officers' mess just today, during lunch."

"Maybe you could build a show around them, sir," Mordecai offered. "Put 'em on every afternoon."

"Why not?" the Lieutenant agreed, "It's a start. I'll talk to Army Transportation about it tonight. See?" He smiled amiably. "It pays to consult the hoi-polloi."

Martin nodded and smiled back. Mordecai grinned. The Lieutenant, pleased and reassured by the conversation, winked and withdrew.

Back at the bridge windows, he stood quietly again, contemplative once more, gazing out into the darkened vista of ocean beyond the quietly rising and falling bow of the *General Simon P. Bliss*. . . .

The images in his mind for the moment, however, are not of the shifting seas before him, nor of the bow of the ship dipping and cleaving into the dark waters. Instead he is contemplating a vision of the graceful arches of the Golden Gate Bridge, burnished and glorious in the full late-afternoon sun as they approach it from the west, then pass under it into San Francisco Bay with the marvelous alabaster city rising from its southern bank, bathed in that same late golden light, then the docking, and the shore strangely solid under his feet again, the mission completed, his wife waiting and then in his arms, the wordless embrace and the warmth and the completeness, and later, together, whole again, the past and the future abiding in their re-union, the continuance of their life and love assured, melting into a fullness of now.

—CODA—

A light rain fell on the USS *General Simon P. Bliss*, starting around midnight and continuing fitfully, at times in brief gusts, through the early morning hours. By dawn it had stopped, but the cloud cover remained with them well into the next day.

When the troops were roused that morning, they woke to the usual sudden glare of the overhead bulbs being turned on in their sleeping compartments. They emerged shortly into the dim, gray light of the deck for their first formation, conscious of little difference from the routine beginnings of all the days they had been aboard the *General Bliss*. Their officers, however, were wideawake, apparently having been up for some time. The morning roll call that ensued, name by name, unit by unit throughout the entire ship, was conducted as usual by the company non-coms, but the entire procedure was overseen by teams of their officers who stood by in attentive surveillance.

Instead of the routine early morning slump as they normally scratched and yawned their way into the new day, the troops were brought into strict ranks at full attention. Instead of their usual half-hearted "hee-o" or "ee-yep," as their names were called, they were instructed to respond smartly, as they did at the military pay table, with their rank and serial number. The process was loud, lengthy, and cheerless—a distressful, though temporary, return to strict military accounting.

Late that evening, after the results of the muster had been accumulated from all units, tabulated, double-checked, and endorsed at each successive level of command, the total count of the troops was brought to a final reckoning against the records of the Army Transportation Officer-in-Charge. To the considerable consternation of all, it revealed nine enlisted men recorded as among the transient personnel of the USS *General Bliss* who were missing and unaccounted for.

For the troops themselves, and for the crew of the ship, the matter of the man overboard in mid-Pacific remained a popular topic of conversation for a few days. With the return of good weather, references to the incident grew less frequent.

The steady progress of the troopship toward the U.S. mainland continued. Each day, its course and position were plotted and marked on the big world map mounted on the main deck, right below the superstructure of the bridge. There the circulating troops could check it any time, along with the bulletins and teletype tearsheets of world news.

Announcements were also posted there, calling attention to the ship's recreational program and to the schedule of religious services on Sunday mornings and at various other times.

Two days after the ship had resumed its course, posters appeared announcing a series of variety shows being scheduled for the remainder of the voyage, featuring the Roy Warner Trio with GI talent of all kinds recruited from the troops and ship's personnel. A temporary stage for the shows began to go up against the aft bulkhead, off the main deck. Looking out over the broad fantail which would accommodate its audiences, the performers would be able to enjoy an unrestricted view of the ship's trailing white wake as it marked their passage across the broad Pacific.

A week later, a second muster of all transient personnel was taken. On this occasion, it was held in full daylight at a special formation scheduled between the two daily chow calls. The final record this time showed thirteen names listed aboard the ship who were missing and unaccounted for.

The succession of days continued and the ship plunged ahead on its course. Day and night, as if unendingly, the churning white wake of the *General Bliss* played out its undeviatingly straight line behind the fantail to the western horizon.

For its GI passengers and crew, however, looking back occasionally in lone moments over the way they had come, their common wake had, if not an ending, at least the recollection of an interruption, back there, far beyond their sight now, back where they had all drifted together without power, dead in the water, for an interval they would carry along, appropriately submerged, wherever the future directed them.

It was done, of course, back there. But as they looked out at the wake in those succeeding days, and over the circular sweep of ocean on which it made its mark, any chance moment could unaccountably carry them, in an instant, backward or forward along the line of that continuous wake. In that larger sense, they knew it would never be done.